LEt tHE
RubbLE
faLL

Mandi [signature]

LET THE RUBBLE FALL

Let the Rubble Fall

MANDI LYNN

THE ROAD TRIP SNAPSHOT SERIES:

Meet Me at the Summit

Let the Rubble Fall

NOVELS ALSO BY MANDI LYNN

Essence

I am Mercy

She's Not Here

To anyone who has climbed a
mountain to find peace.

SIGN UP FOR MY NEWSLETTER

Be the first to know about new book releases,
see behind the scenes content, and more!

https://bit.ly/MandisNewsletter

CHaPteR 1

O ctober 11th was the day my world came crashing down. I was waiting in my dorm room for my parents to show up before I finally noticed the dozens of messages on my phone from family members panicking, trying to get in touch with me.

I remember that day in sections. The last phone call I'd ever have with my dad as he let me know they were on their way. Then running across campus with Lori to get to her car so we could drive to the hospital. And lastly, stepping through the doors of the hospital to see the broken faces of my family, everyone present except the two most important people in my world. I knew my parents were gone before anyone told me.

Today marks 365 days without my parents—days I didn't think I would survive, but here I am. I spent most of the last year with my head in the sand, refusing to look up at the life that had been ripped away from me. But now I'm saying goodbye. It's time for a fresh start.

I don't make it a habit to visit my parents' house. Even six weeks ago, when I came to the house with Dylan to get photos, I found it hard to step through the doors. I want to sell the house. I want to rip it away like a Band-Aid that's falling off from wear, get it over with and never look at it again. It's my Aunt Cora who insists I keep it, even if I move away to Colorado.

Since my road trip in the VW bus ended, I've been staying in Lori's apartment, avoiding my parents' house. But I promised myself today I'd say goodbye, folding up a piece of my life and storing it for later.

When I pull into the driveway, there's a layer of frost on the roof and grass, the sun reflecting tiny rays of light off the bits of ice. At this time last year, I was waking up in my dorm room, planning out my day, trying to think of ways to convince my parents to visit. As the day would go on, they would get eight phone calls from me before deciding to call into work sick to take a day trip to visit me.

Like today, the air was cold, but instead of white frost, everything was clear ice. The roads were coated in a thin layer of black ice, just enough to cause their car to spin out of control at an intersection.

"You there?" It's Dylan's voice that pulls me back into the present.

I'm sitting in the driveway, my phone on speaker with Dylan on the line. We've been talking the entire drive from Lori's apartment to my parents' house. He was telling me about work, and I let myself focus on that instead of where I was going. He had been saying something about a new client at the marketing agency he works for, how they're rebuilding a landing page. I could understand the gist of it, enough at least to not think about what happened a year ago.

"Yeah, I'm here," I say. I put the bus into park and turn off the engine. It's the same VW bus I drove from Washington to New Hampshire. After coming home, Ethan transferred the title and registration to me, and I promised him I'd go on another road trip, but first I needed October 11th to go by. The date was like a ticking time bomb as almost two months went by. I'm eager to go to Colorado, but this day has been lingering in the back of my mind.

"Tell me about your parents," Dylan says when I've been quiet for too long. We're both tired. I've been up since 6:00 a.m., but for Dylan it was 5:00 a.m. His voice is low and muffled on the phone, but he's here, even if it's not physically.

"I've already told you so much," I say. Ever since Dylan joined me on the road trip, it seems like all I've done is talk to him. And when he came to New Hampshire and combed through some of my parents' photo albums, he only had more questions about them. Talking about them used to be hard, but when I tell Dylan the stories from when I was a kid, part of me feels like they're alive again — or at least the memory of them.

"Tell me something I don't know yet," he says.

I stare at the entrance to the house. "My dad painted the front door of our house red without asking my mom first," I tell him.

"She didn't like it?"

"She hated it. I remember her face when she came home from work that day. Her mouth was hanging open. She was too shocked to say anything at first, but once she gained her bearings, he was in for it. My mom went into a full rage. I'm not even sure if it was the color she disliked. I think it was the surprise of having a piece of the house changed without her oversight that distressed her so much. I was at the hardware store with him when he picked out the color. I told him she wouldn't like it." I laugh a little, remembering how I tried to contain my judgment while he was painting the door.

"And he still went for it?"

"Yup." I shake my head, remembering how excited and sure of himself he was when he painted on the first coat. He made fun of me for not helping, but I told him I didn't want to be his accomplice.

A wave of emotion comes over me, and tears form before I can stop them. My throat closes, and it feels like I can't breathe. I feel like I'm going to cry, but I take a deep breath, leaning my head back into the seat. Dylan waits quietly on the other end. I smile in a sad, forced way, trying to focus on the memory rather than their absence.

"She was so angry that he almost went out and bought another can of paint to put it back to the original color. My mom told him not to worry about it."

"Did she end up liking it?"

"I think so," I whisper, feeling tears gloss over my eyes. I take a breath again, but this time it doesn't help. The tears don't sway, and the emotions shift from grief to anger. I thought it would be easier. I convinced myself that the worst was behind me, that the hardest thing was hearing Aunt Cora tell me they were gone. Or seeing them in caskets at the wake, even though they didn't look like themselves at all. Or watching as their bodies were lowered into the ground. The first holidays without them. My first birthday without them. Walking into this house for the first time and knowing they wouldn't be there on the other side of the door. Each time a new first happened, I told myself that was it, the hard part was over. But there's always going to be a new first to face without my parents.

"I wish you were here," I whisper into the phone.

"I wish I were there too." His voice is low and soft. Hearing him makes me feel safer, like maybe I can walk through the door of my house again. I long for him in a way I never have before—for him or anyone I've met. In this moment, I wish I were wrapped in his arms, being held close so I don't fall apart. I've never felt like this toward anyone before, and it terrifies me. I've always thought of love as a very concrete thing. With my family, it was always that way, something natural that I didn't need to think about. I loved my parents, not by default, but because of who they were. But how does love work with someone who doesn't feel like family, someone who's more than that? With Dylan, it feels like I'm free-falling, and I refuse to let go. I'm scared what may happen if I do.

"It gets easier, right?" I say, staring at the bright red door.

"I know it does," Dylan says, his voice firm. "Because a few months ago you wouldn't go to the house by yourself."

"I'm not by myself." I sit in the bus, my phone clutched in my hand while I stare at the front door.

"Progress, Marly, not perfection," he says.

I let out a gasping breath and hold the phone farther away in hope that he doesn't hear me. I unbuckle my seat belt and push the bus's door open. The air is cold when I step outside, and my breath steams in front of me as I walk. Dylan waits on the other end of the line, patient as I make my way across the yard. How many times have I walked to this front door in my lifetime?

I pull my key out of my pocket and unlock the door. The house is a frozen time capsule. The only people with keys are me and Aunt Cora. She doesn't go inside unless she needs to find something. For the most part, she just handles the landscaping, making sure the house at least doesn't appear to be abandoned.

"Cora is getting the house winterized," I say. The door shuts behind me with a soft click. We should have winterized the house last year too, but Cora didn't want to in case I decided to move in. So instead, she paid to heat the house just enough to keep the pipes from freezing. It's heated now, but the temperature is kept low. Next week workers will come by to winterize and lock up the house until I choose to come back to it.

"Are you grabbing anything today?" Dylan asks.

"I don't know," I say, suddenly overwhelmed by how empty the rooms feel. I know it's my house, but it feels like I'm walking through a stranger's home. I keep expecting to see my dad's wallet on the counter or my mom's bathrobe slung over the side of the couch, but everything is too clean. I step down the hall, trying to find some sign of my parents, but all the counters and surfaces have been wiped down. The house is a showroom, perfectly neat and organized. But it's not my home.

I slowly make my way through the first floor, my eyes watering as I walk. I try to ignore how staggered my breathing has become.

"Just take a deep breath and remember why you wanted to come," Dylan says.

The truth is, I don't know why I wanted to come. I suppose most people go to a grave to visit someone on the anniversary of their death, but the one time I went to their graves, there was no trace of my parents. I couldn't sense them in the way some people talk about feeling the presence of their loved ones after they die. I couldn't feel my parents at the hospital, the wake, the funeral, or even their graves. It made no sense to me to grieve there. But they aren't here either. This house is full of memories that burst before my eyes no matter how hard I try to ignore them. But that's all they are: memories. The story stops there, without a continuation in sight.

My dad is hunched in the corner fixing the vacuum for the tenth time. My mom is in the kitchen cooking up dinner. They're both at the table, laughing and arguing over the rules of a card game. The memories are so clear, I swear I see them until I blink and it's gone.

"Where are you right now?" Dylan asks.

I take a few steps forward and wrap my hand on the back of a dining room chair. There's nothing on the table, which was a rare occurrence when my parents were here. The table was more of a dumping ground for projects and the occasional jigsaw puzzle than it was for eating. A tiny sense of déjà vu overcomes me, but it feels wrong—like my brain is confused and doesn't know how to place me.

"In the dining room," I say, my voice only a whisper.

"Do you want to be alone?"

"No," I say.

We're both quiet for a long time. The sun shines through the back windows of the house, the world shouting hello. It feels like goodbye. Tomorrow I leave for Colorado, having no idea when I'll come back. This house will be here—I don't think Cora will ever let me sell—but I don't know when I'll step foot through here again.

I thought I'd be relieved to never have to visit the place that reminds me most of my parents; instead, it feels like they're being ripped away from me all over again, except this time I'm choosing to leave it all behind. I want to be excited for the life I have ahead of me, but right now, all I feel is longing for the life I would have had if my parents were still here.

Would my parents have given me the bus and pushed me to travel? I'm almost certain my dad would've insisted on going with me for some of my adventures, my mom tagging along to do any sightseeing that didn't involve hiking.

It's so easy to picture how my life would have been. How it *should* have been.

"I don't want to leave," I say, my voice edging into a cry. I cross into the other room and sit on the couch. I sink into the cushions and pull one of the old throw pillows to my chest. I expect it to smell familiar, like home, but it doesn't. It smells clean. I'm tempted to throw it across the room, but I grip it closer instead, feeling myself become unhinged.

"Really?" Dylan says. His voice is soft, but there's a hint of worry there that most people would probably miss if they didn't know him well enough. "You don't have to."

As he speaks, I can hear the disappointment, which makes me remember why I wanted to go to Colorado in the first place. My heart's being pulled in two directions.

We've been apart longer than we've been together. We had almost three weeks together during my road trip, but now it's been six weeks since I've seen him. I shouldn't miss him this much, but I do. I want him here, sitting next to me now, only for the most selfish reasons.

"It feels final," I say, having no other way to describe it. "Like if I leave, then so will the last bits of my parents. I hate coming to this house, but what if . . ." I linger on the words.

"What if what?" Dylan coaxes, but I don't say anything. "Marly, please talk to me."

"This house already doesn't feel like home. What if I never come back? Or what if I do and it's even worse?"

"It's not the house that holds the memories, Marly. It's you."

I nod my head, biting my lip to keep myself from crying.

"And you'll be back. I'll come with you next time."

I smile even though I feel like I could crumble at any moment.

"Okay," I say. A few more seconds pass of Dylan sitting on the other end of the phone, his breath a soft reassurance. "I'm going to walk around for a bit."

"Do you want me to stay on the line?" he says gently.

"I think I want to be alone."

"I'm here if you need me. I'll see you soon."

The reminder is a soft encouragement that the loneliness is temporary, and when the line ends, it feels like my breath echoes across the empty house.

I've spent so long terrified to feel the pain of losing both my parents in one fell swoop, but now I let myself cry. I sit on the couch, gasping for air, alone. On the other side of the living room is a rocking chair that my mom always sat in while she read her latest book. If I close my eyes, I can almost imagine her there. I can practically see her lifting her face from the pages to look up at me and smile. But then I open my eyes, and she's gone.

It feels masochistic, going through every memory of this room. How many Christmases did we have together? How many Sunday mornings did we eat waffles while watching a movie in our pajamas? Not nearly enough. The shells of all the memories are here, but the details are gone. The pillow my dad used for his back. The blanket my mom wrapped herself in. It's all gone, split between family members who treasured the items most. I have a few tucked away in boxes I'm too afraid to open.

The boxes sit in a closet in Lori's apartment. They're sealed shut with duct tape, but not because I don't want to see them — the opposite. My mom's blanket is in one. When she first died, I slept with the blanket every night, relishing her smell, which had been left behind. But all too quickly, I noticed it started to change. The more I slept with the blanket, the less it smelled like her, so I tucked it away for a day when missing her was too hard, when that familiar scent would be the only thing that would bring me comfort.

I promise myself that when I get back to the apartment, I'll find the blanket and bring it with me to Colorado.

It feels like I'm in the house for hours, sitting in an ocean of memories. In every corner of every room, there are countless images of my parents. The love is overflowing through the rooms, but with love comes loss, and some days the loss feels like too much.

By the time I step out the front door, I feel drained, like I've walked hundreds of miles. When I lock the door behind me, it feels surreal. How can I come back to this house again if those I love will never be inside?

I walk away from the house of memories, promising myself that whatever lies ahead, walking away will allow me to breathe easy again.

CHAPTER 2

i'm taken aback when I see Aunt Cora's car pull into my parents' yard. She waves as she steps out of her car and meets me in the driveway.

"I was hoping you'd be here," she says, holding something small in her hand.

"I was just leaving," I say. Cora smiles at me, but her eyes are red and tired like she's been crying. It's easy for me to get lost in my grief and forget that I'm not the only person who's lost someone, but seeing Cora forces me to remember that all of my family is grieving today.

"There was something of your dad's that I've been searching for to give to you. I was digging through some boxes today and finally found it."

She holds out a small box and I take it, opening it carefully to find an old keychain that looks vaguely familiar, though I can't place where I've seen it before. The keychain has a few charms on it: a compass, plane, and suitcase. The metal looks like it should be silver in color, but it has a brassy tone to it from use.

"Where is this from?" I ask, turning the charms over in my hand.

"Your dad gave it to your mom when she decided to move to New Hampshire. I think he just bought it as a cheap gift from a souvenir shop, but she kept it for years."

The memory clicks into place, and I remember why it looks so familiar. This keychain is the same one that was always on my mom's car keys. I'd gotten so used to seeing it, I barely noticed it, but now it feels like I'm holding a small piece of home.

"I thought you should have it since you're going to Colorado."

I pull out my keys and add the chain to my set. While growing up, I could always hear my mom coming because the keychain would jingle with every step. Even as an adult, I always wondered why she kept the keychain, but as I place my keys back into my purse, the sound is a tiny bit of comfort.

"Thank you," I say.

Cora smiles back at me, but her eyes glance past me, to the house. Her gaze rests on the door, perhaps she's waiting, just like I am, for my parents to come stepping through. Cora always puts on a brave face around me, but in moments like this, I can see how much my parents' deaths have impacted her. There are lines on her face that I didn't notice before, and the spark in her smile is dimmer. Most days she's the aunt I've always known and loved, but today she's just as lost in her grief as I am.

"You all packed?" she says suddenly, turning her eyes back to me.

"Just a few last-minute things, and then I'll be ready to go."

She nods, the movement automatic. Cora has stepped up

ever since my parents died, but especially once she heard I wanted to move to Colorado. While the rest of my extended family was wary of my decision, Cora was helping me plan the logistics. I'm not sure if it's because she's the only one in my family who has met Dylan or if it's because her brother—my dad—fell in love with a girl who was willing to move across the country as well.

Cora hasn't said it, but I can tell she thinks I'm just going to Colorado to be with Dylan. Sometimes she looks worried when I talk about Colorado, and I'll wait for her to say something, but she never voices her thoughts. Perhaps because she's thinking the same thing I am: What would my parents do?

My mom would have loved Dylan the same way Lori does. I like to think it would have been her telling me to move across the country to be with him—that's what she did after all. It would have taken her days, weeks even, to realize that she's supposed to be the parent warning me to be cautious and not uproot my entire life for a boy. Right before I left, the parental part of her brain would have clicked into place, and she'd have started backtracking, trying to tell me to stay.

My dad was the wild card. He loved adventure, but only when those adventures were planned and appropriate. Although he usually sided with me, he was much too practical in his life to condone me moving for a boy. At least I think that would've been the case.

"Text me when you leave," Cora says, looking me over with genuine worry. Is she questioning letting me go?

"I'll text you every time I take a driving break," I tell her.

That seems to give her some relief, and she reaches out to hug me.

"Be safe," she says, her arms tight around me. "And remember I'm always a phone call away."

She pulls back to look at me, her eyes tearful. Given she has her own kids to take care of, I'm astounded by how she's taken me under her wing when I need her most.

"I will," I promise her.

And just like that, we part ways, my parents' house fading in the background as I drive off.

§

I get back to Lori's apartment at 8:00 a.m. I made it a point to leave before she was awake for the day. I knew she would want to come to the house with me, and part of me wanted that as well. It was the reason I needed Dylan on the phone with me when I first got there. I was afraid if I didn't have someone there, I never would have stepped inside. With Dylan, all I needed to do to be alone was hang up the phone.

I was hoping to get back before Lori woke up, but when I walk in, her head pops out from her bedroom doorway.

"Hey, where'd you go?" Her voice is gentle. She knows what day it is today.

I take a deep breath, sitting on the couch. "My parents' house."

She steps out from her room and joins me in the living room. She sits next to me, throwing a blanket over our legs. My body is exhausted as I sink into the couch, and it feels like I poured all of myself over the confines of my house.

"You okay?"

I shrug. "It just feels final."

"Why?" Lori asks, her gaze curious.

"I don't know. I guess I just keep thinking, 'What if I don't go back?' "

Lori frowns, hesitating before giving me a small smile. "You'll be back. Can't get away from me that easily."

I smile, but it doesn't reach my eyes.

"You know you don't have to come back, right?" Lori says softly. I look up, my eyes tired. "I mean, I want you to come back and visit, of course, but this is about what makes you happy. A lot of people want a fresh start, so if you have the opportunity, take it."

"I know," I say, the words coming out as a sigh. The thought of going to Colorado now seems exhausting.

"And if you fall in love with Colorado . . ." She gives me a faint smile, elbowing me in the ribs lightly. We both know she's not just talking about Colorado.

I shake my head, smiling for the first time today.

"It's just weird," I say. "I'm going to Colorado. No plan. Just a destination."

"That's not true," Lori says. "You'll be staying at Stacey's place, plus you're going to be a second shooter for weddings. And don't even get me started about how you'll be selling your prints at Snapshot Café."

I smile, knowing it's all true. After I made the decision to go to Colorado, things started to fall into place. Dylan's sister, Stacey, was looking for a new roommate after her friend Charlotte moved in with her boyfriend. Charlotte is also a wedding photographer and needed a second shooter for a few upcoming weddings. Without even looking, the opportunity manifested itself, and I took that as a sign from the universe that it was all meant to be.

But now the whole thing is starting to feel wrong. When my parents were around, I wasn't one to be overly cautious. As long as I had approval from my mom or dad, I'd take on just about every challenge. Without them here, I feel like I'm walking in blind. I didn't realize how many times I'd turned to them for reassurance until they were gone. Even when I moved into the dorms at college, I'd needed their approval, and it didn't occur to me until very recently that that was why I'd been so insistent on having them visit me that day.

For the past couple of weeks I've found myself tossing and turning in bed, wondering what my parents would say if they were here. I allow myself to imagine a different life, where my parents gift me the renovated VW bus like originally planned and tell me to take the summer off for a road trip before college. What if I had met Dylan then? Would I have given up everything to go to Colorado, or am I just doing it to run away from the memories of everything I've lost?

"I don't even know how long I'll be there," I say. When I told Stacey I'd be her roommate, it was under the condition that it was temporary and on a month-by-month — or even week-by-week — basis.

I know I'll be in Colorado October through November, but beyond that is a mystery. Even with the wedding photography, I only have three weddings I'm scheduled to shoot. I don't exactly have a career lined up. I'm making money selling stock photos, but eventually I'll have to figure something out long-term. I have more than enough money from my parents' life insurance to live worry free for a couple years, but it seems foolish to sit around without any sort of plan.

And I can't ignore the constant pestering thoughts in the back of my mind: *you're moving to Colorado to be with a boy.* It feels like I'm living someone else's life.

"You didn't know how long your summer road trip was going to last either," Lori reminds me.

I let out a laugh. "That's because I didn't have a choice. If it had been up to me, I would have flown home, and there wouldn't have been a road trip."

"And you wouldn't have met Dylan," Lori says, softly elbowing me with a grin.

I shake my head in disbelief. The thought of seeing Dylan again makes me antsy, like I need to take a few laps around the living room to get the extra energy out. I'm not sure if I'm nervous or excited; all I know is that the six weeks leading up to going back to Colorado have felt like they've dragged on. I imagine what it will be like to see him again, and all I can picture is jumping into his arms. But that feels like a dream.

"What if it's not the same?" I ask Lori. "I mean, it's been weeks since we've seen each other. What if the only thing that made us work was the fact that we were always traveling or going on hikes? What happens when it's just the two of us, with no rhyme or reason?"

"Then you go to Colorado, take photos, and come home."

I pull a blanket on the couch closer to me, tucking it under my chin as I sink deeper into the cushions. Lori sits next to me, but my eyes are trained on the door across the room. I close my eyes and can almost picture my mom stepping through the door, ready to sit down for one of her famous mother-daughter talks where she tries to reason with me. What would she say if she were here today?

"Marly, you deserve a fresh start," Lori says, interrupting my thoughts. "Dylan or no Dylan, you should go to Colorado. Take photos, go to strangers' weddings. Meet new people. Give yourself the chance to live the life your parents always wanted for you."

I glance at Lori and realize my eyes are watering, the tears bursting over and trailing down my cheeks.

"How am I supposed to know what they wanted?" I say quietly.

Lori frowns and reaches out to hug me. "They would want whatever *you* want."

I lean back on the couch, letting my head fall backward until I'm staring up at the ceiling. The possibilities of my future loom around me, none of the options seeming clear or understood. When I first started telling my family I was going to Colorado, they all assumed I was moving there permanently. And I think part of me thought the same thing for a while. It wasn't until I actually started to plan my trip back to Colorado that the idea of moving there terrified me. Anything permanent feels too serious. The only thing that keeps me going is telling myself it's just another trip.

In so many ways, New Hampshire is home. But in much harder ways, it's impossible to feel at home when the two people I love most are gone.

"What do you think my parents would say if they were here right now?" I ask Lori. It's not a question I've ever dared myself to say out loud. It's been a year—a long, hard, unforgiving year. Sometimes it feels like no time has passed at all, yet it somehow feels like it's been a lifetime since I've seen their faces, making it hard to properly remember life before they were gone.

Lori sighs, and the cushions shift as she adjusts herself. "I think they would refuse to tell you what they think. They'd want you to go to Colorado because that's what you want to do. Or they'd want you to say here in New Hampshire because it's what you want. I think you being happy was always the priority."

I smile, fighting back tears, wondering how I can keep crying. "So, you're saying they probably wouldn't have forced me to go on a cross-country road trip."

"No, your dad would have made sure you went on that trip, your feelings be damned."

We both let out a laugh. I push myself off the couch and make my way toward the closet Lori and I share for storage.

"Where you going?" Lori asks.

"There's something I forgot to pack."

The closet is mostly storage for the overflow of small kitchen appliances we've collected. The shelves are full of things like an air fryer, panini press, Crock-Pot, and even a couple of blenders. What I'm looking for is stored away in a box at the back of the closet, behind Lori's large griddle. There are four boxes hidden away in this closet, but today I only intend to open one of them.

I pull the smallest box out and peel the duct tape away. My mom's blanket is folded perfectly inside. The yarn is a pale pink, and the blanket has cream-colored tassels at the edges. When I pull it out, I'm almost afraid to touch it, worried that interference from me will disturb the memories it holds.

With the lightest touch, I pull the blanket to my nose and take a deep breath. The scent is subtle, but there are slight traces of lavender in the blanket. I exhale, tears welling in my eyes. It still smells like Mom.

CHAPTER 3

It takes three days to get from New Hampshire to Colorado. It was easier to say goodbye to everyone than I thought it would be, perhaps because I said my goodbyes over the course of the last month. After the anniversary of my parents' deaths, everything else felt easier in comparison.

I drive at least ten hours each day, making for a total of thirty-two hours. When I stop, it's only to get gas or food or take a bathroom break. Overnight camping spots are nothing more than Walmart parking lots with a highway close by. By the third day, I'm convinced I'll never want to drive the bus again, but as I pull into Colorado Springs, a few familiar roads come up, and I'm eager to make the final stretch.

I've never been to Dylan's apartment before—never had a reason to—but that's where I'm going now. It's 7:00 p.m., and the sun is already starting to disappear behind the tall mountains circling the town. It feels surreal to be driving, knowing I'm just a few minutes away from seeing Dylan after spending almost two months apart. The last ten minutes, I find myself growing overly anxious and antsy. Tiny bits of worry form as I wonder if Dylan will be different from the last time I saw him.

I follow the directions on my GPS and pull into an apartment complex parking lot. There are apartment buildings on three sides of the lot, each with a single door that leads into the building. I park the bus in the spot closest to building B. My stomach jumps with nerves as I pull my phone out to text Aunt Cora I made it. The text goes through right as there's a knock at the window. When I look up, Dylan's hand is resting against the glass, a huge grin across his face. I open the door quickly, and he pulls me into a hug before my feet have the chance to hit the ground.

I expect myself to feel surprised, maybe more nervous, but I find myself completely at ease in his arms. Most of all, there's a sense of relief, not just to be here in Colorado, but to see Dylan in person again, to know he's real and not just a summer dream I imagined.

"You're early," he says, leaning back just enough to look at me.

"I was trying to surprise you," I say.

He kisses me, pulling me closer, and my body melts into his. It feels like a lifetime since we've seen each other, but just like that, it's like no time has passed at all. He smiles against my lips before he pulls away, his hands keeping me drawn to his body.

"You're going to need a quieter vehicle if you want to accomplish that. I could hear the bus from a mile away."

I laugh, realizing that after three straight days of doing nothing but driving, I've tuned out the loud drone of the engine.

We disentangle each other until we're just holding hands, his palms acting like an anchor as my stomach spins from excitement.

"Let me see what the bus is looking like these days," he says, walking around to the other side of the bus, his hand still wrapped in mine.

The VW bus is a camper van, meaning it acts like a tiny RV. It has a backseat and table that can be folded down into a bed that's a little smaller than a full-size mattress. There's a tiny sink, minifridge, and cabinets where I store my belongings. The roof also pops up to give a little more standing room in the middle. The part of the roof that doesn't pop open has a solar panel, making it possible to have power without needing to be hooked up to anything. The bus was a perfect companion when I was doing my road trip, but the past three days it's been nothing more than a place for me to crash every night.

Dylan opens the side door, revealing the mess I managed to make. During the drive I never bothered to convert my bed back into a couch, opting to eat my meals in the front seats or while sitting on the mattress. The cabinets alongside the bed are closed, hiding the balls of clothes I threw in at the last moment. My mom's blanket is rolled up in the corner since I've been sleeping with it every night.

The tiny sink in the bus is where the true chaos lives. The sink is just big enough to fit one bowl, but I've managed to stack it with all the utensils and plates I never bothered to wash. Most embarrassing, though, is the trash that has been sitting in the sink rather than being thrown out.

"Little messier than usual, I see," Dylan says, poking his head in.

"I was in a rush," I say, leaning forward and pulling the sheets taut in a sad attempt to make it look more presentable. I climb into the bus and grab my duffel bag from where it was shoved behind the driver's seat.

"Is that all you need for tonight?" Dylan asks, watching me reach out to grab my mom's blanket, tucking it under my arm. I climb out of the bus and shut the door behind me.

"I pack light," I say as Dylan takes my bag and slings it over his shoulder, grabbing my hand as he leads me to his apartment building.

The first night in Colorado I'll be sleeping at Dylan's apartment. Stacey still works at the hospital, and tonight she's working the night shift. I thought it'd be best to move in when she's home and awake.

"Trent's out with some friends, so it's just you and me tonight," Dylan says, opening the door to the building and guiding me forward.

"You didn't want to join them?" I tease.

Dylan lets out a low chuckle, wrapping his arm around my waist and kissing the top of my head.

Inside the building is nothing but hallways and a set of stairs leading to the second floor. He leads me up the stairway and down a narrow hallway.

"Do you want to stay in and relax for the night or come with me for a surprise?" he says as we walk.

I glance over at him and notice the grin on his face. Truthfully,

I'm exhausted after so many long days of driving, but curiosity gets the best of me.

"What's the surprise?" I ask.

"You'll see." He leads me to the end of the hall and opens the door to his apartment.

The apartment is small, maybe a little smaller than the place Lori and I are used to sharing. It opens into the living room, with the dining table directly to the right of the front door. A little farther to the right is the kitchen, which is all shoved together in a corner. Despite the small size, the countertops are clean, but I suspect that has to do with the smell of fast food in the air.

The apartment is older, and the kitchen cabinets look like something from the nineties, but otherwise the apartment looks like a typical bachelor pad with almost no decorations and plain white walls.

"That's Trent's room." Dylan points to the doorway to my left across from the couch. "That's the bathroom." He points to the door a few feet from the edge of the kitchen counter. "And this is my room." He walks through the doorway directly next to the bathroom. The walls are all white with a few maps of the mountains and hiking trails hanging on the walls. His bedsheets and comforter are a solid dark blue, and his bedside table has a photo of him and an older man, who I assume is the grandfather Dylan always went hiking with. Other than that, the room is plain. It feels practically empty compared to how Lori and I decorated the apartment in New Hampshire.

"I'll be on the couch tonight so you can have the bed to yourself," Dylan says, dropping my bag by the bedroom doorway.

I make a face, sitting on the edge of his bed and putting my mom's blanket down.

"What?" he asks.

"We've slept in the same bed multiple times," I say, referring to how we managed to share the tiny bed in the VW bus without any issues.

He grins and sits next to me. "Well, I wasn't sure if you needed to warm up to me again."

I kiss him quickly. "I'm all warmed up."

He grins. "Good. Now that we dropped off your stuff, let's go to your surprise." He takes my hand and leads me back out of his apartment. I know I should be more tired, but I follow Dylan eagerly, my steps rushed as we make our way across the parking lot. He opens the passenger door for me, and I get into his truck.

He walks around to the driver's side and gets in, starting the engine with a low rumble.

"Where are we going?" I ask.

"You'll see," he says, backing out of his parking space. The last of the sunset fades from the sky as we drive, the mountaintops in the distance shifting from orange to yellow and then, finally, to a light soft blue before fading darker and darker. We've only been driving for ten minutes when it starts to feel like we're getting farther and farther away from civilization rather than getting closer to whatever our destination is.

Dylan pulls the truck off to the side of the road, driving a little way off the road before parking. We're sitting in a large open field, nothing around us except mountains and a singular long road.

Once the engine is off, Dylan hops out of the truck and comes to my door to open it. He offers me his hand as I step out.

"Is this the part where you hide my dead body in a field?" I joke as I scan the area. There isn't another building in sight and while there is a road, it seems to just be Dylan who's on it.

He lets out a low laugh. "Come here."

He leads me to the back of the truck and opens the tailgate. With the bed of the truck open, I can now see that he's piled it full of blankets and pillows, and a cooler is shoved in one of the corners.

Dylan steps up into the truck bed effortlessly and offers me a hand. I take it, putting one foot on the tailgate as he pulls me up until we're both standing.

"I wanted to officially say welcome back," he says, wrapping his arms around me as we gaze off over the horizon. "I've got dinner packed in the cooler, and with enough time, the stars will be out for our entertainment."

He kisses my temple quickly before dropping his arms and walking toward the cab of the truck bed and sitting against a pile of pillows. He opens the cooler and starts to pull out crackers, cheese, and fruit—basically everything needed for a charcuterie board.

"When did you come up with this?" I ask, practically giggling as I move to sit next to him.

"I've had a couple weeks to come up with a game plan." He assembles a sample of cheese and cracker and hands it to me. I take it, still in awe. "You didn't have to come out to Colorado, so I wanted to make it my mission that you have a good time, no matter how short or long your stay is." He gives me a knowing smile, already trying to coax me to stay as long as possible.

"So far it's seeming to be a good choice," I say, leaning into his shoulder.

We continue to snack on the food Dylan packed until the sky grows so dark that we can't see the mountains off in the distance. With the darkness come the stars. They appear scattered in the sky, but as the minutes tick on, the entire sky blooms with them. We take turns pointing out constellations, and every now and then a shooting star darts across the sky so fast that I almost miss it.

We're lying on our backs in the bed of his truck, the blankets and pillows padded around us. My body is pressed close to his as I lie tucked under his arm. The minutes pass on, and our voices grow softer and softer as we talk.

"What do you think you're going to do while you're here?" Dylan says, his voice so low it's almost a whisper.

"I want to capture all this," I say, spreading my arms out over my head.

"Night photography? Have you tried that yet?" he asks, curious.

"Yes. No. I mean, that's not what I mean." The words come out mumbled, my lack of sleep catching up with me now. I shift into Dylan until my head is resting on his chest. He moves to wrap his arm around my shoulder.

Dylan laughs, and his chest rises and falls with the movement.

"I'd love to try to learn night photography. I haven't done it yet. But I mean this feeling of peace. I want to encapsulate all of this in a photo."

His arm tightens around me and he kisses the top of my head. I close my eyes and let myself exist in this peace and wonder how I'll ever capture this feeling on camera. All I know as I lie here with Dylan is that this is everything I want Colorado to be.

CHapteR 4

"**H**ey! How was your drive?" Stacey meets me in her apartment parking lot while Dylan fishes my suitcase out from where I shoved it in the back of the bus. I didn't bring a lot with me to Colorado. It's mostly clothes, hiking gear, camera gear, and various other necessities.

"Long," I say as Stacey pulls me into a hug. She texted me as soon as she was awake from working her night shift. By that point it was almost noon, and Dylan and I had all morning to sleep in after staying out to stargaze for most of the night. Once we got Stacey's text, it took us about fifteen minutes to get to her apartment, but I'd guess she's already had her first cup of coffee based on her energy level. Or perhaps this is how she always is in the mornings. As I walk with my duffel bag of clothes, it occurs to me how little I know Stacey.

"Your room is all cleared out and ready for you. Want me to carry anything?"

I hand her my duffel bag and sling my heavier camera bag over my shoulder. Dylan follows close behind with my suitcase, which has 90 percent of my belongings shoved inside.

Stacey's apartment complex is a lot bigger than Dylan's, with multiple buildings stretched across the property and parking spaces staggered throughout. Each apartment has its own front door, but all the buildings are built close together, mirror images of one another. Stacey's apartment is on the third floor, making hauling everything up the stairs feel a bit more challenging.

"Here it is!" Stacey says, opening the door for me and letting me in. Her apartment is much bigger than Dylan's and even a little bigger than Lori's. The front door opens into the living room as well, but the space is big enough for a large L-shaped couch. Off to the right is the dining table and a kitchen with an island and stools. The entire kitchen looks brand-new, like it was recently remodeled. Framed photos and decorations hang on the walls, giving the apartment a cozy lived-in feel that Dylan's apartment lacks.

"The bathroom and bedrooms are down this hallway." She leads the way, showing me to the bathroom at the end of the hall. "My only request is to wait to shower until I'm awake from working the night before. The pipes are loud."

"Sounds good to me."

"This is my room." She points her thumb to the room at her back. Still standing in the hall, I can see photos scattered across her walls, all framed neatly and arranged symmetrically. Her bedspread is a floral purple pattern, though the bed is still unmade. Her room is perfectly clean and decorated otherwise, looking like something straight out of an IKEA showroom.

"And this is your room." She walks ahead of me, leading

me into a room that has nothing other than a mattress, a bed frame, and an old side table. "I didn't know if you had one or not, but this is my old full-size bed. I upgraded to a queen a couple months ago, so this is all yours if you want it."

"That's perfect actually," I say, realizing I forgot I'd need something to sleep on that isn't the mattress in the bus. I bought a few things when Lori and I shared a dorm room, and then the apartment, but I left it all with Lori, assuming travel would be easier if I bought the things I needed once I got here. Looking at the empty room and knowing I have nothing to fill it with, I have a small bit of regret.

Dylan and Stacey help me unpack my bags, though it doesn't take long. There's a drawer in the nightstand where I'm able to put some things, but other than that, all I can do is hang a few outfits in my closet. Stacey offers me storage areas around the apartment, like a shelf and drawers in the bathroom, but otherwise all my things stay in my suitcase.

Living minimally in a bus makes sense — is even required — but in an apartment where everything I own fits in a few bags? It's a little barren.

"Might need to go furniture shopping," I say, standing at the foot of my bed and eyeing how empty the room is.

"We'll get you settled in before you know it," Dylan says, giving me a quick hug from the side. "I have to head out and meet up with Trent. Do you need help with anything else before I go?"

I shake my head. "All set for now."

"I'll call you later," he says, leaning forward to kiss me

quickly before leaving. Once Dylan's gone, the room feels even emptier, if that's possible. I pull my laptop out and begin to get some work done, sorting through photos that I hope I can sell at Snapshot Café. That's part of the reason I'm here after all. Of course, a huge part is to see Dylan again and to give our relationship a real try, but it feels like if I want to launch my career as a photographer, this is the place to be.

A couple hours later, the sound of pots and pans coming from the kitchen pulls me from my focus, and I wander out to find Stacey cooking dinner.

"Need an extra set of hands?" I offer.

Stacey lifts her head from the cutting board full of raw chicken. "Sure! I wanted to make some pasta on the side if you want to get that going." She nods to a box of pasta sitting on the counter.

"Which one's the pantry?"

"All the cabinets to the right of the fridge."

Stacey finishes cutting the chicken and places it in a baking dish before putting it in the oven.

"Charlotte says you have a wedding this weekend," Stacey says.

"Yeah, it's at some old church about an hour away. It's my first wedding as a photographer, so we'll see how it goes." I told Charlotte when I first talked to her, but she didn't seem too concerned. She'd been looking to find someone to work as a second shooter while keeping to a budget, and I guess I fit the bill. She loved all the portrait work I've done in the past, and with the hours I've spent on YouTube researching wedding photography, I feel at least mildly prepared.

"I'm sure you'll do fine. Charlotte will show you the ropes."

After we eat dinner, I offer to clean up. Stacey lingers in the kitchen while I clean, but she doesn't say anything. Our living situation is odd. We aren't strangers, but it would be hard to say we're friends — at least close friends. When we find something to talk about, the conversation comes easy, but the second we've overstretched a topic, we're both left sitting in uncomfortable silence.

"I'm going to my room if you need me," she says, dismissing herself.

I feel more at ease once she's gone and we're both left in our own spaces, not having to worry about small talk. It will be easier in time, I'm sure. Stacey was eager when I first arrived, but I could tell as the day went on that she realized I wasn't a lifelong friend moving in — I'm mostly a stranger to her. When I went home to New Hampshire, it was Dylan I stayed in touch with, not Stacey.

After I finish the dishes, I retreat to my room. I almost wish it were smaller so the place wouldn't feel so empty. There's a faint echo in the room, and I make a mental note to myself to at least buy curtains.

I'm watching a video on my laptop when Dylan calls.

"Hello?" I say, cringing a little at the echo the room creates.

"Stacey drive you insane yet?"

I laugh, keeping my voice down. "Not yet. She made me dinner though."

"So, I was wondering . . ." He has a mischievous tone. "I

wanted to hike this weekend, and I was hoping I'd find someone to come with me."

I frown. "I have a wedding."

"What day?" he asks, his voice still eager.

"Saturday. We're booked for six hours. I probably won't be back until eight."

"What about Sunday?"

I sigh. Hikes usually mean waking up early, and waking up early means going to bed early. "Where?" I ask, hoping it's something small and local.

"Longs Peak. It's on my list. I haven't hiked it yet, and trust me, the views will be better than anything you've seen in New Hampshire."

I smile despite myself. "What time?"

"Four a.m. start?" His voice is persuasive. He's seen the chink in my armor, and he's going for it.

I frown, wondering if that'll be enough time for me to relax and get ready to hike after the wedding. "We can't do a later start?"

"There are storms in the late-afternoon forecast. Better safe than sorry."

"If there are storms, maybe we'll wait for another time."

"There are always storms," he says, though I know that's not true at all. "We'll be fine, I promise."

I eye my hiking pack sitting in the corner of the room. Dylan sent me links to the hiking trail for Longs Peak when I was in New Hampshire. He told me all about it, saying it was the next peak he was going to cross off his list.

I sigh, realizing I don't want to turn him down. "Can we camp out in the parking lot the night before so I can sleep in just a little longer?"

"Come to my place after the wedding, and I'll drive us there."

I can already imagine the wide grin on his face through the phone.

CHAPTER 5

the next morning I drive to Snapshot Café. Though it's no longer the weekend, the parking lot still manages to be half-full, and through the window I can see tables overcrowded with people. When I walk through the door, the scent of maple syrup fills the room, and there's a quiet murmur of voices and dining ware.

The walls are covered in framed photographs, each image different and unique. At the edge of each frame is a small sticker stating the price of the photo. Photographers from the area bring their photos here to be sold, and my photo was one of them. It's impossible to tell where my photo was before it was sold because the walls are already full again, not an inch of space to spare.

I called Riley, the owner of the café, before I left New Hampshire. She told me I could bring more prints in when my photo first sold, but that was weeks ago. I hope there's still space for my work to hang.

"Table for one?" the hostess asks me when I linger in the doorway.

"Uh, no." I shift and pull a large tote bag off my shoulder. Inside the bag are three more prints I've brought to be sold. "I'm a photographer. I'm here to pick up my check and drop off more prints."

"Oh!" The girl's face lights up when she notices my bag. "I'll go get Riley."

The girl disappears into the diner, and I'm left to scan the walls. There are a few photos I recognize from the last time I was here, but most of them look unfamiliar. With so many photos coating the walls, it would be near impossible to memorize every image.

"Marly, you're back!" Riley comes out from nowhere, her short blonde hair curled and tucked behind her ear almost exactly as the last time I saw her.

"I have more photos," I say, gesturing to the bag slung over my shoulder.

"Come to my office." She motions for me to follow.

Her office is past the kitchen in the back of the building, and the room is huge, the walls lined with shelves. However, instead of keeping books on the shelves, she's filled them with frames, filed and stored so all you can see are the edges of the frames, not the photos. The shelves are labeled, but other than that, the prints and frames are in varying colors and sizes.

"Welcome to our art collection," Riley says. She makes her way over to one of the shelves that still has some space on it. A label on the shelf has my name on it in small print. "What've you got for me today?"

I pull the bag off my shoulder and hand her the frames one

by one. She looks them over as she smiles.

All the photos are from New Hampshire. They're older photos, taken when my parents were still alive, but they're some of my favorites. The first image is Sabbaday Falls, the water pouring over mossy rocks like silk. The second image is the sunrise from The Horn, a mountain my dad and I backpacked. And finally, the last photo is of Mount Washington, as seen from the summit of Mount Jackson. My dad and I did the winter hike together, and when we got to the summit, we had a perfect view of Mount Washington. There was a fresh layer of snow covering everything, but the sky was a perfectly clear blue.

"Are all of these from New Hampshire?" Riley asks, sifting through the images.

"Yeah, a few favorites." The last time I talked to Riley on the phone, we chatted for a long time about where I'm from and how I ended up on my road trip. I only called Riley twice while I was in New Hampshire, but I learned quickly she loves to talk. The first time I called it was to get more details on the types of photos she was looking for. About forty-five minutes later, the call ended, and I'd heard at least six stories of photographers who come to her café to sell prints. It was like she memorized each photo that came through the door.

"I'll add these to the lineup." She puts them on the shelf with my name written on it. "You said you went on a road trip too, right? That's the last time you were in Colorado?"

"Yeah," I say. Riley moves over to a tiny desk in the corner of the room and begins rifling through a drawer and pulling out an envelope.

"Did you get any good photos out of it?"

"I did. A lot of good ones from Yellowstone especially."

Her face perks up, interest piqued. "Can you bring some in next time? Until then, this is all yours."

She hands over the envelope, my check inside.

"Yeah, of course," I say, already mentally sorting through which photos would be worthy of printing.

She turns to my photos on the shelf and pulls out the one of the sunrise on The Horn. "Now, what's the story behind this one?" she says.

I smile, knowing it may be a while until I'm able to get out the door.

§

The next few days I spend mornings cataloging photos, sorting out potential prints for Snapshot Café. I come up with a long list of photos but only print five of my favorites, all from the road trip over the summer. Later in the week I drop off the prints, and Riley eagerly takes them.

"Gorgeous," Riley murmurs, her eyes cast on a print from my time at Clingmans Dome. Dylan and I had woken up early to catch the sunrise as it peeked over the Smoky Mountains. Riley moves to add the photos to my shelf, and it looks like two of the ones I brought in earlier in the week are already gone.

"Are the other photos hanging already?" I ask, gesturing to my shelf. I didn't search for my photos when I walked through the café. I assumed it would take longer for a spot on the wall to open up for me. The café is especially busy today, and I can tell this visit will be a quick one, because every now and then a waiter pokes her head into the office looking for Riley, but she keeps her attention on the photos.

Riley smiles. "One sold, one hanging."

"Oh, wow," I say, a little bewildered. It's been less than a week, and a print has already sold.

"Employees get first dibs on all the photos before we hang them. One of our waiters is a sucker for waterfalls and snatched the photo up before anyone else could." She turns to add the new prints to my shelf. "We do inventory of sales at the end of the month, so you won't be able to get the check until then, but if things keep going the way they are, you'll have more money to pick up than for just one print."

I smile, and Riley leads me out through the crowded café. As we walk, I can see my print of Mount Washington hanging high up over one of the tables, the bright white a stark contrast against the colorful beach sunset photo it's placed next to.

"I forgot to mention it last time you were here, but bring your business card next time. Customers love to come to us when they're looking to hire someone for private photo sessions."

"Oh, I don't have a card," I say, the words coming out automatically.

"Well, if you get one, let us know," she says with a wink before turning away and getting lost in the business of the café.

On the drive back to Stacey's apartment, I toy with the idea of taking on individual clients for portrait sessions. Before my parents died, it seemed like I had almost every weekend filled with some sort of photography gig. I never got around to making a business card because I didn't need to; I had an endless amount of people being referred to me by clients.

Now it's been over a year since I've worked one-on-one with clients. I know it would be simple to step back into the swing of photography, but it feels wrong somehow. In my head, there's a clear before and after. Before my parents died, I was in school taking photos every weekend with clients. After my parents died, I went on a road trip and began selling stock photos and prints. After my parents died, I went to Colorado. A fresh start. A clear *after*. And I'm not sure if I want my after to include something from my old life. At least not yet.

I video chat with Lori in the mornings before she has to leave to go to class. In a way, it's just like when we shared the dorm together for that brief period of time before my parents died. We may live hundreds of miles apart, but we still manage to fit in an hour or two of talking to each other every morning.

Lori insists I decorate my room or at least buy cheap used furniture somewhere, but I'm never in the apartment anyway. The only time I'm in the apartment is when I call Lori for our morning check-ins. In the few days I've been here, I've made it a habit to bring my laptop to the local coffee shop and work there. Then once I'm done for the day, I head to Dylan's place to spend the evening with him after he finishes work. Stacey's apartment is mostly a place to sleep. Even the bus feels more like a home base than my empty bedroom does.

"Got your bag packed for Sunday?" Dylan asks while we're watching a movie together on Friday night, a pizza laid out on the coffee table in front of us.

"Good to go!" I say. It didn't take long for me to pack for the hike since half my belongings are still in bags.

"What about the wedding? Nervous?"

I nod, easing back into the couch. "I'm assigned to the groom and candid photos for the day, so it shouldn't be so bad, but I don't really know what to expect besides constantly taking photos."

"I'm sure you'll be fine," he says, pulling me closer to his side.

"How's the weather looking Sunday? Is there still a storm in the afternoon?"

"I haven't checked yet." He moves to reach for the phone in his pocket. I wait while he pulls up the website we use to check the forecast for Longs Peak. He frowns.

"What?" I ask, sitting up so I can see.

"Freezing rain is predicted to start at two o'clock, with the possibility of snow in the afternoon," he says, letting out a disappointed sigh.

"We can't hike in that," I say.

Dylan is silent next to me, trying to pull up another website for a more detailed forecast. "If it does snow, it's the first of the season, so it won't be much. The real storm won't start until five at the earliest. We'll be showered, clean, and sitting back on this couch again by then." He's still looking at his phone as he talks.

I eye him, cocking one brow. "You want to go out in that? I don't think you want to deal with slippery rocks on this type of hike."

He looks at me, and the disappointment is palpable.

"I don't want to risk it," I say, sinking back into the couch, leaning my head on his shoulder. He lets out a low sigh, kissing the top of my head before turning his gaze back to the TV. The conversation ends there, the evening continuing without argument.

CHAPTER 6

during the wedding, I go through two SD cards and three batteries. From the moment I meet the groom until the last minute of my and Charlotte's scheduled time, I don't stop taking photos. Charlotte assured me when we got to the venue that there was nothing to worry about. The groom is always the easy one. And he was. I told him and the groomsmen where to stand and how to pose, and it was as simple as that. The men were tossing jokes back and forth, pulling their focus from the task at hand, but I quickly learned to work with them, taking photos even when they didn't realize it.

Lucky for me, there were only four groomsmen and the groom. They were a rowdy bunch, but they listened well once they got their fix of jokes.

I must have taken at least one hundred photos before the wedding had even started. The bride had emailed Charlotte a shot list, and I copied it onto my phone to keep track of which shots I was responsible for. The bride didn't have a lot of requests for the men, but Charlotte had her hands full with the bridal party and the copious number of poses they wanted to try.

A couple minutes into the ceremony, I could tell Charlotte and I had found our stride. She stood on the opposite side of the aisle, taking photos from every angle while also ensuring we didn't step into each other's shots. When the ceremony ended, we both glanced at each other, and Charlotte gave me a quick thumbs-up.

"How'd you do?" she asks me while the guests make their way back to their cars; they'll drive to the next location for the reception.

"Good," I say, switching out a full SD card for an empty one.

The next thing I know, Charlotte is rounding everyone up for the family photos. I hold my phone out for Charlotte so she can see the list of names, and she asks for the appropriate groupings to gather in front.

Charlotte takes most of the formal photos while I help her keep track of who is who and which photos we haven't taken yet. Within a couple minutes, we've finished with formals, and the extended family members leave to enjoy cocktail hour.

We have fifteen more minutes with the wedding party for photos, and we go through them quickly before we're left with just the bride and groom.

"I've got this," Charlotte says. "Head over to the reception to start getting candids. The hardest part of the day is over." She smiles at me before pointing the bride and groom where to stand.

The rest of the night moves in a blur. Between the groups of people and the music, I lose track of time, taking photo after photo. It isn't until Charlotte taps me on the shoulder that I realize we're done for the day.

"So what did you think?" Charlotte asks as we walk back to our cars.

"I don't think I've ever experienced something like that before." I shake my head as we walk. I pull the last SD card out of my camera and put it in a small plastic bag before handing it over to Charlotte. From here, my job is done. Charlotte will sort through the photos, edit them, and send them off to the bride and groom.

The entire day feels like one long, hazy event. When I took photos one-on-one in high school, it felt easy. Simple. Photographing weddings feels like something I'll need a couple days to recover from.

"Yeah, weddings are a lot of fun, but they're tiring. I'll probably sleep for the next twelve hours so I can be at least a little refreshed before the hours of photo editing begin." She holds up the plastic bag with my SD cards before adding it to her camera bag.

I get back to the apartment later that night, wondering if I'm cut out for the job of being a wedding photographer. Sure, I can do it, but what's the point if all it does is make my head spin?

When I finally get into bed that night, I fall asleep almost immediately. Waking up the next morning, I can hear Stacey out in the kitchen making breakfast.

I peel myself out of bed and walk into the kitchen. Stacey's back is to me as she flips a pancake on the pan.

"Need any help?" I ask. At the sound of my voice, she jumps

and lets out a little yelp.

She turns quickly, holding the plastic spatula up toward me like a weapon. When she sees it's me, she relaxes a little, dropping the spatula onto the counter.

"Oh my god, I didn't know you were still here." She lets out a nervous laugh. "I thought you were hiking with Dylan today?"

"No, it's supposed to start raining soon," I say, reaching into the cabinet to grab a coffee mug.

"What do you mean?" Stacey asks.

"The forecast had rain and snow in the higher elevations." I shrug, pouring myself a mug of coffee from the pot Stacey already started. When I glance over at her, she pulls her pan off the stove and goes to her bedroom without a word.

"Stacey?" I say, following behind her.

She opens her laptop on her desk and pulls up a website. A map loads onto the page, and a single point pings on the screen. It's a typographic map, the same kind I use when I'm hiking to see how steep the elevation is on a trail.

"What is that?" I ask, looking over her shoulder. But I already know what it is, because it's the same GPS system my mom used when she wanted to check in on me and my dad when we were hiking. She made us purchase one of the expensive GPS devices in case of emergencies, so she could always check our location.

"Dylan still went on the hike. I didn't know he went without you. He didn't tell me about the rain," she says, zooming in on his locator beacon. "This was his location ten minutes ago."

She zooms in until we can see the location better. All along the trail are little dots signifying when his GPS locator went off to pinpoint his spot. They wind all the way up the trail for seven miles, right to the summit of Longs Peak. There are more dots signifying he's already started to descend and is on his way back.

"He wasn't supposed to go without me," I say, stunned.

"Well, Dylan isn't exactly known for his ability to sit back and relax." She runs her mouse over his locations until she reaches where the trail starts. A number pops up reading 2:53 a.m.

"He left the trailhead at 2:53 a.m. Seems like he's been keeping up a pretty good pace." She hovers her mouse over all the dots on the map, making note of the times.

"The plan was originally to start at four o'clock. Maybe he wanted to play it safe and start even earlier because of the weather," I say, mostly talking to myself.

I pull my phone out and dial his number quickly, my eyes fixed on Stacey's computer screen. She scrolls back to his most recent location and reloads the screen. Another locator beacon pops up on the screen, showing his newest pinpoint.

"He's on his way down," she says, pointing to the beacon on the screen. She lets out a small huff of frustration before closing her laptop. "He'll be fine. I'm just annoyed he didn't tell me he was going solo."

My phone continues to ring, but he doesn't pick up. I shove the phone into my pocket, trying to stop myself from panicking. Dylan's done plenty of solo hikes. I remind myself that this one should be no different, but a pit forms in my stomach, and I can't push it away.

"Why would he go without me?"

Stacey turns and gets up from her desk. "I'm sure he'll

be fine. He goes hiking alone all the time when he can't find someone to go with. I mean, since you've been in New Hampshire, I think he's hiked four peaks solo." She thinks about it and then corrects herself. "No, I think it's five. He's gone hiking almost every weekend while he's been waiting for you to make the drive back here."

"Every weekend?" I ask, my hand still clutching my phone.

Stacey shrugs. "He can't hold still. He always has to keep moving."

I knew Dylan had gone on at least one hike in the weeks I was away, but only because he sent me photos. But it was just one set of photos from his hike up Mount Princeton. There were four other hikes he didn't tell me about?

Stacey begins to walk away. Whatever worries she had before are now gone since seeing his locator beacon update.

I pull out my phone again, this time opening the website I use to see the forecast for mountain peaks. I type in Longs Peak and wait for it to load. The temperature is estimated to be forty-two degrees with winds of thirty miles per hour. The rain hasn't started, but it's supposed to start sooner than planned, with the temperature dropping as the day goes on. I try to let myself relax, knowing it's not raining as of right now. But how long until it starts? Will he be off the exposed part of the trail by then?

I try to think back to the many times I looked at the trail details with Dylan. Most of the trail is exposed. Half the hikes in Colorado are exposed, the elevation too high to allow trees to grow, making the terrain all the more dangerous during storms because there's nowhere to hide.

"What do we do?" I ask, walking out to the kitchen, where Stacey has gone back to making pancakes.

"Nothing." Stacey shrugs, unbothered. "He's not injured. His GPS is still pinging, and it should update us on his location every ten minutes or so. He turns his phone on airplane mode when he hikes to conserve the battery, so no point in texting him."

Stacey watches me, but she must see that her words do nothing to soothe me. She reaches over the counter and writes something on a sticky note before handing it to me.

"Here's the website you can go to and his GPS number to track him. Just keep an eye on his pace and make sure he never stops for too long. He can send an SOS signal if he needs to, and it sends a text to his emergency contacts that he needs help. But he's fine. I promise. This is just Dylan doing his weekly hike. When he gets back, we can yell at him for not giving us the full details."

I grip the sticky note and grab the bus keys from the hook on the wall.

"Where are you going?" Stacey asks, following me.

"To the trailhead parking lot. I'll start hiking and meet him on his way down." I grab my hiking bag off the floor by the front door, where I left it Friday night when I thought I was still going on the hike.

"Marly, you can't go hiking alone," Stacey says, stepping in front of the door to block my way.

"Why? If Dylan can hike solo, so can I." I wait for her to move out of my way.

"Dylan knows these mountains and has more experience

solo hiking in Colorado, whether I endorse his solo hiking or not. If I let you go after him, I'll have two solo hikers, and Dylan would kill me if I let you go alone. Besides, Dylan has hiked thirty-five of the 14ers, and you've hiked one. If he's in danger hiking alone, then it's too late to do anything about it, but I'm not going to let you go out there by yourself too."

"Then come with me," I offer, pulling my bag onto my back, my impatience growing.

"Are you kidding me? I know my limit, Marly, and Longs Peak far exceeds my limit. The trail Dylan's on now covers more than five thousand feet of elevation gain, not to mention the trail is fourteen miles with freezing rain on the way. If we go out there, we'll need to be rescued next."

I feel myself waver, and I drop the bag. "Then at least let me go to the trailhead so I can wait for him in the parking lot. The drive there will give me something to do while I wait."

Stacey watches me, perhaps wondering whether or not she can trust that I won't go running off into the woods. With a dejected sigh, she takes a small step to the side so I can open the door.

"Just wait in the parking lot. And when he finally gets back, be sure to yell at him for not letting any of us know he was planning to hike solo."

I grip my keys in my hand as I open the door. "Oh, I'll let him know."

CHAPTER 7

I've been driving for an hour, and I'm only halfway to the trailhead for Longs Peak. I should be closer, but every half hour I pull off to the side of the road to open the website for Dylan's GPS to check his location to know he's okay and still moving. His pace is slowing down as he goes downhill, which is unusual for him, but I don't let myself think about it too much. The closer to the bottom he gets, the easier—and safer—his hike will be. But the clouds in the sky are growing darker, and small raindrops start to fall onto my windshield. I've been telling myself I'm overreacting, but as soon as the rain shows up, panic kicks in. This drive feels all too familiar to the drive I made to see my parents in the hospital.

Not again, I dare to scream in my mind over and over as I drive. I attempt to push the thoughts away, thinking if I ignore the possibility, it can't happen. Not again.

I ease the worry away, remembering how I've hiked in the rain before and walked away without any injuries, but I can't ignore the anxiety bubbling to the surface. I remind myself over and over that I'm being irrational. Driving to the trailhead gives me something to do to pass the time at the least.

I pull off to the side of the road for the third time. I load up the map on my phone, and this time his locator beacon is to the side of the trail slightly — enough that maybe the satellite is just off — but it makes the pit of worry in my stomach grow.

"Deep breath," I say to myself. He hasn't signaled that he needs help, so he's probably fine. It's just an error on the GPS. As long as he keeps moving, it means he's fine. Before I know it, he'll be back below tree line.

I tuck my phone away and get back out on the highway. The rain begins to fall harder as I drive, coating the roads and cars in front of me. I'm only driving for about ten minutes before I pull off at another exit and load up my phone again, hoping when the screen loads it will show him back on the trail.

When his locator beacon loads, it's in the same spot. The breath exits from my lungs, and I remind myself to think before jumping to conclusions. Maybe it's the same locator beacon and I pulled over too soon for his location to update again. I tap on the beacon to display the time: one minute ago. I zoom in on his location, and that's when I see two locator beacons side by side, which means he hasn't moved in the past ten minutes. Maybe longer.

I dig into my glove box and find a clean napkin I stuffed in there from my last fast-food run and fish out an old pen. I write down his GPS coordinates and the time. According to the map, he made it past the Boulderfield campsite, which is a flat portion of trail before it zigzags to lessen the steep descent that brings you back down to tree line. He's about nine and a half miles into his hike, with five miles left to go. I write as much information down as I can about his exact location before I start dialing Stacey's number.

"Hello?" she answers.

"I've been looking at Dylan's GPS, and he hasn't moved in the past ten minutes." I try to keep myself calm, needing Stacey's reassurance so she can talk me out of my panic.

I hear rustling on the other end of the line as she pulls up his location online. "He's probably just taking a break to eat or something. I'm sure he's fine."

"It's raining, and he's off-trail," I say, voicing the words out loud to see if my worry is valid.

"Hold on," she says. I hear her move again and then the faint noise of her typing on her computer. "He's right next to the trail. He probably moved to the side to take his break. Just give him a couple minutes. There's nothing to worry about."

I let out a shaky breath, trying to convince myself that she's right. Maybe all this is just because I'm usually the one on the hike, not the one left behind to worry.

"Okay," I say, urging myself to calm down.

"Are you still on your way to the trailhead?"

"Yeah, I pull over every now and then to check on his location though."

"Okay, just keep driving. I'll check his location every few minutes, and I'll call back if he doesn't get going soon."

"Okay, sounds good." I sit up straighter in the seat and imagine Dylan sitting on some rock somewhere just grabbing a bite to eat. That's all this is. "I'll text you when I get there."

"Bye," Stacey says, and then I'm left to sit in silence.

I spend the rest of the car ride promising myself I won't pull off to the side of the road again to check on him. I turn my radio on, blasting some of my favorite songs, but it doesn't do much to distract me. The rain only falls harder, and all I can think about is how much more slippery the trail will be in the rain, regardless of whether he's below tree line or not.

It feels like an hour later when Stacey calls me, but when I check the time, it's only been another fifteen minutes.

"Hello?" I say, reminding myself to think positive.

"I just got an SOS from his GPS. I called search and rescue, and they're on their way. They have his location, and they're going to hike up to retrieve him." Stacey's words come out in a rush, and I slow my car down, letting the others on the highway speed past me.

"What?" is all I can say as I grip the steering wheel. My mind starts reeling, the worst-case scenario jutting forward, and then the thoughts begin again. *Not again.*

"I don't know the details, just that he signaled that he needs help."

"They can't bring in a helicopter? He's still above tree line. That would be the fastest way."

"Not in this weather. They have to hike up."

I keep my breath even and focus on the road. It feels like the world tilts at odd angles, and I pull off to the side of the highway. Cars rush past me, the movement shaking the bus as they drive by. Water comes down in sheets, filling the bus with noise, so I have to hold my phone close to my ear to hear Stacey.

"It will take hours to reach him," I say. Panic is nipping at my back.

"I know." Stacey hesitates. "I have to go. Someone from the rescue team is supposed to call me soon. I'll meet you in the parking lot, okay?"

"Okay," I whisper. There's a soft click, and Stacey hangs up. I sit in white noise as the rain pelts the roof of the bus. I count to ten, trying to ignore how my hands are shaking, and put the bus back into drive.

I merge onto the highway and push the fear away. For now, all I can do is drive. I don't give myself permission to worry. I don't let myself wonder or ask what could have happened. Instead, I drive, urging myself not to speed. The faster I get there, the longer I'll have to wait without answers.

An hour later, I pull into the parking lot, flashing lights making it clear I've found the right place. Rain is still coming down, though not as much as it was when I got the call from Stacey. The clouds are dark as they hover over us.

There's an ambulance, a cop car, a handful of national forest vehicles, and a few dozen other vehicles in the parking lot. A group of hikers are on the edge of all the commotion, standing at their cars, glancing over to the flashing lights. A few of them are pulling their backpacks off and stuffing them into their cars, but they linger and stare despite the falling rain.

I park near them and jump out.

"Hey," I say as I jog over. One woman in the group glances over and waves. "Did you guys just get back from hiking Longs Peak?"

"We were hiking Chasm Lake," a man in the group says, his eyes lingering on the commotion a few feet away from us.

I look toward the first responders. There're only four people, and most of them are talking on their radios.

"My boyfriend is hiking Longs Peak, and he put out an SOS signal from his GPS," I say.

The woman standing closest to me goes soft as she glances at the ambulance, probably assuming the worst.

"We hiked Longs Peak Trail and saw the search and rescue team hike up with a stretcher," she says.

I perk up a bit. "How long ago was that?"

"Maybe when we were three miles or so away from the trailhead? They were running up. There were six people there to help. They didn't seem bothered by the rain. We were just trying to get out of there as quickly as possible without tripping."

"Okay, thank you," I say, turning away from the group.

"I hope he's okay," the woman says to my back as I head toward the bus.

I spend the next hour talking to the search and rescue team waiting at the trailhead. They keep me as updated as possible, but it doesn't take long for me to realize they only know as much as I do, which isn't much. We know Dylan's location and when he stopped moving, but that's about all we know. I continue to load the GPS signal, but it never moves.

Despite the rain, we're all standing outside our cars. A few people have umbrellas, but I duck in and out of the bus, refusing to hold still, my clothes getting soaked. At some point it occurs to me I'm cold, but when I start pacing in the rain, the thought is forgotten.

"Excuse me, can I talk to someone? My son is the missing hiker," a woman says after barreling out of her car. She's visibly shaken as she makes her way over, and one of the police officers meets her halfway, guiding her to a canopy tent they set up next to the ambulance.

The woman's resemblance to Dylan is obvious. She has the same curly brown hair, but her face is rounder and softer, like Stacey's.

"What's your name, miss?" the officer says.

"Janet Ellis. Dylan Ellis is my son. I spoke to someone on the phone on the way here."

"Yes, that was me. The rescue team is on their way to retrieve your son now. They're about a mile away. Once they locate him, we'll be able to give you more information about his injuries."

"I thought you knew his location?" she asks.

"We do. His location continues to update every ten minutes, and he hasn't moved since his SOS signal. Once our rescuers have eyes on him, they'll let me know."

"Mom!" a familiar voice shouts across the parking lot. I turn and see Stacey running out of her car. She goes straight to her mom, hugging her.

I step away, moving farther from the crowd now forming near the flashing lights. I pace near the entrance to the trailhead. The trees offer a little solace from the rain, but not much. I keep close enough to the police officer that I can hear his radio whenever an update comes through, but just barely over the sound of the rain. The air gets cooler as time goes by, and the rain shifts into sleet, covering the ground in slush.

"We're at Granite Pass now. EMTs are running ahead to see if they can spot him while the rest of us carry up the equipment," the muffled voice comes over the radio.

My ears perk up, and I pull out my phone. The map for the trail loads, and I scroll until I find Granite Pass. They're four and a half miles in now — less than a mile away from Dylan — but they're also about to encounter the steepest part of the trail.

"Marly!" a voice shouts, and I glance up to see Stacey running toward me, her mom watching from a distance.

Stacey wraps me in a hug, and I welcome it, now realizing how cold I became standing out here just waiting. My jacket is soaked through, but Stacey is mostly dry.

"They're at Granite Pass," I say, clinging to those words.

"I know," she says. "They'll have him soon." She pulls away and grabs me by the hand. "I guess if Dylan isn't going to introduce you, then I will. This is our mom." She waves at Janet, who gives me a quick kind smile despite looking panicked.

She wraps herself tighter in her thin jacket as she walks over to meet us, an umbrella in her left hand.

"Hi," I say, putting my hand out to shake. Her grip is soft and cold in my hand.

"Marly?" she asks, her voice a little uneven.

I nod.

"Not the best way to meet, I know," Stacey says, voicing the same thing we're probably all thinking.

"Stacey says you were supposed to go with Dylan on this

hike today?" she asks.

"I didn't trust the weather," I say, wondering how soaked I am. Dylan's mom had the sense enough to bring an umbrella.

"Dylan didn't tell her he planned on going without her," Stacey chimes in.

Janet nods, seeming unsurprised.

"You said he hikes solo all the time," I say.

"Apparently, even a storm doesn't sway him. He's gotten a little more daring in the past year or so since he broke his leg. He acts like he has something to prove," Stacey says, eyeing the police officer as he talks to the team on the other end of the radio.

"At least he was with his dad last year," Janet mumbles. She crosses her arms and rolls her eyes. I'm left to wonder what more there is to that story. Dylan mentioned once that he'd broken a leg winter hiking with his dad last year, but he said hiking Mount Elbert was the first 14er he'd hiked since his injury.

"We've got him. Looks like he took a nasty spill. His leg is pretty banged up. Can't put any weight on it, but I don't think it's broken. Arm looks dislocated. Working on rescue now."

Our heads dart up as the words come over the radio. I hear Janet's breath hitch as she stands there in silence. The three of us wander closer to the police, waiting to hear more.

"What does that mean?" Janet mumbles. When I glance over, she appears to be just on the edge of hysteria. Maybe hearing his status straight from the source isn't a good idea.

"They're going to put him on a gurney and carry him out," I say. If Dylan's GPS is correct, then he fell on the flatter part of the trail. Hiking Longs Peak is dangerous because of the Keyhole section. I saw photos online and felt dizzy just looking at the last assent you have to make to reach the summit. It's not for the faint of heart. So, why is it he got hurt on the less challenging part of the trail?

Stacey glances over to her mom, a line of worry creasing between her brows. Her mom is clutching herself, shivering, but I can't tell if it's out of fear or cold. "Marly, do you have anything in the bus to keep us warm while we wait?"

I try to think of everything I keep in the bus, but my blankets and clothes have been moved into the apartment.

"I think I can make us some hot cocoa," I offer, pointing toward the bus.

"Mom, you want to go with her?" Stacey asks.

Janet is hesitant, seeming torn between going with me and staying to listen to updates on her son.

"I'll let you know anything important," Stacey reassures her. Janet nods and walks over to the bus with me. We walk in silence, but as the sound of the radio softens in the distance, Janet seems to automatically calm, which I'm guessing is the real reason Stacey wanted her mom to go with me.

The table in the bus is already set up when we get there, and I motion for Janet to sit while I fish out my camping stove to heat up water. She relaxes into the seat so much that I contemplate moving the bus to park closer to the police so we can all sit and get some solace from the rain.

I'm waiting for the water to boil when I glance over at Stacey as she stands with her lone umbrella. She's watching us with a worried look on her face. I step out of the bus, about to cross the parking lot to talk to her, but she shakes her head no, signaling for me to stay put for now. Stacey's starting to pace, the worry evident while we wait in the bus, but Janet seems distracted, watching as the water rolls to a boil in front of her.

I pull some cups out of one of the cupboards and pour us each a mug before scooping cocoa mix into each one. By the time the cocoa is made and we walk back over to Stacey, it's been less than ten minutes, but there's a buzz of energy around everyone, especially the police.

"What'd they say?" Janet asks, gripping her cup.

"They have him strapped to a gurney, and they're carrying him down now. He'll be okay," Stacey says, taking the cup of cocoa I offer her.

"I'm going to go talk to them." Janet starts to walk toward one of the police officers, but Stacey puts out a hand to stop her.

"I already did. He has a dislocated arm, and his leg is in bad shape, but they won't know details until he gets to the hospital. Other than that, he's just really bruised up. He'll be okay."

"How long until he's off the mountain?"

Stacey shrugs, but the worry is still there on her face, even if she's trying to hide it.

"Three hours. Maybe more."

I stare out at what should be mountains, but all I see are dark clouds in the sky, blocking out any sort of view. I reassure myself that it's just three more hours. That's all I need to wait until I can see Dylan and know he's okay.

He'll be okay. At least that's what I promise myself.

CHaPteR 8

n o one talks. I move the bus closer to the ambulance and open the doors so we can all sit and listen to the radio as updates come in. There's not much to hear. The rescue team rarely has anything to say except to give their current location. At first, it's a relief to hear updates, but then when I look on the map to see where they are, it's always discouraging to see how little ground they've covered. Hikes down always take me the least amount of time. In fact, I usually make it a habit to nearly run down mountains. It's taking the rescuers much longer to hike down carrying Dylan on a stretcher than it did to hike up.

Stacey sits next to her mom at the table, staring off into space, her eyes sparking whenever the radio static turns on again. I'm in the front seat of the bus, my head resting back against the chair, trying to stop myself from looking at the map again and counting how many more miles.

"We're almost down to the smooth portion of the trail." The radio comes alive, and our heads turn.

"There's an ATV waiting for the handoff," the officer says to whoever's waiting on the other end.

Janet perks up, eyeing the entrance to the trail. "What do they mean?"

"When I first got here, they sent an ATV as far into the trail as they could go. They're going to drive him out once they meet up with the ATV," I say.

It's only a few minutes later that we hear static on the radio again, but the voice on the other end is different. "Loaded up and heading out."

"Does that mean he's on the ATV?" Janet asks, standing up from the table and walking out of the bus. Stacey follows her as she makes her way over to the entrance of the trailhead. As they walk, a police officer motions for them to follow him. The sleet has nearly stopped, leaving just a misting in the air.

I stay back, sitting in the bus, waiting for the minutes to pass by. I'm not sure how long I've been sitting alone before I hear an ATV off in the distance, but as soon as I do, I jump out of the bus.

Stacey and Janet are there standing at the sideline, waiting in anxious anticipation. The sound grows louder until the ATV is a bright highlight of orange in the span of green and brown of the forest. A gurney is strapped to the back of it. Janet breathes a huge sigh of relief as Dylan is pulled out of the woods and unloaded from the vehicle. I barely get a glimpse of him before a rush of people emerge around Dylan and unstrap him.

Everyone crowds around the ambulance until I can't make out what's going on. I'm lost in a sea of people, and all I can do is step back and hope I'm not in the way. My eyes search for Dylan, but when I find him, all I can see is blood.

I'm transported back to the hospital, walking into the room to see my parents, their bodies beaten, nearly unrecognizable. I collapse to the floor, gasping for air, crying until it feels like I can't breathe. I don't want to look at them, but I can't pull my eyes away. I know it's my parents in front of me, but all I see are strangers. They're someone else. These people have to be someone else.

Aunt Cora is the one holding me. She's talking, but I can't hear a word she says. I'm pushing her away, screaming, crying. I can't breathe.

I blink, but when I look up, it's Stacey who's holding me. Dylan is in the ambulance, and he glances over, frowning when I meet his eyes.

"He's fine, Marly," Stacey says.

I'm gripping Stacey, my eyes darting around. I'm gasping for air, and one of the EMTs makes his way over to us. Janet stands a couple feet away, her gaze worried, but it's me she's looking at, not Dylan.

"She okay?" the man says.

No one answers as all gazes turn to me. My heart is hammering out of my chest, and I have to take a few more breaths to remind myself where I am. I pull away from Stacey, realizing how tight my grip was on her.

I nod, too afraid to speak.

"Why don't you come sit down for a bit?" one of the EMTs says.

I glance over at Stacey, and she gives me a small nod. My body feels heavy as I make my way over to the tent and sit in one of the fold-up chairs. Stacey follows me, and someone hands me water and a granola bar. I take it, sinking into the chair. The ambulance pulls away, and Janet leaves to go to her car.

"You want me to drive you home in the bus?" Stacey asks.

I shake my head. "You have to drive your own car."

"I'll come get it tomorrow."

"It's fine," I say, trying to make myself sound surer than I really am. "I just need to sit for a bit. I'll meet you at the hospital."

She looks me over, opening her mouth like she's going to protest, but she doesn't.

"Call if you need me," she says with a weak smile.

I watch as she walks away, and before I know it, I'm alone, my mind reeling, left to wonder what just happened.

CHaPteR 9

I miss the call from the ER. I miss a lot of calls the day my parents died. I'm too busy hanging out with friends to notice my extended family trying to get in touch with me. When I finally answer the phone and my aunt tells me to come to the ER, I run out the door, Lori following close behind me.

"Marly, what's wrong?" She's putting her jacket on as she follows me into the stairwell of our dorm building. I could've taken the elevator but waiting for the steel doors to open feels like a lifetime.

"My parents got in an accident on the way here. My aunt called and said they're both in the ER."

It occurs to me that if I make one tiny misstep, I'll tumble down the stairs, but I'm beyond caring.

"Are they okay?" Lori follows close behind, and we both run out of the stairwell and into the lobby area.

"I don't know," I say, tears blurring my vision.

There are a few students hanging out in the lounge, and I feel the room go eerily quiet as we run through. I rifle through my purse, trying to find my keys.

"I'll drive," Lori says, taking the keys from my hand when I pull them out.

I don't have a chance to respond. Lori runs out ahead of me, and we both sprint out the door and across campus. My car is parked in the eastern lot for residents, a walk that normally takes me five or ten minutes. I remember being annoyed when they first assigned me a spot so far away from my building, but now annoyance is replaced with utter rage.

It's like one of those dreams where I'm trying to get somewhere, but no matter how hard I try, I never seem to get any closer to my destination.

But this isn't a dream, and everything about the drive feels like a nightmare.

Lori doesn't talk to me once we're in the car, her focus on the road. My eyes linger out the window, and I beg my mind not to focus on the worst-case scenario. I tell myself they're okay, because that's the only outcome I can live with. Somehow, I feel in my gut that they're gone, but I push it away, clinging to hope even though it's already slipped through my fingers.

It takes an hour and a half to get to the hospital, and no other phone calls come in. I clutch the phone in my hand, wondering if answering the phone would have made a difference. How long did I waste hanging out with my friends before it occurred to me to look at my phone? Or realize that my parents were supposed to arrive at my dorm by then?

We drive up to the ER, and Lori pulls the car up to the side of the building.

"I'll meet you in there once I find a parking spot."

I hold my breath, suddenly scared to walk through the double doors. I step out into the cold air, my breath fogging in front of me.

Once I step through the doors, there's a false sense of calm. A woman is sitting at the front desk, a phone held up to her ear. I take a few steps toward her, wondering how in the chaos of an ER the lobby can be so untouched.

"Marly."

I turn when I hear the voice, and Aunt Cora wraps me in a hug before I have a chance to say anything.

When she pulls away, her eyes are a bright, brilliant red, tears soaking her face. She won't look at me. Instead, her eyes roam around me, her hands gripping my shoulders.

"Are they okay?" I ask. My eyes flicker past Cora and out the door. I can see Lori in the parking lot, running toward the front entrance of the ER. "Can I go see them?"

Aunt Cora shakes her head before she finally looks at me. I can see the agony before I hear it in her voice, and that's when I realize she's not holding on to me for my comfort, but to hold herself together. When she does speak, I feel myself buckle and fall.

§

A horn honks, and I'm brought back to the present. The stop light is green and has been for who knows how long. I glance in my rearview mirror and see a man shaking his head impatiently. I put my foot on the gas, pulling forward through the intersection.

After half an hour sitting under the tent, the EMT who'd witnessed my breakdown felt comfortable enough to let me drive. By then, most of the rescue team had left, leaving only a small group behind to make sure I was okay.

It takes me longer than anticipated to drive to the hospital. I slow down, focusing on the present rather than letting my mind wander to the past. The memory was so clear, as if my parents had died yesterday. When I finally get to the ER, I find an open spot in the parking garage before taking slow, measured steps toward the entrance of the hospital. It feels like déjà vu as I walk, and I remind myself over and over this isn't the same. This is different. I saw Dylan. He was okay. And this isn't the same.

I can see Cora standing in front of me, teary-eyed, telling me my parents are dead.

"They didn't make it." Her words were soft, so soft, that I wasn't sure I heard her correctly. I refused to hear her. "I'm so sorry," she said over and over again, clutching me like I could bring them back. And then she fell to pieces. We both did.

I'm in a fog as I pass through the hospital doors. Dylan and his family are nowhere in sight.

I stumble to the front desk, forcing myself to push the memories away. The woman sitting at the desk is distracted when I first walk in, her eyes glued to the computer screen.

"I'm here to see my boyfriend, Dylan Ellis. He was in a hiking accident," I say, my words growing uneven. The woman on the other side of the desk gives me a soft smile and starts typing, pulling up his information.

"He's with a doctor now. It might be a while before he's able to see anyone."

I nod, trying to reassure myself that this is good. Hers aren't the same sad eyes Cora gave me when I asked if my parents were okay.

Dylan is fine. At least I tell myself that.

The woman points to a set of double doors off to my left. "There's a waiting area over there. Dylan's other family members are through those doors," she says.

I nod, aware of the shakiness of my steps as I walk. I push through the doors and see Stacey sitting in a corner of the room. She notices me almost as soon as I walk in. She makes quick strides across the room and brings me into a hug.

"I was about to call and make sure you were okay," she says. When she pulls away, I can see tears in her eyes, but she seems more relaxed than when I last saw her before Dylan came in on the ATV's stretcher.

"How is he?" I ask.

"They're doing X-rays now, but they think he has a bad sprain in his ankle. He had a dislocated shoulder, but they already popped it back into place." She looks me over as she talks, perhaps waiting for me to break down again.

"What about all the blood?" I say, trying to keep my voice even.

"Head wound. Nothing major. Just a few stitches. They don't seem to be concerned about it."

I nod, trying to find relief in the news, but all I can feel is sheer panic, like I'm still waiting for the ball to drop.

"Come and sit. My mom is with the doctors right now,"

Stacey says, ushering me to the corner where she's been sitting.

Just like that, we're waiting again. It's a different type of torture, to be standing by, having no way to help but to sit and wait.

Stacey is calmer than I am, seeming relieved to be in the ER now, whereas sitting here in this hospital feels worse than it did in the trailhead parking lot. Good news never comes to those waiting in a hospital ER. At least not for me.

"Did you call your dad?" I ask in an attempt to keep my mind from wandering.

Stacey freezes, taking her time to choose her next words. "I don't think Dylan would want me to do that."

I open my mouth to say something, then pause, waiting for her to elaborate further.

"Dylan hasn't spoken to our dad in over a year. They don't get along very well."

"Oh," I say, a little surprised. Dylan has never gone out of his way to talk about his dad. I only heard Dylan mention him once when he was telling me about how he had broken his leg hiking with his dad. I assumed he and his dad were close, but perhaps I only assumed that because that's the relationship my dad and I had.

Stacey chews on her lip, thinking. "Did Dylan tell you why he got hurt last time?"

"He slipped when he was hiking with his dad."

She nods, looking down at her phone in her hand as she speaks. "Our dad's always been jealous of our relationship with our grandpa. Dylan went hiking with Grandpa all the time, so our dad wanted to go hiking with Dylan. When Dylan and I were kids, our grandpa took us camping, fishing, skiing—you name it, we did it. Our dad, on the other hand, has always been MIA, since long before our parents divorced. That's why our grandpa stepped into our lives more and more, to fill the spots our dad was supposed to. That just made our dad pissed." She shrugs.

"He went hiking with Dylan. Isn't that a good thing? He was trying to be a good dad."

"It wasn't really like that," she admits. "It was more like he was trying to sabotage Dylan. Make him never want to hike again. He complained the whole way, and on the way down, he took off. Dylan says he *ran* down. And of course, Dylan was carrying all the gear in *his* bag. Our dad barely carried anything. Dylan kept up. He was in far better shape, that's for sure. But a heavy bag throws off your balance, and it only takes one slip to break a bone. It was in the winter, so hiking conditions weren't perfect, and it got foggy on the trail, so Dylan only hiked faster because he couldn't see our dad anymore. The faster he went, the sloppier he got. Dylan broke his leg because our dad was too busy running down the mountain and Dylan didn't want to lose sight of him in case he got hurt, which is ironic since Dylan was the one who got injured." She shakes her head, rolling her eyes.

"Then what happened?"

"Our dad thought he could use the entire thing as a 'teaching moment' and said Dylan's injury was a perfect example why he shouldn't be going hiking. All it did was teach Dylan why he doesn't need his dad in his life. As soon as his leg was healed, he was back on the mountains, and he hasn't been in contact with our dad since."

I'm about to ask another question, but Janet steps into the waiting room, her face tired but calm. "They said they can release him soon. They just want to observe him for a little longer," she says, coming to sit on the other side of Stacey.

"Which leg did it end up being?" Stacey asks.

"Nothing broken this time. But he messed up the left ankle pretty good," she says with a tiny laugh. "That boy is lucky to be alive." Relief floods her voice. "The team that rescued him said if he'd had the same fall farther back on the trail, he'd have been a goner. He shouldn't have even been out there if he knew a storm was coming."

In the next hour, Janet comes and goes, talking to nurses and doctors and signing paperwork. Eventually, Stacey goes to see Dylan, leaving me alone in the waiting room, sitting in my own anxious bubble. I'm not sure how much time has passed when Stacey comes back to the waiting room.

"Marly, come on," Stacey says, motioning for me to follow her down the hallway. As we walk, all I can hear is the sound of machines beeping and the rushed murmurs of nurses. When we're almost to the other end of the hallway, Stacey takes a left turn into a room. I follow, hesitant as I walk through the door. Dylan's face is the first thing I see. There're stitches and bruises on his forehead, but he looks like himself. He smiles when I step into the room, and his gaze scans me as if I'm the one who's been injured. When our eyes first meet, there's a hint of worry, but the longer he looks over me, the more relieved he seems.

I take a few more steps in, relieved to see just a cast on his foot and a spattering of bruises and scrapes. Otherwise, it's the same old Dylan. For the first time in hours, it feels like I'm able to take a full breath of air.

"Look who I found," Stacey says, ushering me in.

"Hey," he says, his voice rough. "You might have had the right idea skipping out on this one." He laughs in a quiet way, and a knot of tension loosens in my chest. I let out a deep sigh, realizing how badly I needed to hear his voice.

"Maybe take my advice next time," I say, walking closer to him. I pull up a chair near his bed to sit. "How are you feeling?"

He stretches out the arm that's not in a sling. "Like I fell off a cliff." He laughs.

Stacey is still standing in the corner, shaking her head. "I'm going to go find Mom."

We're left in silence. I stare at the sling and boot his ankle is in until my eyes wander to the stitches on his forehead. Dylan sits in the silence with me, his good hand reaching for me. I take his hand in mine. His skin is rough and covered in scrapes.

"Are you okay?" he asks me softly.

I almost want to laugh. Dylan is the one lying in the hospital — cast, stitches, and all — yet he's asking me if I'm okay.

"I'm fine," I say quietly.

"I saw you when they put me in the ambulance. I heard you scream and when I looked over, you were kneeling on the ground, and Stacey was holding on to you." His voice is low, a sound so soft that I'm almost unable to hear him.

The words feel like a knife. I'm not entirely sure what

happened back in the parking lot, but hearing it from someone else's perspective makes my breath catch.

"I'm fine," I repeat, the words feeling a little more unhinged.

"But—"

"I don't want to talk about it."

He gazes back at me, his eyes full of unspoken questions.

"What happened?" I ask, desperate to change the subject.

Dylan looks away from me, down at the cast on his foot. "I don't know. Everything was going perfectly. I mean, the entire hike getting to Longs Peak was amazing. It's an adrenaline rush to be up there. You look to the right, and all you can think is, 'Holy shit, I could die up here if I slip.' "

I cringe, and Dylan seems to notice, softening his tone.

"I did fine on the way up. The way down was a little trickier because of how steep it is, but I took my time. It started to rain a little, so I tried to get out of the steep portion as fast as possible. Then I got past the Keyhole, and I knew the worst was behind me. The trail flattens out, and you're just navigating the boulder field, but the rain started picking up. I didn't realize how tired I was until the adrenaline rush went away, and then the rain just made me move a lot slower than I wanted to. I must have slipped or something. I tried to catch myself, which is how I ended up with this." He points to his arm in a sling. "And then I landed badly, obviously." He points to his ankle. "I fell into some sort of crevice in the rocks. Nothing too bad, but I couldn't get out on my own because of my arm."

I nod and close my eyes, begging the panic to go away.

Dylan gives my hand a small squeeze. "I'm okay," he says.

I let out a sad, tired laugh. Dylan's in the ER bed, yet he's the one comforting me.

"I know," I say, hoping that now I will finally believe it enough to let the panic diminish.

I glance over at Dylan, and when our eyes meet, a smile lights his face. I want to reprimand him, but I can't.

"Why didn't you tell me you were still planning on hiking without me?" I ask. The words have been in the back of my mind since I discovered he'd gone alone.

Dylan glances away, looking at his casted leg rather than at me. It's a long moment before he speaks. "I didn't want you to tell me not to go."

I wait for him to say something else, to have a better reason, but it never comes. I want to ask more, like why he never told me about all the other hikes he did while I was in New Hampshire, but Stacey and Janet walk into the room, followed by the doctor. I let go of Dylan's hand, stepping out of the chair to get out of the way. They look at his charts while talking about medicine for his pain and when he needs to come back in to have his ankle looked at again. He'll also need physical therapy for his arm and ankle, and in the next few weeks the stitches will need to be removed as well. Janet takes it all in, writing it down in a tiny notebook that she pushes into her purse once she's done.

The hospital room feels small with all of us in here at once, and I almost take the opportunity to step out until Dylan stops me before I can.

"Marly, can you drive me back to my apartment?" he asks.

"Sweetie, why don't you stay with me in your old room?

There won't be any stairs to worry about, and I can make sure you get all your medicine," Janet says.

"I'll be fine," Dylan says quickly. "I'd rather sleep in my own bed anyway."

She thinks about it for a long moment. After everything, I'm sure she'd rather be right there with him to make sure he's okay, but there's no reason for him to be anywhere but home.

"Okay," she says, still unsure. "I'll go get your prescriptions so you can be discharged."

Janet slips out of the room, leaving Stacey standing beside Dylan.

"She's getting a wheelchair rental too," Stacey adds in a joking tone.

Dylan lets out a low laugh. He moves a little, trying to sit up more in bed, but he flinches and relaxes back into the mattress.

"By the looks of it, you may want the wheelchair. Dislocated shoulder means crutches aren't an option."

"I don't need a wheelchair," Dylan says, annoyance in his voice.

"You can't walk on your foot or put weight on your arm for at least a couple weeks."

"I'll be fine," he says, his voice firm.

Stacey shakes her head, a mix of dark humor and annoyance. "You know you could have died out there, right?"

Dylan looks away from her, refusing to meet her gaze.

"I mean, Marly had the good sense to know not to go hiking. Why didn't you?"

Stacey points at me, but Dylan keeps his eyes on Stacey.

"Relax, Stace. People get twisted ankles all the time from hiking."

"This is the second time in two years we've had to rescue your ass off a mountain. Who's to say next time you won't be as lucky?"

"So, what, you don't want me to go hiking at all? I suppose you'll give it up too, right? Don't want to be a hypocrite." He rolls his eyes.

"No, what I'm saying is learn to listen to your gut. If something feels dangerous and stupid, it probably is. When the forecast says rain, you take a rain check, not a challenge."

"It wasn't supposed to rain until later in the day."

"You know as well as I do that rain can come at any time, regardless of what the forecast says. What you did today was reckless."

"I didn't think it was reckless."

"Marly did!" Stacey says, gesturing toward me.

"Marly's not used to these mountains." He glances over to me, trying to say the words kindly, but they still sting.

"It's class-three hiking, for God's sake. Frankly, from what I've heard about that trail, I'm surprised it's not class four," Stacey shouts.

Dylan watches me, and I can tell he wants to say something, but he holds back. Hiking is categorized into five classes that define how challenging the terrain is. Class three usually involves scrambling up rocks, but without assistance from a rope.

In fact, I try to hike below class three because I've never been a fan of hiking trails that require climbing rocks. Class three is the last hiking level before you need rock climbing equipment to safely complete the trail.

"I just slipped. I was tired or something. But I'm okay now, and it won't happen again."

"Yeah, pretty sure that was the sentiment when you broke your leg too."

"You know that wasn't my fault!" he fires back quickly.

Stacey rolls her eyes and walks out of the room, clearly done with the conversation. Even though she's gone, the tension still lingers, and Dylan refuses to look up at me, his eyes trained on the boot on his leg.

I want to say something, to add on to what Stacey was already saying, but I keep to myself. The stillness in the room isn't broken until his mom steps back in with Stacey in tow.

"They said you can be discharged in the morning. We're going to go home, but I'll come by in the morning. I'll have your wheelchair rental ready. They said you can't use crutches because of your shoulder, so please be careful and let people help you in and out of the wheelchair."

"Sounds good," he says, voice flat, anger still present in his tone. His eyes never lift from his ankle.

Janet lets out a relieved huff of air and gives me a quick wave. "It was good meeting you, Marly." She walks away, Stacey following close behind until it's just me and Dylan. Once she's gone, Dylan drops his head back against the pillow and closes his eyes.

"You okay?" I ask.

He lets out a low laugh and flinches a little. "Ten bucks says

82

I wake up to at least half my body covered in bruises."

"They're already there," I say with a small laugh.

I reach for his hand, and a tiny smile creeps in at his lips. He opens his eyes and meets my gaze.

"I'm sorry I went without you," he whispers. For the first time, I see how tired and beat up he is. It makes me wonder how much of the conversation he had with Stacey was genuine or just him jumping to defend himself.

I suck in a breath, and thousands of words fly around in my mind, but I can't get myself to speak any of them. I want to be here with Dylan, but a part of me longs to run out the hospital doors and forget any of it happened.

"I'm just glad you're okay," I say, letting a light laugh coat my words, trying to brush off the conversation. But I am so glad to be here, holding his hand, no matter how scratched and torn his skin may be. "I'm going to head back to the apartment."

I try to pull my hand away, but before I can, his grip tightens. Our eyes meet, and I wait for him to speak, but he doesn't.

"I'll come by first thing in the morning," I promise, leaning down to kiss his forehead before I slip out of the room and down the hall. By the time I get close to the glass doors, I'm shocked by how dark it is. When I pull my phone out of my pocket, it reads 1:23 a.m. I make my way quickly across the brightly lit parking lot. Once I get to the bus, I enter through the side door, fold the table down, and make my bed. There's no point in driving back to Stacey's apartment just to come back here again in the morning. I close all the window shades, but light from the parking garage seeps in. My arms search for my mom's blanket, a tiny piece of comfort, but it's still in my room at Stacey's apartment.

As soon as I'm lying down, my chest heaves open, and I begin crying in a way that's become all too familiar.

CHAPTER 10

the lights in the parking garage never turn off, so it's a constant menace all night, even with my shades closed. I think of driving back to Stacey's apartment, but I'm too exhausted to peel myself out of bed. I fall asleep quickly after crying myself into exhaustion, but I awake multiple times. Each time I'm reminded why I'm in a parking garage, and I pull my sweatshirt over my eyes to block out the light. The sleep is never restful, because even when I am able to ignore the lights, a car drives through the garage, making the entire bus rumble.

I wake up when the morning shift arrives at the garage. Every few seconds another car drives by, the entire building shaking with it. Then there is a honk of a horn as someone locks their car and walks away. I abandon the bus at 6:48 a.m. after giving up on sleeping.

When I get back to Dylan's room, Janet is already there, her hand resting on the handlebar of a wheelchair. There are dark circles under her eyes as she reads something off her phone.

"Marly, you're here early," she says when she sees me

walk in. I retreat to the plastic chair closest to Dylan, my body sinking in.

"I slept in the bus last night."

Janet seems satisfied with my answer and turns back to her phone, but Dylan eyes me, waiting for me to elaborate. I shrug, hoping I don't look as tired as I feel.

"So absolutely no stairs," Janet says. "Just because it's not a broken leg doesn't mean you can go about your life like nothing happened. You need to let the ankle heal."

"That's not what the doctor said," Dylan says.

"I know, but the doctor doesn't know you," Janet says, giving him a face that says, "Try me."

"He said I could walk in my boot after three days."

"Okay, fine. Three days. How are you going to get around until then?"

"Marly can help me up the stairs, right?"

He glances over to me, and I stir awake, realizing I started to zone out during the conversation.

"What?" I ask, trying to sit up, but the plastic makes me slip forward and slouch in the chair.

"Dylan, just take the chair for three days. That's all I'm asking," Janet says before I have the chance to say anything. She pushes the wheelchair forward, offering it to Dylan.

A nurse walks into the room, bubbly and bright. "Okay, Dylan, you're ready to head home."

The nurse sees the wheelchair and takes it from Janet, wheeling it closer to Dylan. Janet stands by, satisfied as he moves to sit up without complaint.

He makes a face at the wheelchair but doesn't fight with the nurse as she helps him out of bed. The blankets are pushed away, revealing dark bruises scattered across his legs, leading to the boot on his foot. The scrapes along his arm look better today, less red and inflamed. He winces when he leans forward, but he moves slowly, relaxing into the seat.

"Now, you can't use crutches because of your arm. No walking for the first three days to let things heal a little. After three days, you can walk with the boot if you feel up to it, but take it easy. It's not just your ankle you hurt."

"He'll be in a wheelchair," Janet adds, and I catch Dylan rolling his eyes.

The nurse smiles. "Perfect. If you want to run ahead and pull your car up to the side of the building, we can meet you there."

"Marly, can you drive me back to my place?" Dylan asks, trying to shift to see me.

"Yeah, I'll get the bus," I say, fumbling through my bag for keys as I walk out the door. As I walk away, I can hear Janet talking to the nurse, asking questions she already asked the night before.

I get to the bus quickly and pull it out, moving it to the front of the building. There's a small line of cars, each one waiting to pick someone up or drop them off. When it's finally my turn, I can see Dylan smile as he sees me, his mom still hovering over his shoulder.

I put the bus into park before jumping out to help the nurse on the other side.

"Well, looks like you'll be leaving in style," she says, opening the passenger door.

The woman wraps her arm around Dylan's waist, helping him lift himself, but once he's standing, he's able to turn until he can sit in the bus. Dylan scoots back in the seat, settling in and resting his head back. His face is tense, and I wonder how sore he still is.

The nurse folds the chair and hands it to me so I can put it in the back of the bus.

"Just call if you have any more questions," the nurse says, turning to face Janet.

The two talk for a few more seconds as I turn to get inside the bus. Dylan laughs as I buckle up.

"She won't stop asking questions," he says, running his hand down his face in frustration.

We sit there for a few more seconds until the nurse finally waves a quick goodbye before walking back into the building.

"I'll meet you back at your apartment," Janet says, turning to us now. She rests her hand on the door of the bus, her head poking through.

"Mom, I'll be fine. Marly and Trent will get me all settled. Go home and get some sleep."

Her gaze jumps from Dylan to me, and I try to give her a reassuring smile.

"Okay, call if you need me," she says, giving his hand a light squeeze before she turns away. "Here are your prescriptions for the pain." She hands over a small white bag. Dylan mumbles a quick thank-you before Janet walks away.

I put the bus into drive, happy to leave the hospital behind us. Dylan is silent beside me, so I'm the one to break the tension in the air.

"Does Trent know you've signed him up to be your home nurse for the next couple weeks?"

"I was actually hoping you'd sign up for that job." He gives me a weak smile, and I get a glimpse of the Dylan I've been missing. A second later, the smile drops, and he closes his eyes.

He sits beside me quietly, and when I glance over again, his gaze is out the window.

"You've barely said anything since the accident," I say.

"Because I don't know what to say," he says, the words slow and tired. I feel his gaze on me, but I keep my eyes on the road. "I got hurt. I'm in a cast. It's over."

"It's not over. You can't just go back to normal like nothing happened."

He doesn't say anything, so I continue.

"You could've died." The words are firm. "Do you know what it's like to have to wait for hours for rescuers to find you, and then more hours for them to get you in the ambulance? And then *more* hours to drive to the ER and wait? Not to mention all I can do while I'm waiting is think, 'Hey, last time I was in an ER, I was told my parents were dead.' "

"Do you want me to apologize for getting hurt?" Dylan says, his voice picking up. I'm shocked by how quickly he snaps to attention. "Or should I go back in time and undo the entire thing? Because I could certainly do without all this." He gestures to his body.

"You were irresponsible." I try to stay calm, but I can feel myself losing my temper.

"There was nothing irresponsible about that hike. I go hiking alone all the time. I've gotten caught in the rain before. Just because you're here now doesn't mean you get to tell me when I can and can't go hiking."

"How often do you go hiking alone?" The words come out sharp. This isn't the way I wanted to have this conversation, but now it feels too late to turn back. "I was talking to Stacey, and she told me you went hiking almost every weekend while I was gone, but you never told me about any of them."

"Why does it matter?"

"Because I'm your girlfriend. You're supposed to tell me these things."

"Okay, fine. I did five hikes while you were gone. All of them solo. None of them involved getting injured. I always made sure my mom or Stacey knew where I was."

"But you didn't tell *me*," I say.

"It didn't matter. You weren't here."

"It matters because I'm your girlfriend. We talked almost every day on the phone, and none of those phone calls involved you telling me about how almost every weekend you went hiking. You don't need to ask me permission to go; I just want to know."

Dylan lets out a sigh, burying his face in his hand, elbow propped up against the edge of the window.

"I didn't tell you because I honestly didn't think it mattered. When we were on the phone, I was way more interested in hearing about what you were up to than telling you how I walked in the woods alone for hours again. All that mattered to me was that you were coming here and eventually I wouldn't be alone."

"But then you went hiking alone," I say, my words softer.

"I know," he says, shaking his head. "I was just being stupid."

There's more to the story — I can feel it — but he lets the words linger there, shutting the door to the conversation.

"I just need to know you're safe," I say, trying to hide the waver in my voice.

I wait for Dylan to say something, but he doesn't, so we sit in silence most of the drive. An hour later, I turn on my signal and merge off the highway, turning down an intersection and toward Dylan's apartment. When I park the bus, Trent is waiting for us since Stacey already called and filled him in on everything. Trent meets Dylan at the passenger door, pulling it open.

"Looks like you managed to survive the night," Trent says. "How you feel?"

I open the side door and pull out the wheelchair and unfold it.

"Like a million bucks," Dylan says, pushing himself up with one arm. Trent leans down and wraps his arm around Dylan's waist, helping him stand and pivot into the wheelchair. I push him across the parking lot, following Trent to their building. Trent and Dylan launch into their own conversation, talking about some show they watched together.

Trent holds the door open for me while I wheel Dylan into the building. There's no elevator, so Trent helps pull Dylan up, taking him up the stairs one by one. I cringe while watching them go up the stairs. Dylan's bad foot hovers, and Trent tries to take most of the weight off of him. They make it up eventually, but it's slow going. I take the wheelchair up, following close behind.

Trent lets out a big sigh when we finally make it to their apartment, and he helps Dylan sit on the couch.

"I have to leave in a bit to go to work. Do you need anything before I go?" he asks Dylan, glancing over to me as well.

I pull everything out of the bag that Janet gave Dylan before we left. There're two prescription bottles and a folded piece of paper that Janet used to write down instructions on when to take everything.

"No, I think we're good," Dylan says. I put everything on the table and sit next to Dylan on the couch.

"I'll be honest, Dylan, you're making hiking look like a dangerous hobby," Trent says, moving to grab some of his things off the table. The words are meant in jest, but Dylan looks more annoyed than amused.

"Says the guy scared of hiking even the little mountains," Dylan says.

Trent chuckles and shakes his head. The two continue their joking while Trent moves in and out of his room, getting ready for work and dragging everything he needs along the way. Dylan is watching TV by the time Trent makes it out the door to head to work.

We spend the entire day watching TV, and I fight to stay awake. I'm curled up next to Dylan on the couch, leaning on his good shoulder while the other sits in a sling. Dozens of questions still go through my mind, but I'm too tired to bring any of them up, practically falling asleep on the couch as the television drones on. We're into what's probably the fifth movie of the day when Dylan gets a phone call.

"Hello?" he says, pausing for a few seconds. "Yeah, that's fine. Okay. See you in a bit." He hangs up and puts the phone down on the pillow beside him.

"Who was that?" I ask.

"My mom. She said she's coming over to drop off some food."

Sure enough, about an hour later there's a knock at the door, and Janet pokes her head in, holding a casserole dish.

"Hey, how are you feeling?" She lets herself in, making her way toward the kitchen.

"Same," Dylan says, a tiny hint of annoyance coating the word.

"Marly, do you mind helping me out at the car? I have a few more things to bring up," Janet says as she puts the casserole into the fridge.

"Sure," I say, pulling myself up from the couch. I glance over at Dylan, and he gives me a shrug. I follow his mom out the door, and we make our way back to her car.

"Thank you again for helping so much," she says as we cross the parking lot.

"Yeah, of course."

"I was actually wondering if you could do me a favor. Dylan isn't one to let injuries stop him from doing things. When he broke his leg, he tried too much too soon, and we ended up back in the hospital for more X-rays."

We reach her car, and she hits the button on the remote to pop the trunk. There are five bags of groceries, and she hands me two. She pauses, holding the third bag.

"I just wanted to let you know in case he tries to convince you he can start hiking again next week. I swear, that boy would run a marathon with a broken foot just to prove a point."

I let out a nervous laugh. He wouldn't really do that, would he?

"I'll keep an eye on him," I say, taking the third bag from her, and she smiles. "What are all the groceries for?"

She takes the last two bags and closes the trunk of her car. "Grocery shopping isn't Trent's strong suit, and I didn't want you or Dylan to have to worry about food. This should be enough to get the boys through the week without ordering pizza."

We head back to the apartment, and when we step through the door into the living room, Dylan is exactly where I left him. He gives a weak smile.

"You don't need to grocery shop for me, Mom." He straightens himself a little as we take the food into the kitchen.

"Either I grocery shop or there will be takeout littering the place whenever I come to visit."

Dylan shrugs, not seeming put off by the idea.

Janet doesn't linger. She unloads the food and then goes over everything the doctors and nurses said about Dylan's recovery. A few minutes later she makes her way home. Once she's out the door, Dylan motions for me to join him on the couch. I sit down next to him, and he wraps his arm around my shoulders, pulling me to his chest.

"Now what?" I ask.

"We sit and watch movies until I can walk so my mom doesn't feel the need to nurse me back to health." He wiggles his casted foot slightly.

"What's your plan for dealing with this?" I point to his leg that's propped up. His mom's words linger in my mind, and I wonder what Dylan's thinking.

"Well, I'm out for the count for at least a month or two. I have to do physical therapy for my arm and ankle, but when I broke my leg, it healed up pretty fast, so I suspect we'll be able to continue our weekend hiking adventures soon." He pulls me closer to his side, kissing the top of my head. I'm sure he means the words as reassurance, but all I can feel now is an edge of anxiety.

I swallow, trying to think of how to put my next words. The questions that have been lingering in the back of my mind for the past twenty-four hours come to the surface. "Stacey was telling me about the first time you got injured," I say. He looks at me, his gaze curious. "Well, when you first told me about it, you made it sound like a big part of the reason you got injured was because of the weather. Stacey made it sound like that wasn't the case."

His demeanor changes as I speak, his gaze drifting away. "It was part of it."

"What's the whole story?" I ask.

He shifts, pulling himself up a little more before he speaks. "It was winter. My dad went on the hike with me, and it wasn't going well from the beginning."

"What do you mean?"

"My dad and I don't have the best relationship. Right from the start, my dad was extremely opinionated about how . . . idiotic he thought the entire thing was. I thought about just canceling the hike and calling it a day, but he insisted on going. He was complaining about his bag, so I carried it, along with my own. Since he didn't have a bag anymore, he was a lot faster than me. Eventually, the weather got so bad that we could barely see anything. I told him we needed to turn back, so we did, but he just took off without me. I was running to catch up to him when I tripped and fell. I was worried he was so far ahead that he wouldn't even know I was hurt, but he heard me shout when it happened."

"Why didn't you just tell me that over the summer? When you first mentioned getting hurt hiking with your dad?" I ask.

"Because it's easier to tell myself I got hurt because of the weather rather than believe that if I was with anyone else, I never would have been injured in the first place." As he talks, a mix of anger and frustration boil up to the surface. "My dad likes to tell me I would have gotten hurt even if the weather had been perfect, that it's the hobby that's the issue, not the conditions. I had a bad feeling about the hike the entire time, but I ignored it because I thought the hike was my dad's way of showing a peace offering. Instead, he used that hike as leverage against me."

He's quiet, and all I can hear is his soft breathing in the still room.

"You said you had trouble hiking after the accident," I say, thinking back to how he mentioned Mount Elbert was the first

14er he'd done since his injury. "You told me you had an anxiety attack the first time you went hiking after getting injured. But your mom and sister didn't mention anything about that. They just keep saying how you pushed yourself too hard after you got injured."

He seems embarrassed, his eyes darting away and glancing at something on the other side of the room. As he looks away, I'm forced to question again whether Dylan is telling me the full truth.

"They don't know about that," he says, looking down. "I did have an anxiety attack. I went alone on my first hike after my injury because my mom and sister didn't want me to go. They thought I wouldn't go if no one went with me, but it was just a short walk. It was barely even a hike, but I slipped and hurt my leg and started freaking out, thinking I'd broken my leg again, but this time I was alone. I was able to finish the hike, but I went back to the doctor to get more X-rays. My leg was fine, but for a long time, I thought every hike was going to end in injury. I figured the only way to get past that fear was to dive headlong into it until it didn't bother me anymore. Mount Elbert *was* the first big hike since that injury."

When he finishes, he looks over at me, his eyes full, begging me to understand.

"Then why, after everything you've been through, did you go out there when you knew a storm was coming?"

He opens his mouth to speak but pauses before he finally finds the words. "I don't know," he admits.

I bite my lip, frustrated with the answer. "This summer, you told me to know when to turn around, so why didn't you follow your own advice?"

This time he doesn't have an answer for me. He blinks, staring at his cast, perhaps wondering the same thing I am.

"Dylan," I say, pushing him to speak.

"I didn't feel like I needed to," he says, the words coming out sharp.

I lean away, surprised by his response.

He closes his eyes, frustrated. "I didn't know the weather was going to turn so fast," he says, his words seeming tired. The seconds hang between us, neither of us willing to break the tension in the air just yet.

"When you were in the ambulance and ER, it . . ." I pause, wondering how much I should tell him. "It felt like I was seeing my parents in the hospital again. It was like I was standing there again, hearing the news about my parents for the first time. And I couldn't stop myself from thinking, 'Not again. Not him.' "

The words come out strained, and Dylan looks over at me. His eyes go soft, and now it's him with questions.

"What happened in the parking lot?" he asks softly.

I try not to think of how I may have looked, Stacey holding me up as I collapsed to the ground screaming.

His eyes dart from me to the room, worry painted clear across his face. "I didn't know what was wrong."

I open my mouth to speak, but all that comes is a tiny gasp for breath. I don't know what to say, so I pull myself closer to him, hiding my face and leaning into his chest, tears coming in silent streams down my cheeks.

"I'm sorry," he whispers. He kisses me, and I remind myself he's here. I haven't lost him, and I shouldn't have to worry about losing him. I shift until my lips meet his, and I let myself fall into the kiss, pushing any worries away. For now at least.

CHAPTER 11

d ylan says goodbye to his wheelchair three days after coming home. He only used it every now and then to get around his apartment, so when the third day arrives, he puts on his boot and takes his first steps.

"Are you sure?" Janet asks, her hands still gripping the wheelchair. Dylan takes a few paces around his apartment, testing his foot.

"Yeah, it feels fine. My arm hurts more than my ankle does. The wheelchair was just a precaution anyway. I never needed it."

Janet frowns, folding it up. Dylan has a limp when he walks, but that has more to do with the giant boot on his foot than the injury itself.

Three days turns into two weeks, and each day Dylan seems more like his old self. The stitches come out, the bruises heal, and the scrapes along his arms and legs disappear. He even gets used to the boot, walking better and more fluidly each day.

The more Dylan heals, the more eager he is to get back out on the trail. I spend almost every day at Dylan's apartment, making us food, watching movies, and very slowly Dylan starts physical therapy. Sometimes I'll pull my computer out to check sales on my stock photos or edit photos I took earlier in the week. He works from home since he can't drive until his ankle is healed, so most days look the same, with both of us sitting at our laptops working.

At least once a day we roll out yoga mats to stretch. It was Dylan's idea, and it felt silly at first, but it became part of our daily ritual. Trent mocks us whenever he walks in on us stretching in the living room, but Dylan is always quick with a comeback.

It's also become part of my job to drive Dylan to physical therapy once a week, and when we get home, he shows me all the moves so we can do them together. For me, the stretches and strength moves come easily, but for Dylan, it takes a little longer.

"How does it feel?" I ask, watching him scrunch up his face as he tries to extend his ankle. He's sitting on the floor, his leg stretched out with a towel on the ball of his foot and each end of the towel in his hand. He has to gently pull the towel back to stretch his ankle, and I can tell the movement causes some pain.

"Tight," he says, face strained.

"Don't pull too hard," I say. He relaxes his grip, but frustration radiates off him. He doesn't say anything, but I can see how much he's battling his own body in this moment. We haven't spoken about starting to hike again, but it's plain to see just how badly he wants it, even if the thought of him being out there again scares me.

By the time November comes around, it's been three weeks

since Dylan's accident, and I have another wedding scheduled. This time Charlotte picks me up from Stacey's apartment.

"Ready to go?" Charlotte says when I jump into her car. I put all my camera gear in the back, stuffed in a bag full of lenses and too many SD cards. It's a winter wedding, the snow coating the ground a perfect backdrop for some of the photos we have planned for the day.

"Yup!" I say, buckling up. Truthfully, I've been dreading shooting for the wedding all week. The first wedding was exciting because I had no idea what I was in for. This time I know exactly how much work lies ahead, and I don't feel up to it.

Charlotte puts the car into drive and begins to run through our schedule for the day. "The guys will be getting ready in the basement. The bride didn't have any special requests, so just do whatever looks best. I'll be with the bride in the suite upstairs."

"Are they doing a first look?" I ask, trying to make a mental list of everything I need to photograph.

"No. And their ceremony isn't for another couple hours, so we have plenty of time to get photos separately. And then they've got an hour for photos together after the ceremony."

It's only our second wedding together, but Charlotte texted me some of the photos I took last time, and even I was a little impressed. The first wedding went by in such a whirlwind that I wasn't sure what photos I had taken, but I was happy to hear that not only Charlotte was happy with my photos, but the bride was as well. At this point, I'm not sure if I enjoy photographing weddings, but it's reassuring that at least I'm good at it.

"How's Dylan?" Charlotte asks once we finish reviewing the schedule for the day.

I shift in my seat. I haven't had the chance to tell Charlotte everything, but I know Stacey did.

"Really good, all things considered," I say, trying to leave it vague.

"Stacey called me when he first got out of the hospital. She was pissed." She laughs a little.

I smile in a sad way. "She wasn't the only one."

Charlotte shakes her head, eyes still on the road. "My ex wiped out on his motorcycle once. Took a turn too tight and just slid. He was wearing riding pants and a jacket, so he was okay, just a little bruised up. But once I knew he was okay, I was livid. I put my foot down about the whole motorcycle thing and said it was me or the motorcycle."

"What did he say to that?"

She glances over, raising an eyebrow. "I did say he was my ex."

I sigh, leaning back into the seat.

"What I'm saying is you gotta know your limits. What kind of reckless bullshit are you willing to put up with?"

Charlotte moves on to talking about the wedding again, but her words stick with me for the entire night.

It's much of the same chaos as the first wedding I did, but this time it feels more natural, expected almost. Charlotte and I develop a flow, and we know how to work around each other without either of us getting in the way.

The wedding moves by in a blur. It feels easier the second

time around, but even then, the familiar wave of exhaustion hits me as soon as Charlotte drops me off at Stacey's apartment. I'm only a couple steps through the door when my phone starts ringing and Lori's name shows up.

"Hey, what's up?" I answer.

"You're free from the wedding tonight, right?"

"Yup, just got home."

"Good, I need to vent." She sighs, and then she goes off, launching into some story of a professor who gave a pop quiz on a topic they haven't covered in class yet. Lori calls me a couple times a week, always ready to dish on everything that's been going on. In reality, the worst part about moving to Colorado was losing Lori. But we keep the long-distance friendship going strong with phone calls and weekly video chats.

"I mean, no one knew any of the answers on the quiz. What's the point of quizzing us on something that hasn't even been covered in class yet?"

"Was it something in the homework?" I ask.

"No," she says quickly, then rethinks. "I've been going through all the reading assignments. Nothing on the test was in our homework. Unless I read the wrong chapter?"

I can hear Lori flipping through a book on the other end of the line, before the sound of pages stops.

"Ugh, it doesn't matter now anyway. How's Dylan?"

"He's getting better," I tell her, but my voice is deflated.

"You say that like it's a bad thing."

"It's not. It's just . . ." I think of the conversation I had with Charlotte and how she asked her ex-boyfriend to give up his motorcycle. This wasn't that serious, was it? "This isn't the first big injury he's had from hiking. And, I don't know, sometimes I want him to just give up on these big hikes he has planned. He acts like he has some deadline to meet. Like he has to hike every one *now*, or else."

"Or else what?"

"That's the thing. He won't tell me. I know there's more to the situation, but I don't want to push him, so I just . . ."

"You just let it bother you for a long time without ever saying anything?"

I let out a single laugh. "Pretty much."

"Go talk to him. Corner him so he can't get away from you."

"But I don't know even know what I would ask."

"Why are you in such a rush to finish hiking all these mountains?" Lori says as if it's obvious.

I let the question run through my mind, seeing if I can already predict Dylan's answer, but nothing comes up. The more I think about it, the more I realize I've never once asked Dylan *why* he hikes. It may seem like an innocent question, but after Dylan's reactions to his injuries, it feels like there has to be something else in the works.

"Okay, I'll see what I can get him to tell me."

"Good," Lori says, seeming pleased with herself. "Now I need your help picking out classes for next semester." And from there we spend the next hour sorting through Lori's class options, writing down which classes would create the best schedule while also checking off more of the requirements for her business degree.

The next morning I'm up and out of bed, making myself breakfast quietly in the kitchen. Stacey got home when I was asleep, and her door is shut, a signal to keep noise to a minimum while she sleeps off her night shift.

I drive to Dylan's apartment and let myself in with the key he gave me after his accident — a fact Lori was absolutely giddy over.

"He gave you a key?" she practically squealed when I told her over video chat.

"It's his key. Since I'll be coming and going so much, and he can't exactly get to the door in record time, it just made the most sense."

I tried to push off the significance of that key, but I'd be lying to myself if I didn't admit I'm just as excited as Lori. Getting the key to his apartment was no simple thing.

Trent is already at work when I let myself in, but I spot a light on in Dylan's room and make my way over.

"Good morning," I say, knocking on the door as I walk in. He's still lying in bed, scrolling through his phone. His foot is out of the boot, propped up on a pillow. His ankle is still visibly swollen, but it's getting better.

"Hey," he says with a smile. He puts his phone down and motions for me to come over. I close the distance between us and lie next to him in bed, tucking myself in by his side. It's become my habit to sink into the spot on his good side, resting my head on his shoulder.

"Do you want me to get ice for your foot?" I ask. Normally when his foot is propped up, there's a bag of ice on it, but not today.

"Not yet," he says, wrapping his arm around me tighter.

"What are our plans for this weekend?"

A grin spreads across his face as soon as I ask the question, and I know he already has the entire weekend mapped out. For the past couple weeks we've been trapped indoors and focusing on physical therapy, but Dylan said he needed a healthy dose of vitamin D.

"I'm glad you asked." He pulls up a webpage and shows me the screen. The photo is of a lake with the classic Colorado look of mountains and rugged trees lining the edge of the water. In the foreground of the photo is a bright green tent. It may be one of the most picturesque camping spots I've ever seen.

"That's gorgeous," I say quickly. I take the phone and scroll, looking for more photos, but there aren't any.

"I've heard of Alta Lakes, but I've never gone camping there. It's free to camp, but the campground is first come, first serve. If we want to go, we'll have to leave early in the morning."

I raise an eyebrow. "How early?"

"Up to you. I still can't drive." He motions to his foot.

"Well, how far of a drive?"

"Six hours," he says quickly, trying not to put an emphasis on it.

"Six hours?"

"It will be worth it," he says, kissing my forehead before pushing himself to sit up. I follow suit, standing so I can hand him his boot cast.

"We can't go camping somewhere closer?" I ask.

He shrugs. "There's always somewhere closer, but I figured

we could use a little bit more of an adventure." He grins at me in the way that makes it impossible to disagree. I glance out the window and see the bus parked out in the parking lot, the bright teal a stark contrast against all the other cars around it.

"I guess it's been a while since I've used the bus for camping."

Dylan comes up from behind me, wrapping his arms around my torso until I can feel his breath on my cheek.

"Camping, just like when we first met."

"You'll be sleeping in the tent while I'm in the warm bus?" I ask, turning to face him.

He grins, dropping his arms. "I'm injured, so I get the bus. You can sleep in the tent."

I laugh, rolling my eyes, but he closes the distance between us quickly, kissing me until we're both laughing.

CHAPTER 12

t he apartment is silent when I wake up the next morning. Stacey's still asleep when I slip out the door, so I leave her a note on the kitchen counter, letting her know I went camping with Dylan.

The sun is just barely peeking over the horizon when I get out to the bus. The morning air is cold and dry, my breath visible as I walk. While I naturally hike less in the winter to avoid storms, it's my favorite hiking season. It's when the snow coats the trails, packing down the rocky terrain and making a smooth but steep pathway to the top. Hiking in freshly fallen snow has always been a favorite of mine. The trick is to hike while the delicate shelves of snow still rest on the tree branches. Once it gets too warm, the snow falls onto the ground, and the magic of winter dies off a little. But when it still coats every surface, you feel like you're walking into an untouched world of wonder.

A lot of the cars that are normally in the apartment parking lot are already gone, most of our neighbors having already left for work.

The bus starts up with a soft purr, and I make my way toward Dylan's apartment. When I pull into the parking lot, he's already standing at the entrance of his building, waiting for me.

"I could have helped you get down the stairs," I say as I pull up alongside where he stands.

"I've mastered the art of hobbling down the stairs," he says, opening the passenger door and stepping in. He tosses his duffel bag into the back with a soft thud.

"Hope you packed warm," I say, eyeing the frost that lingers on the grass in front of the apartment building.

"What, you don't want to use my body heat for warmth?" He smiles as he buckles up.

I laugh as I roll my eyes, and we begin the six-hour drive.

The plan is to drive out to the camping spot and hope we can find a place to stay. Our only hope is that there won't be a lot of competition for a spot since it's November. I saw a camping spot online where I can park the bus directly in front of the lake, but I try not to get my hopes up. If worst comes to worst, we have a list of other dispersed camping spots nearby that we can try if Alta Lakes is full.

The six hours of driving goes by slowly. It takes closer to seven and a half hours due to stops for food, bathroom breaks, and hitting a bit of traffic. It's 3:00 p.m. when we pull onto the final road for Alta Lakes. I make my way down a narrow dirt road that stretches for a couple of miles, a light coating of snow over the path.

"Do people camp here in the winter?" I ask, eyeing the road, which doesn't look like it's been driven on in a while.

"I think so," Dylan says, leaning forward to get a better view. He shrugs, the tires making a soft crunching sound as we go.

It feels like we're driving endlessly down a tiny dirt road to nowhere. After a few minutes of seeing no signs, I start to think I'm not going the right way, but I follow the directions on the GPS, crossing my fingers it doesn't lead us to a dead end. It occurs to me as I'm driving that this bus isn't designed for winters, and all it would take for me to get stuck is one good snowfall, pothole, or sheet of ice. I glance over at Dylan. His face is level and even, but I can tell he's concerned by the way he leans forward in his seat, trying to assess the situation. A few more minutes go by, and I'm about to ask if we should turn around when the road opens up in front of us, mountains and a lake off in the distance. As I get closer, I spot the clearing amongst the trees, and I realize we're the only ones here — for now at least.

"Home sweet home," Dylan says. He has a huge smile across his face, a spark coming to his eyes that I haven't seen since we hiked Mount Washington together. The mountains are his home, and it seems like this camping trip is the best medicine I can give him.

I make a few turns around the campground, checking out all the spots, but I already know which one I want. Right by the shore, there's a wide spot that gives a perfect central view of the lake. I drive forward and then back into the spot, turning just right so that the lake and mountains will be our view when I open the side door of the bus. Once the bus is in park, I hop out, and Dylan follows.

The lake doesn't have a beach. The edge of the water begins

right where the grass ends. The lakeshore is scattered with worn logs and branches that line the lip of the lake. The water starts off shallow, but just a few feet in, the water turns a deep shade of green, making it impossible to see the bottom.

On the other side of the lake is a rolling hill speckled with tall pine trees. Where the pine trees end, a tall mountain range reaches out to the sky. The mountains across the lake are coated in a bright blanket of snow. The air is cold but still above freezing, though I wouldn't be surprised if we wake up to frost in the morning.

"Ready to set up camp for the night?" Dylan says, wrapping an arm around my waist. I can feel the energy radiating off him as he takes my hand and leads us back to the bus, opening the side door so we can start setting up for the night.

Dylan puts the pop-up into place while I go searching for the camping stove and pull it out from one of the cabinets. I also search for the folded camping chairs that I stashed under the seats before I left New Hampshire. I pull the chairs out, and since we'll be off-grid, we're set up for the night in no time. I lean forward across the tiny table and flip on my fairy lights. With a faint glow, we settle into our camping spot.

"Want to go for a walk?" Dylan says as I'm pulling out a can of soup that I packed into one of the cabinets. I put the soup on the counter.

"Where?"

"I found a trail. It looks like it goes off to the right and around the lake."

I glance down at the boot still wrapped around Dylan's

ankle. He's been walking in it just fine, but it was always to get from one point to the other, not to go on a walk for the sake of walking.

"Let's just stay at camp," I offer, stepping out of the bus and motioning to one of the camp chairs I set up.

Dylan glances quickly at the chair, and though he doesn't say it, I see his frustration with the idea of sitting when there are things to explore. He doesn't argue, but rather than sit in the chair, he paces toward the lake.

I eye the woods off to our right, wondering where the walking trail is Dylan found.

"Is it flat?" I ask.

He turns to face me, his face lighting up. "Flat, boring, and safe."

I bite my lip, wondering what Janet would say if she knew Dylan was already trying to get out onto the trails. One little walk couldn't hurt, could it?

"A short walk," I say, leaning into the bus to grab my camera. "If the ground isn't flat, we turn around."

Dylan doesn't say anything in response. He just grips my hand, leading me toward the trail he found. I sling the camera strap around my neck as we walk, surprised by Dylan's eagerness.

"You're going to hurt yourself," I say, laughing as he leads the way. He slows down, his balance a little thrown from trying to walk so fast in the boot. And then he stays at a slower pace, making sure to walk in a way that won't bother his ankle.

The trail winds around the lake, the water always just a

glance away. I take photos as we go, capturing nature from every perspective. Since winter is just around the corner, the forest feels a little more barren the usual, the leaves already browned and fallen. The ground is flat and beaten, but there are enough exposed roots and rocks that I'm nervous about walking through the area with Dylan's boot. He goes much slower than he's accustomed to, taking careful measured steps as we go.

We're in the trees, the bright blue water to our left as we walk. To our right, the trees grow more and more dense, making it nearly impossible to step anywhere besides the established walking path. I make short stops as we walk, testing out the macro lens on my camera to get close-up shots of moss, insects, and the intimate texture of the forest that most people miss when they're walking.

"How am I looking?" Dylan says with a smile, lifting his foot and hovering it in the air.

The boot is dirtier than I've ever seen it, with bits of grass and pine shoved into the small crevices. Dylan holds it up with a sort of admiration, like the dirty boot is just another marker in his recovery.

"Definitely not built for this," I say, bending down to brush off a dead plant that got caught on one of the straps. "How you feeling?"

He puts his foot down and glances ahead where the trail continues. The trail is thin, with just enough room for the two of us to walk side by side, but it winds onward and out of sight. We've been walking for about half an hour, but we've barely made any distance from the bus.

Dylan frowns, his gaze trained ahead of us. I reach for his hand and give it a gentle squeeze, making him look at me.

"The mountains aren't going anywhere," I remind him.

He gives me a smile, but it's forced.

"Let's head back to camp."

He lets go of my hand, making the air feel even more cool in his absence.

He's quiet on the way back, his mind gone to some far-off place I can't reach. It isn't until the bus is back in sight that he speaks up.

"We've got neighbors," he says softly. I follow his gaze and see a couple in the campsite next to ours. They're standing next to their truck, unloading their things as they work together to build a tent. Rather than on the ground, their tent sits in the bed of the truck, a perfect fit. As we walk closer, the girl notices us and puts up a hand to wave. Once we make it back to the bus, the girl walks over, her eyes on the bus.

"Hey! Have you ever stayed here before?" she asks as she greets us with a friendly smile.

"No, he found it online," I say, gesturing to Dylan.

"Oh," she says, seeming a little disappointed, but she perks up again quickly. "My name is Naomi, and that's my boyfriend, Jim." She points to Jim, who's settled into one of the camping chairs at the edge of the water.

"I'm Marly." I smile. "And this is my boyfriend, Dylan." As I say the words, they surprise me. We've been dating for a couple months now, but this may be the first time I've ever introduced Dylan as my boyfriend. It causes a bundle of nerves in my stomach, saying the words out loud, but I'm soothed the instant I feel Dylan's hand brush up against the back of my arm.

"We're from Georgia. New Hampshire?" She points to the bus and its license plate. I almost forgot the bus was registered under my name after I got home.

"She's from New Hampshire. I'm from Colorado," Dylan says.

"I'm staying in Colorado until further notice," I say. The words come out bold, far surer than they feel. Even Dylan looks over at me with a sly grin, excited by the notion of "until further notice."

"Oh, cool! We're just traveling for a few months. We graduated college in the spring, so I guess this is our victory lap before we figure out what to do with our lives. Has the bus been good for camping? We wanted to get one but opted for the truck tent since we already had the truck."

"Yeah, I've been in and out of the bus since summer. My uncle renovated it for me."

Her gaze flits back to the bus, eyes curious.

"Do you want a quick tour?"

Naomi's face lights up. "I'd love that."

I lead her over to the bus, letting her peek in at the setup. It's not much of a tour since the bus is so small, but Naomi's eyes are wide as she falls head over heels.

I put my laptop away and fold the table down so I can make the bed. It only takes a couple seconds to transform my eating and work area to my sleeping space.

"This is so cute!" She pokes her head into the bus more to see farther back, where I have a few cabinets for storing my clothes.

"Do you live out of this full-time?"

"We were living out of it for about a month, but now we have an apartment in Colorado Springs." I slip up with my words, insinuating that Dylan and I are living together. Naomi doesn't care about the details of our living situation, of course, but when I look at Dylan out of the corner of my eye, his eyebrow is raised with a half grin.

Naomi takes a few steps back and glances over at her tent in the back of the truck. "Here, come meet Jim, and we'll show you our setup. It's mostly a glorified tent, but it's something."

I follow her back toward her camping spot, where Jim is crouched down on the ground, trying to get a fire started.

"This is Jim. Jim, these are our neighbors for the night, Marly and Dylan," Naomi says.

Jim looks up and smiles. Even though he's crouched on the ground, I can tell he's a tall, lanky sort of guy. His hair is long and curly, pulled up into a bun on top of his head.

"We were admiring your bus," he says, standing up to shake my and Dylan's hands.

"All credit goes to her uncle," Dylan says.

"I was going to show them our setup," Naomi says, turning to Jim.

"Oh, yeah." Jim steps over and unzips the tent so we can look in. "It's not much, but we've got an air mattress, our minifridge thing, and this." He pulls out a giant battery. "It has a solar panel charger, so we recharge every day. It keeps the cooler cold and our phones on."

Their air mattress is pushed to the far right side of the tent, piles of blankets and pillows covering the bed. Off to the left is about a foot-wide section of space that's just big enough to fit the fridge and battery charger. In the back corner of the tent is a duffel bag. Every inch of the tent is taken, but overall, it doesn't seem that bad. If Lori were here, though, she might not agree.

"Unfortunately, we don't have a heater," Naomi adds, pointing to the pile of blankets.

Jim turns to go back to making a fire. "Yeah, we're heading back home now. We said we'd wait until first snowfall."

"*He* wanted to wait until first snowfall," Naomi whispers to me, smiling.

"Where'd you go?" Dylan asks.

"The goal was to hit as many national parks as possible. We ended up visiting twenty-two in about five months. We're on our way to visit our last one of the trip, Hot Springs in Arkansas," Jim says.

"Oh, wow," I say, a little jealous. "I did a trip from Washington to New Hampshire, but I didn't do as many stops as I should have."

"If you want to join us for a campfire, feel free," Naomi says, gesturing to the tiny fire Jim has started. "It's all we've got for heat until we retreat for the night under a couple dozen blankets."

I smile, realizing this is the sort of thing I was supposed to find when I was driving solo across the United States. It's the simple connections, even if I never see Naomi or Jim again.

Dylan helps Jim build the fire, and while they're busy, I make a quick trip to the bus to grab the soup I was going to heat up for dinner. I cook on my grill, bringing it to a quick boil before pouring it out into two bowls. By the time I make the walk back to Jim and Naomi's campsite, the fire is going strong, and Dylan has already brought over our chairs to circle around the pit. I hand him the bowl and pull my chair up next to him.

Naomi's at her grill, heating up what looks like some sort of freeze-dried meal I usually use for backpacking trips. Jim mans the fire, slowly adding more and more wood. As the fire blazes, the sun begins to set, orange rays of light streaking through the trees. The sky glows with the last light of the sun, the water reflecting the light onto the Rocky Mountains in the distance. By reflex, I pull my camera out from around my neck and begin to take photos from my seat at the campfire.

Jim, Naomi, and Dylan are talking—I can hear their murmurs off in the background—but my eyes are pulled away from the fire until I can't help myself. I get up from my chair, taking small steps toward the edge of the water. I move slowly, my eyes scanning to see what angle would be best to capture the moment. I crouch down at the water's edge, trying to make the camera lens level with the lake. The water is so calm, the mountains reflect perfectly off the surface. I angle the camera so the water to cuts straight through the middle of the photo, two perfect halves. With a soft click, I capture the photo.

"You do photography?" Jim asks, his voice pulling me back to the campfire. I turn and see Jim's and Naomi's faces trained on me, curiosity in the air. Dylan watches me, leaning back in his chair with a small smirk.

"Sorry," I say, making my way back toward the fire. Dylan

takes my hand as I sit next to him, and even though I feel embarrassed to have been caught in my creative process, when I look at Dylan, all I see is pride beaming from him.

"Nothing to be sorry about. If anything, I'm sorry I took you out of the zone."

I shrug. "It's no big deal. I sell stock photos and prints."

"You do?" Naomi lights up, her eyes curious.

"Yeah, mostly landscape photography. Excuse to travel, I guess." I laugh a little as I say the words, knowing I practically had to be forced to travel. But now that I'm here, it feels impossible to imagine myself going home again and not taking the bus out for adventures.

"Can I see some of the photos you've taken?" she asks.

"Sure." I take my phone out and show her some of my favorites. When I get to my collection of photos from Yellowstone, she perks up, having just visited the park herself a couple weeks ago.

Between the four of us, we launch into conversations of all the places we've been, pulling our phones out every now and then to show photos. As the conversation continues, the forest turns to darkness, and soon our little fire is the only source of light. Even the moon is gone, leaving us to only see the stars in the sky.

Naomi is in the middle of showing me photos from Redwood National Park when I feel Dylan shift next me. He leans forward to whisper to me.

"I'm going to head to bed," he says softly. The words take me by surprise; it feels like our night has only just begun.

"Oh." I shift, about to get up, but Dylan puts a hand on my shoulder.

"You can stay out. My ankle is bothering me, so I want to lie down and elevate it."

"I can go with you," I say.

"No, stay up. Have fun." He leans down and kisses me quickly. With the soft glow from the fire, I see a faint smile on his lips.

"Are you sure?" I say, surprised by Dylan wanting to go to bed.

"Yeah," he says, standing up. "Good night, guys." He waves, and Jim and Naomi echo back a quick good night. I watch Dylan walk back to the bus in the soft glow from the fire, a slight limp in his step as he walks.

CHAPTER 13

It's late by the time I make my way back toward the bus. Naomi and I talked all night, sharing stories of travels and hikes until we ran out of wood to burn. I pull the bus door open quietly, hoping not to disturb Dylan while he sleeps, but he's already awake when I open the bus door. He's sitting up, massaging his ankle.

"You're still awake?" I whisper, climbing in the bus. I close the door behind me and it shuts with a loud thud. It's warm inside compared to the night's chilly air thanks to the small space heater I brought along.

"Yeah, it's been hard to sleep with my ankle. It's hurting a little extra today."

I lean forward and switch on the fairy lights that hang along the ceiling of the bus. It's still dimly lit, but at least now I can see Dylan's face, which is currently in a grimace. I look down at his ankle, and it looks like it might be a little more swollen than before.

Did he hurt himself while we were walking? I try to think

back to earlier today, to notice if he was limping on our walk or doing something that might have irritated his ankle, but I can't think of anything. My mind wanders, daring to think if this is just how it will be for Dylan from now on.

"Have you taken anything?" I ask, pulling my jacket off and tossing it into the front seat. The bus is tight when the bed is out. While I'm thankful the bed is big enough to sleep the two of us, it becomes nearly impossible to move around when the bed is converted.

"I don't have anything."

"Lie down," I say, kneeling on the bed to reach one of the cabinets in the back of the bus by the foot of the bed. I pull out spare clothes from the cabinet, tossing them to the side to reach the first aid kit I have stashed away. The kit is small, the same type of kit I bring hiking, but it has exactly what I'm looking for: a small bottle of Advil.

I hand Dylan two small pills and my water bottle, which was sitting on the counter, and he takes them in one gulp. He lies out across the bed, and I reach back to the front of the bus and grab my jacket from where I tossed it. I fold it and the spare clothing I just took out of the cabinet into a tall pile.

"Put your foot here," I say, guiding Dylan's foot onto the pile so it's elevated. The pile of clothing sinks, barely elevating his ankle, but it's better than nothing.

"It will be fine by morning," Dylan says in protest.

I ignore him and reach down to the small fridge behind the driver's seat. The fridge is nearly bare since we didn't stock it before leaving. There's an apple and a small carton of orange juice, but then I see what I was hoping for: an ice pack.

The fridge is just that: a fridge. I don't have a freezer and have never needed a freezer, but I like to keep an ice pack in the fridge in case I ever lose power and need to keep the food cool. Joke's on me, though, because the ice pack isn't even frozen. I pull it out, and though it's not as cold as I wished, I hold it gently to Dylan's ankle.

"You don't have to do that, Marly. I'll be fine."

I glance over at him, wanting to tell him it's not fine. He needs to stay off the ankle, because if he doesn't, things will only get worse. The words almost tumble out of my mouth before I'm able to catch myself.

I let the ice pack drop. It's one of the hard square ones full of blue liquid. The liquid is already melted, and in a couple minutes, the square will be too melted to offer Dylan any sort of help.

"How long has it been hurting?" I sit up next to Dylan, my eyes examining him as he lies down across from me.

"It was bothering me a little when we were walking." He shrugs.

I feel my eyes widen in surprise. "Why didn't you say anything?"

"You were having fun taking photos. I didn't want to ruin it."

I want to protest at his words, but I hesitate, trying to think back to our walk earlier today. Was I really so consumed by working with the camera that I didn't notice Dylan was hurting?

"I'm sorry," I say.

"It's fine," Dylan says, reaching his arms out to pull me to him. I crawl closer until I'm lying down next to him, the fairy lights giving the tiny space a warm glow. I move until my head is resting on his chest, his arms wrapping around my shoulders. "This ankle will be up and running in no time."

When he says the words, I feel myself stiffen. If Dylan notices the change in my posture, he doesn't say anything. The thought of Dylan being back out on the mountains terrifies me. I want to convince myself that the thoughts of him getting hurt again are irrational, but I can't. He broke his leg the first time. He sprained his ankle and dislocated a shoulder the second time. Who's to say there isn't going to be a third time?

"Even if it takes longer to heal, the mountains will always be there," I say, trying to comfort myself in the thought that it may be another year before Dylan's able to hike anything big again. I mean, that's what happened when he broke his leg after all.

Dylan's silent for so long, I think maybe he's fallen asleep, but then he shifts slightly.

"Yeah, but I want to finish soon, and I still have twenty-three summits left."

I wait for him to say more and explain himself, but he doesn't. "Why?"

There's another long pause of silence. "Because I told myself I'd finish in the next two years."

Again, I wait for more of an explanation that doesn't come. I shift and sit up, leaning on one elbow so I can look at him. His face is dim in the small bus, but even then, he keeps his eyes trained away from me.

"Why two years?"

"Because it will be my grandfather's eightieth birthday. Or at least it would have been." His gaze is still far away, but he continues. "He had this goal of finishing the 14er list before he turned eighty, but when he found out I wanted to finish the list too, he stopped summiting new mountains and began repeating summits with me. He was at fifty-one summits and then stopped seven summits away from his goal so I could catch up with him."

"You want to finish the list for him," I say, knowing in my gut that's all Dylan's ever wanted. He nods his head and then finally turns to look at me again.

"It's more than just crossing something off a list. I can spend my whole life working, making money, buying a house, doing whatever it is I'm supposed to do, but when I get up there, I feel like I have reason, like I'm meant to stand at those summits and witness the world at my feet. I know it sounds cheesy and dramatic, but it's the truth. My grandpa told me once that you can live a million lives and never truly know what it means to live. Well, when I'm out there, I feel like I know what it means."

He turns to me, his eyes full of wonder, emotions that I've never seen from him before. He's like an injured bird trying to take flight but falling over and over in a panic, only getting himself more hurt trying to live free.

"Marly, I need to finish this list," he says, his eyes locked on mine.

His eyes are pleading, and all I want to do is tell him yes, that he'll finish the list and be able to do this monumental thing that his grandpa wanted for him. But then the selfish part inside me begs and pleads to keep him safe here beside me.

"What happened?" I ask. Dylan looks at me, confused. "When your grandfather died."

"He had a heart attack." He pauses, his words coated in a type of pain that feels familiar to me now: the pain of losing a loved one. "It was a shock. We always joked that he'd outlive all of us because he always seemed so healthy, until one day he wasn't."

"I'm sorry," I say, because I don't know what else to say. How many times have people told me they're sorry when there's nothing to apologize for? I hate that—people telling me they're sorry when they find out my parents died. Saying sorry doesn't fix anything.

"We were hiking to cross off Redcloud and Sunshine Peak. The weather was perfect, there was almost no wind, and there wasn't a cloud in the sky. Right before we hit our second summit of the day, he had a heart attack. I called for rescue and did chest compressions until rescue arrived, but he was already gone."

Dylan's looking away from me again, and though it's hard to tell in the light, his eyes look glassy, like he's fighting back tears.

"You were there when it happened?" The words come out so softly, I'm not sure he hears me.

He gets choked up for a minute, like he wants to say more but can't. I drop my arm, letting myself lean back into him, my head resting at the top of his shoulder. At first, it feels like he wants to slip out of my grasp. He hesitates, his body pulling away, but then he surrenders into himself and lets the emotions flow.

I move closer, putting my head to his chest, hearing his heartbeat loud and clear. His breathing is jagged and uneven. I don't say a word as I wrap my arms around him.

I wait for him to cry, to let the last bit of resistance go, but it never happens.

CHapteR 14

We part ways with Jim and Naomi the next morning. By the time Dylan and I make our way out of the bus and into the cold November morning, their tent is already packed up. We say goodbye quickly, exchanging phone numbers, having no idea if we'll ever see one another again.

The friendship is fleeting in this way, but I can't help but marvel at how quickly we were all able to connect and then leave feeling as if we've met new friends.

Dylan is talkative on the drive home, more animated than he usually is, like he's making up for how upset he was last night. He doesn't bring up his grandfather or hiking on the way home. Instead, he takes it as a personal mission to sort through fan theories of a TV show we've been watching together. When I drop him off at his apartment, he seems exhausted, his shoulders slumping forward more than usual, but he doesn't say anything.

By the time I kiss him goodbye, it feels like the chance of us finishing our conversation from the night before has long come and passed.

A few days later, we go out for dinner at a local Italian restaurant, and I pick Dylan up since he still can't drive. When he comes to the passenger door, he's a little off. Normally when I pick him up to drive somewhere, he kisses me quickly before he buckles up and we head off, but this time he just gives me a smile before settling into his seat.

The entire drive to the restaurant, I have a pit in my stomach, thinking something's wrong or that I may have done the wrong thing during our camping trip. When we're seated at the restaurant, I hear Dylan's phone buzz a couple times but he never answers the messages or notifications coming in.

We're sitting, and the silence feels heavier than usual while we wait for our food to arrive. I'm about to ask Dylan what's wrong when my phone lights up with a text from Stacey.

Are you with Dylan?

I open the message and show it to Dylan.

"You'd better answer her texts. Now she's hunting me down," I say jokingly.

He looks at my phone quickly before giving a short chuckle. "She doesn't like to be ignored."

I wait for more, but he leaves it at that. I respond to her message with a quick yes, hoping that will be enough to satisfy her.

Where are you???

The next text comes in quickly after I respond, and Dylan lifts his gaze.

"Please don't answer that," he says, his words defeated.

"Why does she want to know where we are?"

"Probably because I won't answer the couple dozen texts

she sent me." He shrugs as he talks.

I open my mouth to speak, then pause. He watches me, waiting to see if I'll respond to her text. I put my phone on the table between us. When we were camping a few days ago, it felt like we were so close, like I was finally starting to see the real Dylan, but now it feels like we're starting over again.

"What's going on?" I ask.

Another text comes through on my phone, but I leave it unread. Dylan glances down and sees Stacey's name pop up on the screen.

"My dad is in town to visit."

I lean back, not seeing the point. "Is your dad texting you?"

He gives a short sarcastic laugh. "He never texts me. Stacey wants me to go see him. She acts like she doesn't care about him, but she's always the first to fall for his 'fatherly' act. Every couple months he tries to insert himself into our lives like he doesn't ignore us 360 days out of the year. Stacey is planning a family dinner, and she's trying to corner me into going."

"Why not just go?"

He looks down and opens his mouth like he's going to speak, but our dinner arrives. The waiter passes us our food and gives us a small wave before walking away. We're left in an awkward silence, both of us sitting, neither talking nor eating.

"What's wrong with seeing him for just one night?" Most of what I know about his dad is based off what Stacey told me, but I can't imagine their relationship is so bad.

Dylan looks up at me, and I can tell there's more he isn't revealing.

"It's not just about one night of dinner," he says. He turns to his food and begins to eat as a sign that this conversation is over.

Another text comes in from Stacey.

Marly, please. It's important. Tell Dylan to check his texts.

I sigh, pushing my phone away.

"I'll go with you," I tell Dylan, hoping that might help. He pauses from eating and looks up at me.

"Marly, he's just not a good guy. Even when my parents were still married, he was never around. He was always too busy working to even bother to remember when our birthdays were. He only showed up in our lives again after he realized our grandfather was doing everything he was supposed to. Then he tried to be dad of the year just so he could take a few photos and post about it on Facebook to give himself a pat on the back."

"But if he's trying to connect now —"

"He's not trying to connect," Dylan interjects. He takes a moment to catch himself and lowers his voice. "He either heard about my accident and wants to rub it in my face, or he feels like he needs to save face and post about what a great dad he is on Facebook again."

"You don't know that," I say, but I've already lost the battle.

Dylan sighs, but not in frustration. "I know you want me to see him again. And I know part of it is because of what a great relationship you had with your dad, but I need you to understand that's not the case here. It never was. It never will be."

He reaches across the table and takes my hand, giving it a gentle squeeze. I nod my head, not fully understanding the situation but choosing to at least accept it.

"Okay," I say.

Dylan gives me a weak smile in silent thanks, and we both turn to our food.

As we eat, our phones continue to go off, but I turn mine on silent, tucking it away into my purse. Dylan never turns his off, his eyes wandering back to it every time Stacey's name lights up the screen. We're only halfway through dinner when he takes his phone out and texts a reply to her.

"She always gets her way," he mumbles as he shakes his head.

§

It's Thanksgiving. Well, it's a week before Thanksgiving, but Stacey decides it's close enough to Thanksgiving to call it that. She seems elated with the idea of hosting Thanksgiving and spent all week preparing—shopping for supplies, decorating the table, and cooking up just about every classic Thanksgiving dish imaginable.

Dylan gave me the option of missing the dinner, mentioning that I could fly home for the week if I wanted to avoid the family drama, but I assured him family drama feels easier to deal with than family grief. Truthfully, the more unfamiliar and different the holidays, the easier it is to ignore who's missing from the dinner table. My parents grew up with a Thanksgiving tradition where we say what we're thankful for before we eat, but without them here, it feels like a wasted tradition.

I could still make it home in time for my family's Thanksgiving next week, but I'm more than happy to stay in Colorado and avoid the holiday this year. I kept my mom's baking tradition alive, digging up my mom's old apple pie recipe and baking it at Dylan's apartment since Stacey laid claim to the kitchen all week to cook. She was in a frantic spell of cooking, and I was afraid of what might happen if I stepped in her way.

Dylan's quiet when I pick him and the apple pie up from his apartment, not saying anything more than small talk on the way over. He holds the pie in his lap, but I can't help but feel a little disappointed. The crust burned the tiniest bit, so I already know it's not going to be anywhere near as good as what my mom used to make.

Stacey's head lifts when we walk through the door of the apartment.

"Oh, good, you're here. Marly, can you set the table?"

I step into the kitchen and put the pie down while Dylan makes his way over to the couch.

"Where's Mom?" Dylan asks, propping himself into a seat.

Stacey makes a face. "She got called in for work."

Dylan raises his eyebrows and looks at me. I can tell right away he thinks this is his excuse to leave. If his mom isn't here, why should he be?

"Give him a chance," I whisper to him quickly.

He opens his mouth to retort, then glances at me and decides against it.

Stacey is a bundle of nervous energy as she moves around the kitchen making a Thanksgiving meal that's more fit for a family of twenty rather than four. Stacey points out the dishes and utensils she wants to use, and I work to lay them out nicely — though Stacey steps in and rearranges everything a few minutes later.

"What time is he supposed to be here?" Dylan says when Stacey pulls the sweet potato casserole out of the oven.

"One o'clock," she says, her eyes focused on other tasks.

Dylan pulls his phone out and shows it to me. The clock reads 1:09 p.m.. I glance over at Stacey, but she doesn't notice. Dylan leans back, an annoyed look on his face. I move to sit next to him.

"This is why I don't bother with him," he says in a voice too low for Stacey to hear.

"If he doesn't show up, there's nothing for you to worry about," I say quietly.

"It's not me I'm worried about," he says, his gaze trained on his sister, who looks one burnt dish away from a mental breakdown.

We watch in silence as Stacey finishes laying out the dishes. She gives herself a minute to admire the spread of assorted foods before she finally has a moment to check the time. Her face drops when she looks at the clock on the microwave.

"We can wait a few more minutes," I say. Stacey looks over and smiles, but I can see the worry hidden behind it.

She moves, pulling her phone out and dialing a number. Dylan and I sit quietly while she paces the kitchen, phone held up to her cheek.

It seems like the phone rings for a long time before Stacey

eventually gets sent to voicemail and hangs up. She starts over, dialing again. This time when she reaches voicemail, she leaves a message.

"It's Stacey. The food is ready. I was just wondering where you are . . ." She pauses, her words hanging. "Bye."

The room fills with silence again, and after a few moments, Dylan gets up to meet Stacey in the kitchen.

"Why don't we eat?" he says, his voice gentle.

"No, no. It's fine. The food has to cool anyway," she says, her voice a little peppier than usual. Forced.

Stacey paces, anxiety rubbing off of her and filling the room. Dylan is the opposite. Where Stacey is anxious, Dylan is mad. Without saying a word, I can tell he's already upset at his dad, and he hasn't even stepped through the door yet.

Another fifteen minutes go by. Stacey has finally stopped pacing when there's a knock. We all turn toward the sound, a little stunned. Stacey is the one to open the door.

"Stacey!" their dad says, stepping inside and wrapping Stacey in a hug.

"You're late," Dylan says.

His dad takes a few more steps in. He's tall, with broad shoulders and short cropped hair. In some ways, he looks a lot like Dylan, with the square jaw and brown hair, but the similarities end there.

"Traffic," he says. His gaze moves to me, and he raises an eyebrow.

"I'm Marly," I say, going to stand by Dylan and offering my hand.

"James," he says, shaking my hand. "Dylan didn't tell me he had a girlfriend."

"You'd have to call." Dylan shrugs.

"Come on, let's eat," Stacey says, interjecting between the tension already building, ushering everyone to the table.

Awkward isn't the best way to describe the meal. Dylan sits next to me, seething in his skin. I reach for his hand under the table and give him a gentle squeeze, trying to pull him back. When he glances over at me, I smile, but he doesn't reciprocate.

Stacey spends most of the time talking, telling her dad all about her job. James listens, nodding his head, but he doesn't offer anything. Stacey talks so much, I wonder if she even realizes everyone else is done eating and her plate has barely been touched.

"So, Dylan," James says the moment Stacey pauses. I see her face drop out of the corner of my eye. Next to me, Dylan stiffens. "I heard you got into another accident." The words come out too casually for the parent of a child who had to be admitted to an ER. The words sound closer to gloating than concern.

Dylan's face goes pale, and I brace myself for him to lash out, but he freezes.

"Yeah, but he's fine," Stacey says nervously.

James cocks his head to the side. "I mean, *another* trip to the ER?"

Dylan looks down, licking his lips. It's a night-and-day difference, the Dylan who was angry at his dad when he first arrived to the Dylan who wants to curl in on himself now. I still hold his hand under the table. His muscles were taut before, but now it feels like he's pulling away from me.

"I was supposed to go with him, but I had to back out last minute," I say, leaving out the details.

James turns his gaze to me, an eyebrow raised. "Why didn't you go?" His eyes bore into me, and I reel back, regretting having said anything in the first place.

"The weather wasn't good," Dylan says beside me. He squeezes my hand, running his thumb across my skin.

James nods his head in mock understanding. "It was too dangerous to go."

"No, it just took me longer to hike than I thought, so I got caught in the rain," Dylan says.

James looks up, leaning back into his chair and crossing his arms as he thinks about it.

"I gotta be honest with you, Dylan. I don't like that you go on those hikes."

"This isn't news to me," Dylan says, face deadpan.

"Yeah, well, maybe you should take my advice this time."

"Dad, we don't need to talk about this," Stacey says, her words soft.

"Actually, we do." James uncrosses his arms and leans forward, resting his elbows on the table. I glance over at Stacey, and the nervousness I saw earlier is replaced with embarrassment. "Dylan, you have had not one but two ER visits from hiking in the past two years. Does that not strike you as a red flag? That maybe the hobbies you participate in aren't safe?"

I look over at Dylan, but it's like he's checked out of the conversation. He's looking at James, but his face is blank.

"Was a broken leg not a clear enough sign to find something else to do with your life? What was it this time? Your foot's in a boot, so it wasn't nothing." He gestures to Dylan's leg.

Dylan just gazes back, waiting for his father to finish.

"I don't want you hiking anymore. You're going to get yourself killed. Was losing your grandfather in a hiking accident not enough of a message?"

Dylan laughs and shakes his head. "Why do you care? You'd have one less kid to pretend to care about."

"Dylan," I say, tugging on his hand, but it's like he isn't aware I'm there anymore.

"Do you even care that you were late today?" he says, letting go of my hand. "You realize Stacey has been planning this dinner from the second you texted her that you were going to be in town? And don't pretend you're here because you missed us or because of some stupid holiday. You're here because you heard about my accident, and it would literally kill you to miss an opportunity to give me some self-righteous speech that makes you feel like dad of the year."

"I do care," James says, his voice rising in volume along with Dylan's.

"No, you don't," Dylan says, his voice silencing the room. "If you cared at all about this family, then you would have been at Grandpa's funeral, but you couldn't stand the fact that he was one hundred times the dad you'll ever be. And now you're just here trying to ruin the one thing I have left of him."

"Dylan," Stacey warns, but her voice is wavering. I look over, and her eyes are red, tears ready to burst.

"Stacey, it's okay," James says with a hushing tone.

"Stop it." Dylan stands up, the chair echoing a loud screech through the room. "Stop acting like a dad only when it's convenient to you. And Stacey, move the hell on. He's not going to change, and in a couple days he'll stop answering your phone calls again."

Dylan walks away from the table, his limp more obvious than it usually is. He grabs his coat from where it's hanging and walks out of the room.

I glance over at Stacey, and silent tears are running down her face.

"I'm going to drive him home," I say, rushing out the door to catch up with Dylan.

CHAPTER 15

"**d**ylan?" I run down the stairs, quickly meeting up with him since he hasn't gotten far in his boot. I know he must hear me, but he continues down the stairs. "Dylan, wait."

"I need to get out of here," he says, making his way down the stairs one by one with careful steps.

"Just cool off a minute," I say, taking a few steps in front of him and blocking him from going any farther.

"I can call Trent to pick me up so you don't have to drive me again."

"Just wait," I say, pushing myself in front of him.

"Why?" He starts to move to the side to get around me, but I block his way again. His face is distraught, his eyes looking out to the parking lot like he's ready to jump into any of the cars and drive off.

"Because I really don't want to go back in there, and I need you to take a breath," I say, trying to laugh it off, but tension is still in the air.

He looks back up the stairs and sighs. "I'm sorry about what happened back there." He holds out his hand, and I take it. "That's why I haven't seen him. It never ends well."

I glance up at him, nodding in silence as we walk. We make our way toward the bus, Dylan moving slower the farther we get. He gets in on the passenger side, leaning against the window as we drive off.

I wait for Dylan to say something more, but after a few minutes of silence, I'm convinced he'd be happy to never speak of it again.

"Can I ask a question?" I say.

Dylan looks over, seeming genuinely surprised. "Yeah, of course."

"Did your dad really not go to your grandfather's funeral?"

He lets out a heavy sigh and stares out the window. "Yeah."

"Why?"

He shrugs. "You heard what I said earlier? About him being jealous?"

"Yeah, but you don't actually believe that, do you?"

"Why else would he refuse to go? I've tried making a million excuses for him, but the truth is, he's just too busy caring about himself to notice when the rest of his family is hurting. If you ask me, he's probably happy my grandpa died, because now he doesn't feel like he needs to compete to be a good dad anymore. He only shows up when he wants to."

"Your dad's always been like this?" I glance over at Dylan, and his gaze is fixed out the window.

"For as long as I can remember. Maybe he was better when I was really little. Stacey says he was, which is why she hangs on tighter. She tells me about these memories she has and how we were this picture-perfect family. If that was the case, I guess me being born ruined it all."

"That's not true," I say.

"How do you know?" He glances over, eyes pointed. A beat passes, and his eyes soften. He turns his gaze back toward the window. "I asked my mom what happened, and she was very . . . hesitant to tell me anything. My theory is that all the memories Stacey has of our dad are just things my mom has told her to make her feel better. There aren't any photos or videos of our dad when we were kids. Stacey just has stories that she likes to obsess over."

Dylan shifts in his seat, dropping his hands into his lap like he's giving up. "After my grandfather died, I promised myself I'd never see my dad again," he mumbles. He drops his head back onto the headrest and closes his eyes. "After he missed the funeral, I told myself no more. But he keeps managing to squeeze back into our lives."

"Because he's your dad," I offer, my voice gentle.

He shakes his head. "He's not my dad. You don't get to be someone's dad just because of genetics. You have to earn it. I gave that man a second chance two years ago when we went on our hike together. I was stupid enough to believe that maybe he had changed. Lot of good that did me."

I glance over, and Dylan's forehead is against the glass, his eyes wandering off into the distance. When I drop him off at his apartment, he hugs me in a desperate, longing way, like he can't hold me close enough. I can feel his breath at my temple, uneven and ragged, but he doesn't say a word as he pulls away and disappears into his apartment.

I take the long route to get home, hoping James will be gone by the time I get back. When I pull into the parking lot, I realize I have no idea what James drives, so the only way to know if he's gone is to go in.

When I get to the apartment door, I stand with my hand on the knob, listening closely to try and hear if there are any voices on the other side. There's just silence.

I take a slow step in and hear pots and dishes being moved. When I look around the corner, I can see Stacey standing at the sink, cleaning up dinner.

"Hey, I'm back," I say as I step in. Stacey glances at me quickly, revealing her red-rimmed eyes. She turns back to the sink after giving me a sad smile. "Did your dad go home already?"

"After you guys left," she says, grabbing a dirty dish to clean. It slips out of her hands and into the sink with a splash of soapy water.

"I'm sorry things didn't go as planned," I say. I take a few steps closer, and all I can see is how Stacey's hands are shaking the tiniest bit. She drops the same dish again. "I can help clean up." I step forward without letting her answer. I grab the sponge out of her grasp and stand in front of the sink until Stacey moves out of my way.

She's defeated when I take the dish, but she retreats to one of the dining room chairs to my right.

"Sorry you had to witness our family drama," Stacey says,

rubbing a tear away.

I finish scrubbing one of the dishes before rinsing it off.

"It happens." I shrug.

"It just feels like our lives are nothing but drama." Stacey sighs.

"Have you ever thought of just letting it go?"

Stacey stares at me, perplexed. "What do you mean?"

"Cutting him out of your life," I say, and Stacey frowns.

"Of course I have." She shrugs, shoulders heavy. "But he's still my dad. I just can't stop . . . wishing things were better."

"Dylan says things were different when you were a kid?"

Stacey lets out a low, tired laugh. "It seemed like it at least."

"Can you tell me about it?"

Stacey shifts and leans her elbow on the table.

"He used to play dress-up with me." She frowns in a sad, nostalgic way. "Dylan thinks I'm crazy, of course. He thinks all these memories are made-up, but I know they aren't." She composes herself a little as she speaks, more like the Stacey I know.

"How can you say for sure though?"

She shakes her head, looking down at the floor. "I can't."

I finish cleaning the dish and leave it to dry on the counter. When I look over my shoulder, Stacey's face is buried in her palms as she cries softly. I dry off my hands and pull out the chair next to her.

"Hey," I say, putting my hand on her shoulder, but she doesn't look up. If anything, the contact stirs her, and she cries more. Without hesitating, I wrap my arms around her, the same way Lori consoled me countless times in the past year. It feels off for it to be the other way around — me consoling someone else.

"I think he was right," Stacey says, pulling her head up and resting her elbows on the table.

"Who?"

She shakes her head, her hands clutched close to her mouth like she could begin crying again at any second. "Dylan said our dad just comes around to save face." She reaches for her phone that has been sitting in her lap. She holds the screen out to me.

It's a Facebook post from James Ellis.

Another perfect Thanksgiving in the books. My daughter is such a wonderful cook.

Below the caption is a photo of the table setting, all the dishes and utensils perfectly aligned. I take the phone from Stacey's hand, trying to get a closer look.

"When did he even take the photo?" I say.

"It's the photo I texted to him to tell him he was running late." She takes the phone from my hand. "Was the whole thing just a joke to him?"

I don't know what to say. I watch Stacey tear up again, but this time I have no idea what I'm supposed to do. She cries, her body shaking, before she takes a deep breath, sits up straight, and pulls her phone out again.

"What are you doing?" I ask.

"Deleting him from my Facebook," she says, scrolling to his profile and unfriending him. "He never tags me anyway. I'm just a prop." She closes Facebook and opens his contact card on her phone.

"Stacey," I say, but she hits "block" before I can stop her.

"It's fine," she says, getting up. "I don't want to be a part of his life." She starts pacing, her eyes darting around the room. There are casserole dishes everywhere. She made so much food that there are only a few bites out of each dish. "There's no room for leftovers in the fridge," she says, and it sounds like she's going to cry.

"Maybe we can drop some off at your mom's house for when she gets out of work."

"I made all this food, and no one ate anything." Her voice picks up an octave.

"It's fine. We'll make sure it doesn't go to waste." I move to stand, picking up one of the dishes, wondering what I'm supposed to do to make her feel better.

"No one even stayed long enough to eat the pie." She motions to my burnt apple pie, which is sitting on the counter untouched, and that's when she starts laughing. But then the laughter turns to tears. I cross the room, hugging her again, this time her arms wrapping around me.

"It's okay," I say, mimicking the same words Lori would tell me. I always wondered how Lori was such a solid rock for me to lean on. She was always there to catch me, and I never understood how. But now I do.

It's not about knowing the right words to say or the right thing to do. It's about just being there.

CHapteR 16

"Was it that bad?" Lori asks when I talk to her on the phone that night. I lock myself away into my room when she calls, making sure to stay quiet in case Stacey is close by. I tried to help Stacey clean up the kitchen, but she started to comb through everything in a way I'd never seen before. After the dishes were cleaned, she pulled every pot, pan, and plate out, claiming she wanted to reorganize. She was quiet as she worked, and all I could hear was the shuffling of boxes and bags.

"Yeah, I mean, I've never wanted to crawl out of a room more, and I wasn't even part of the discussion. I was just watching it. Not to mention what happened after James left."

"So, Dylan is pissed, and Stacey is sad?"

I pace the room, putting my ear to the door every now and then to see if Stacey is still out there. I hear a cabinet door close and more pans being clanked together.

"Stacey is currently reorganizing the entire kitchen," I whisper. "She's not even a neat freak. I wouldn't say she's messy, but she's definitely not organized, and right now I think she's trying to rearrange every cabinet out there or something."

"Maybe ask her for tips," Lori jokes. Lori always referred to me as the messy roommate. I can clean up after myself, but only if someone reminds me to.

I roll my eyes and sit on my bed. "Not helpful."

There's a soft laugh on the other end of the line. "Okay, so Stacey is dealing with her problems by trying to reorganize her life. You're hiding in your room. What's Dylan doing?"

I groan, lying down. "Dylan texted me when I got back from dropping him off about a hike he wants to do this weekend."

"Isn't he still in a boot? I mean, I'm not a hiker myself, but I think it tends to be a lot easier to do when you don't need crutches."

"He doesn't have crutches. He can't have them because of his shoulder. He wants to start training now by doing small walks and hikes to build up the strength in his ankle again."

"Sounds like the boy wants to prove his dad wrong."

"Well, if he tries to go hiking now, all he's going to do is prove his dad right."

Lori is quiet on the other end. "What's the hike?" she asks.

"It doesn't matter, Lori. It's not happening. We went for a walk at the beginning of the month, and he was having issues with his ankle."

"Just tell me. I'm on your side, but I have an idea."

I pause, wondering what plan Lori could have brewing. I keep her on the phone as I copy and paste the details of the hike Dylan texted me. The trail is practically flat compared to what we normally hike, but anything feels like too much right now. I sit in silence as Lori reads through the text I sent her.

"If Dylan wants to hike. I say let him hike," she finally says.

"I thought you were on my side?" I say, my voice rising. I sit up, listening, but the muffled sounds of Stacey out in the kitchen still float their way into my room.

"I am, so hear me out. Dylan chose an easy hike. The beginning of the hike is flat. When you get a mile in, you can turn around before it starts to get hard. You both get some much-needed fresh air, and no one gets hurt. *Or* . . ." She pauses for dramatic effect. "You don't even go that far into the hike, Dylan realizes how unprepared he is, and you turn around with Dylan knowing he needs more time to heal."

"And what if he doesn't realize he needs more time to heal?"

"That's what you're there for. To make sure he doesn't push himself too far."

I mull over the idea in my mind, letting the option sit with me. I want so badly for things to go back to the way they were before, when Dylan and I did every adventure together. There was never a worry in my mind as to whether what we were doing was dangerous or not. So, why is it that now I can't let it go?

"Lori, I don't want him to go."

"It's just a mile or two. He walks that much every day. Now he'll just have a better view." Her voice is light.

I'm silent, knowing Lori's right. Every part of me wants to hold Dylan in place, but I feel the control slipping out of my grasp.

Lori hears the apprehension in my silence. "He'll get back

out there, Marly, whether you like it or not."

I know Lori is right; I'm just not willing to admit it.

A couple days later, I pick Dylan up from his apartment, and we make our way to Seven Bridges Trail. The beginning of the trail is flat, then after the first mile the elevation increases, but that shouldn't matter. We won't be getting that far anyway. That's what I have to remind myself the entire drive. It isn't a hike. It's a walk. One mile, and that's it.

I made Dylan promise to not push himself, and that means we have an established turnaround point on the trail, but a part of me hopes he'll ask to turn around a lot sooner than that.

Beside me as I drive, Dylan seems more like his old self, all smiles for the adventure ahead. His hand grips mine as we drive, his thumb running circles up and down my palm.

"I pictured our first hike together back in Colorado a little differently, but this will have to do," Dylan says, motioning to the brace on his foot. It's been a couple days now without his boot—a fact he's proud of. He only wears the brace occasionally; today he wears it out of caution. He walked down the stairs of his apartment flawlessly when I picked him up, but all I can picture is how bad his limp was when he walked out of Stacey's apartment after the unsuccessful family dinner.

When we arrive, I park the truck as close to the trailhead as I can. When I picked Dylan up, we switched to his truck, leaving the bus behind in exchange for all-wheel drive.

The late-November air is crisp, and there's a few inches of fresh snow on the ground. It's not the first snowfall of the year, but in the past few weeks, the snow has been accumulating, creating a light coating over everything.

Tomorrow is Thanksgiving, and this time Janet won't be working, Stacey won't be cooking, and the four of us will hopefully have an uneventful dinner. When I woke up to two more inches of snow, I was excited, thinking perhaps the idea of slippery terrain might be enough to sway Dylan's plan, or even that Janet may ask for Dylan's help cooking, but it never happened. When I texted Dylan this morning to see if he still wanted to go, the idea of fresh snow seemed only to excite him.

Dylan steps out of the truck with a wide grin, and I follow close behind.

"Is your mom going to yell at me for letting you hike?" I ask, eyeing his bad ankle. He smiles as he takes the lead, making his way toward the trailhead. It's been a few weeks since we did the walk at Alta Lakes, and Dylan has reassured me over and over that his ankle is fine, but a pit of worry sits in my stomach.

"She'd be glad I have a babysitter." He turns back and winks but doesn't completely answer the question.

We don't carry much on us today. Since the hike is short, I'm just carrying a backpack with water and extra layers in case we get cold. Dylan is empty-handed and the happiest I've seen him since I arrived in Colorado. I want to be excited with him, but all I can seem to do now is worry.

The hike begins as a wide-open trail. It snowed just enough to coat everything, letting us leave footprints as we walk. The sun is starting to shine through the clouds above us, making the fresh snow fleeting. But for now, it's a magical winter wonderland, each tree branch highlighted in white.

I let Dylan lead the way, and he focuses on his steps as he walks. I watch, waiting to see him limp, but he never does. When we walked at Alta Lakes, I was too consumed with my camera to notice when Dylan was struggling, so today I left the camera at the apartment, promising myself I'd focus on him today.

"How's the ankle?" I ask when we're half a mile in.

He slows down until we're standing side by side. He takes my hand and matches my stride.

"Perfect," he says, taking in the wintry views.

I smile back, but it doesn't reach my eyes. Whether Dylan notices or not isn't clear, but his gaze shifts to the forest around us.

We continue onward, reaching the first bridge when we're almost a mile in. It's nothing more than a long wooden bridge that takes us over the stream of water that runs along the trail, but Dylan is eager to cross it.

"I missed this," he murmurs. I can feel his eyes on me, but I train my gaze on anything else. A tiny ghost of anxiety sits in my core, waiting to come out, but I ease it away, promising myself this bridge means we'll be turning around soon.

As soon as we cross the first bridge, the second bridge comes into sight. I feel a tiny sense of relief when I see it. We're about to reach the end of the second bridge, our agreed-upon turnaround spot. Dylan stops and turns to look at me.

"Let's keep going." He smiles.

I'm unable to hide the shock on my face, and Dylan frowns in response.

"This is where we said we'd turn around," I say.

"I know, but I feel fine. Better than fine. Besides, the views don't start until at least the third bridge." He half turns in the direction of the trail ahead, but I stay firm in my spot on the bridge.

"That's also when the trail starts to get steep, and you can't do that with your ankle right now."

"Sure I can. Marly, I'm fine." His eyes are pleading as he grips my hand, trying to usher me forward.

"There's snow on the ground!" The words are sharp, my voice raised in a way I didn't mean, and I instantly regret it. Dylan raises his eyebrows, seeming more surprised than hurt. He drops my hand and walks past me, back in the direction of the parking lot.

"Dylan, I'm sorry," I say quickly, reaching for his hand. He takes it, but he doesn't look up at me as he walks.

"This is what we agreed on. This was the turnaround point, so I'm turning around." The words come out flat, and I'm not sure even he believes them as he speaks.

"I just don't want you to make things worse," I say.

He nods, his gaze fixed on his feet as he walks.

"Have you done this trail before?" I ask.

"A lot. I just wanted you to see it," he says, finally meeting my gaze. His eyes are sad, like he's given up, ready to succumb to his fate.

We walk in silence on the way back, letting the sound of the stream be the thing that leads us onward. When we finally get back to the truck, I notice a small limp in Dylan's leg.

"Does your ankle hurt?" I ask as we both get back into the truck.

"It's fine," he says, a little frustration sparking through.

My first response is to reiterate why it's important that we didn't go farther than the second bridge, but I bite my tongue and start up the engine.

"We can ice it when we get back," I say, pulling out of the parking lot.

Dylan is silent next to me, and when I look over, his gaze is out the window again, the corners of his lips turned down—the complete opposite of how he was when we pulled into the parking lot.

"You okay?" I ask.

That seems to spark something in him, and he lifts his head to look over at me. "I said I'm fine."

"Dylan, I need you to be honest with me about how your ankle is. You aren't doing anyone favors by trying to gloss it over. You're only going to end up getting hurt again."

"Then it hurts, okay?" he says, dropping his head back against the headrest. "It hurts, and I wish it didn't, because how am I supposed to do ten-mile hikes when a short walk is hard? I want to be out there." He points to the mountains that roll out in front of us as we drive. "I should be planning hikes or a ski weekend with Trent, but I can't do any of that because of this stupid ankle."

"There are other things you can do," I say, my words gentle.

"Like what?"

I glance over, and his eyes are out the window again. I've never seen Dylan cry, but this is perhaps the closest I've gotten. Even when we were in the ER, he put on a smile, but now he's crumbling. He's leaning against the passenger window, his elbow keeping him propped up, but his eyes are red, eyebrows scrunched like he's barely keeping it together.

"I'm sure Trent is dying for a player two on that video game he's been playing."

Dylan doesn't say anything, so I try again.

"Or if you're looking for outdoor activities for the winter, we can try ice fishing."

Dylan lets out an exasperated laugh. "I'm not that desperate. I'll just watch Trent accuse me of cheating when I beat him at his favorite game."

He smiles, and I take that as a tiny victory. The drive continues in silence for a while, not even the music on to keep us company.

Dylan shifts next to me, his voice low. "When we were on the trail and I said I missed it, I didn't mean hiking. I mean, yes, of course I miss it, but I meant I miss hiking with you."

When he says the words, I instantly feel guilty. The entire time I was so focused on turning around that I never bothered to realize that was our first hike together that was more than a mile since Mount Washington in August. Now it's November, an entire season later, and all I can focus on is *not* hiking. I feel a little trapped myself, realizing I'm in much the same situation I was a year ago.

"Me too," I say, but I know it's not in the same way he does. I miss how we were before his accident, before all I could do was worry.

CHAPTER 17

James is leaning against the apartment building when we pull into the parking lot. I don't recognize him at first, having only met him once, but I know it's him by the way Dylan stiffens in his seat next to me.

"What the hell," Dylan mutters, getting out of the truck before I finish putting it into park. He's halfway to the front of the building by the time I unbuckle. Dylan still has a slight limp in his walk, but I can tell he's fighting to hide it from his dad.

"Well, so nice of someone to answer their phone," James says, uncrossing his arms as he stands and takes a few paces forward.

"What are you doing here?" Dylan asks, his voice gruff.

"I'm heading back home, so I wanted to say goodbye before I left. I tried calling." He raises an accusatory eyebrow.

"You've never seemed bothered about leaving without saying goodbye in the past," Dylan shoots back. James's face drops the smallest bit.

"Where have you been?" James says, eyeing Dylan like he's

sizing him up.

"Hiking," Dylan shoots back without hesitation. James glances over to me, noticing my presence for the first time.

"You go too?" he says, turning to me.

I hesitate, unsure how to respond. I glance at Dylan for help, but his eyes are glued to his dad.

"Yes," I finally say.

"Figures," James says, shaking his head. "Boy doesn't have his head on straight, so why would you?"

"Don't talk to her like that," Dylan snaps, his words sharp. James seems surprised by the response, taking a half step back.

"Take it easy, kid." He puts his hands up in mock defense, rolling his eyes. "I just thought once you had a girlfriend, she'd be able to knock some sense into you, but I guess I shouldn't be surprised."

"If you wanted to say goodbye, you can leave now." Dylan takes my hand and starts toward the front door of the building, past where his dad is standing.

"So sensitive," James mutters. His tone shifts, and he takes a few steps toward us. "I'm just trying to look out for you."

"Well, do it the same way you've done it since I was a kid: miles and miles away from here."

Dylan opens the front door to the building, guiding me in, but I pause when James starts speaking again.

"Those hikes aren't safe, Dylan." The words come out like a warning.

Dylan ignores his father and puts a hand on my back, trying to usher me in.

"Marly, right?" James says. I'm inside the building now, but I move to peek around Dylan through the doorway. "You can't support this. I mean, you two went for a hike today, and he's already limping again. Be honest, how do you really feel about him getting back out there?"

James locks me in his gaze, and Dylan pushes on my arm, urging me to go into the building.

"Come on," Dylan says under his breath.

"Hmm?" James says, prodding.

"I'm worried when he hikes," I admit.

Dylan turns quickly, keeping his back to me when he moves to look at his dad. "Get out of here." He says the words slowly, and James rolls his eyes.

"Yeah, love you too," James says. With a final wave of a hand, he turns away and heads back to his car. I'm too stunned to speak, and Dylan keeps his stance at the door, watching his dad get into the car.

I expect the tension to drop once his dad drives off, but it seems to only linger as Dylan turns back into the building, moving around me and toward the stairs leading up to his apartment.

"You okay?" I ask, following close behind.

"Of course I'm not okay!" he snaps at me. His words are loud, his face red with anger. "My dad comes here to gloat, and you tell him exactly what he wants to hear. That's all he'll be talking about now next time I see him." He gets to the top of the stairwell and paces there, running his hands through his hair.

"I didn't know what else to say," I murmur.

"Say that you're happy for me to get back out there." He says the words so quickly that they morph together.

"I can't," I admit. The words sting as I say them, and I want to take them back, but I also can't stop myself from telling Dylan the truth.

His face softens after I speak, but not in a way that says I'm forgiven. The corners of his lips turn down, and it feels like he's hearing me for the first time today.

"What do you mean?" he asks, unsure.

"It scares me to think of you hiking again. I want you to, and I want you to be safe, but it feels like those are two very different things."

He opens his mouth, then shakes his head and turns away, making his way back to his apartment.

"I need to go ice my ankle," he says, walking to the front door of his apartment.

"Dylan." I begin to follow him, but he turns back.

"Just go home, Marly." The words come out gentle, like he's given up on me, and that makes it hurt all the more. I want to say something, but before I get the chance, he opens the door to his apartment and goes inside, leaving me alone in the hallway.

§

Stacey is there when I get back to the apartment, and if I thought Dylan was in bad shape, Stacey is even worse. I've gotten so used to getting home to an empty apartment that seeing Stacey sitting on the couch makes me jump in surprise.

"Sorry, I didn't know you'd be home," I say quickly. Her arms are folded around her knees, which are pulled tight to her chest. Her cheeks are bright red, stained with recent tears.

"I took the day off," she mumbles into the arm of her sleeve. She unfurls herself, putting her feet on the floor and wiping the tears off her face.

"You okay?" I ask.

Stacey gives me a weak smile. "Yeah, my dad just left. I thought he was staying longer."

"He was waiting for Dylan at his apartment," I say, moving to join Stacey on the couch.

"He was?" She perks up, surprised by the news.

"It wasn't a good visit."

She frowns, nodding in acceptance. "What did he say?"

"Mostly he was just there to remind Dylan that hiking is dangerous."

Stacey lets out a single exhausted laugh.

"What?" I ask.

"My dad said he was leaving, so I thought I'd give him one last chance, that maybe he'd hear me if it was just me and him, but it didn't make a difference. The entire time my dad was here, he was just on his phone. I could barely get him to look at me. Meanwhile, Dylan is trying to avoid our dad like the plague, but he just can't stop obsessing over what Dylan's doing." She wipes her face again. "I'm done giving him second chances."

"Why do you think he's always hounding Dylan anyway?"

She shrugs in a nonchalant way. "Who knows. Dylan is a lot like our grandpa, so I assume that's a big reason. Our dad hated

Grandpa, and Dylan is so much like him, so . . ." She trails off, lost in her train of thought. "He couldn't control Grandpa, but he can control Dylan. Or at least he can try."

We both let out a small chuckle, knowing there's nothing that can control Dylan.

Stacey lets out a stronger laugh. "Dylan hikes half for the joy of it and half because it's his way of giving our dad the middle finger. He knows our dad doesn't think he should do it or that he can't do it. Dylan sees it as all the more reason to do hike."

Stacey moves off the couch with a heavy sigh.

"Where you going?" I ask. She grabs her coat off the hanger and slips her arms through.

"Taking a lesson from Dylan and moving on with my life." She takes her purse from where it's sitting on the small table near the door. "I'm going out with a few friends for dinner. I'll be home later tonight."

Before I know it, I'm alone in the apartment, still trying to unravel everything that happened. It feels like I just ran head-on into a decade's worth of family drama without warning. Eventually, I get Lori on the phone, trying to make sense of it all. I've finally finished recounting everything that's happened, but Lori's said very little, which is very unlike her.

"I'm sorry, Marly."

"What am I supposed to do? All I had to do was stick up for Dylan in front of his dad, and I screwed it up. Saying nothing would have been better than what I said."

"He just needs time to decompress."

I lie back in my bed, staring at the blank walls of the room.

"But that's not the only issue," I say. "During the hike today, Dylan wanted to keep going, but I made him turn around. He was already mad at having to turn around, and then on top of it, he was limping by the time we got back to his truck."

"Dylan will be fine," Lori says. "Just give him a pep talk and a little more time to heal, and before you know it, he'll be right back at it again."

My head spins at the thought.

"Can I say something?"

"Yeah, of course," Lori says.

"I don't want him to heal faster." I blurt out the words before I can regret them.

"What do you mean?" Her voice is skeptical and wary.

"The sooner he's better, the sooner he's right back out there on the mountains. And there's a tiny part of my brain that's thinking, 'Strike three, and you're out.' "

Lori lets my words sink in. "You're afraid he's going to die out there?" She says the words slowly, like she isn't entirely sure if she understands what I mean.

I've never admitted the words to myself before, and it stings to hear Lori say it out loud. "I know it makes me sound crazy — "

"No, it doesn't," Lori says, her words soft. "You've lost the two most important people in your life already. Of course you're afraid of losing another one. That doesn't make you crazy; it makes you human."

I nod, though I know she can't see me.

"The way you're thinking is probably the same thing your mom was thinking every time you and your dad went hiking.

I'm willing to bet every time you two went on one of your crazy adventures, she was anxiously awaiting the text that meant you had gotten back to the car safely."

I let out a sad, nervous laugh.

"He'll be okay, Marly. He had a surprising string of bad luck, but he'll be fine, just like you've been fine on every hike you've gone on."

"He just seemed so mad at me when we had to turn back."

"I don't think he was mad at you," Lori says.

"But he just walked away from me like he was giving up," I tell her.

"Marly, if hiking is as important to him as everyone seems to think, then it's not a *you* problem. The issue is that Dylan has spent his entire life doing this *one thing,* and now he can't. He's angry, but not at you. He was just angry at himself because he *can't* do the thing he loves most. His body won't *let him.*"

"I know, but—"

"No buts," she interrupts. "He feels trapped in his body because he can't do the things he wants to. Give the boy some space. Let him have time to process the fact that things are going to take a lot longer than he'd like."

"What do I do until then? What about his dad?"

"There are some things you can't fix. His dad is one of those things. Dylan has to deal with it in his own way. But I'd say a good place to start is giving him some space, and then when he's ready, talk to him."

CHAPTER 18

It's Thanksgiving day, but I can't bring myself to show my face at Dylan's family dinner.

"You sure you don't want to come?" Stacey asks, lingering in the doorway of my room.

"Yeah, I'm not feeling good." I muster the excuse, hiding myself away in bed.

She frowns, but she leaves me in peace, the front door making a soft click behind her.

I don't see Dylan for the rest of the week. The excuse of working late always comes up, but in reality, it feels like work is just a convenient excuse for him to avoid me. We still text throughout the week, but never more than quick updates and to say good night and good morning.

Stacey is a shell of herself in the days following her dad's visit. She comes and goes from the apartment, mostly keeping to herself. She puts up a good front, smiling at me like it's something on her to-do list, but I've gotten to know her enough to see how off she is.

I've grown used to the way she lingers in the living room and kitchen, always cooking up some new recipe, but this past week she's been ordering takeout and retreating to her room. It's Friday night and her first day off for the past few days, and she's barely left her room once. Her typical Friday night ritual when she isn't working is to bake something like cookies or brownies and catch up on whatever episodes she missed of her latest TV show, so when she doesn't emerge from her room, I go digging through the cabinets and pull out a box of brownie mix.

I've never been a baker. I can cook, but only enough to get by. There's always something that I mess up during the juggling process of preparing food, but this time I go through the steps carefully. It probably takes me longer than the average person to bake the brownies, but either way, they end up in the oven ready to go. I'm sitting on the couch, and there's only five minutes left on the oven when I hear Stacey's door squeak open.

"Are you baking?" she says, stepping into the living room. Her hair is tied up in a messy bun, and she's wearing her favorite pair of sweatpants. Despite the fact that she's been up since 8:00 a.m., it looks like she just rolled out of bed.

"Figured you needed a pick-me-up," I say. The smell of the brownies fills the air, drawing Stacey closer until she joins me on the couch. She looks shocked, a smile lighting her face in a way I haven't seen in days.

"You could say that," she says softly.

"Everything okay?"

She looks up and smiles, but when she does, tears break through, and she shakes her head.

"I'm just trying to wrap my head around the idea that my dad isn't ever going to be the person I want him to be," she says slowly, like she's trying to convince herself of what she says.

"Sometimes . . ." I struggle with the words, wondering if they'll be at all helpful to Stacey. "You have to learn to be happy all on your own, because you never know who will be in your life tomorrow."

Stacey glances over, her eyes tired and heavy. "Was your dad a good dad?"

I'm put off by the question, thrown by the conversation being aimed back at me.

"He was the best," I say simply.

"And you're happy now even though he's gone?" Her eyebrows are cinched together, her mind lost in thought.

"I'm happy despite my parents being gone," I say softly. The words feel difficult to say, more complicated than they really are, because part of me doesn't feel happy. It feels impossible to be happy when there are so many points of my life I wish I could change. But I could be happy if I just let myself be.

The timer goes off, and I get up to remove the brownies from the oven. Stacey shifts and turns the TV on, pulling up HBO Max and sifting through the shows we've been watching. I cut up the brownies and hand her a slice, still warm.

"Thank you," she says, and in that moment, we feel like lifelong friends falling into a Friday-night tradition.

We're almost an hour into our show when there's a soft knock at the door. Stacey is the one who gets it, crossing the living room to open the door.

"Hey," she says, almost in a whisper, to whoever's on the other side of the door.

"Is Marly here?"

I recognize Dylan's voice instantly and shift to get up. Stacey leaves me at the door with Dylan as she makes her way back to the couch.

My first thought upon seeing him is confusion. Did Trevor drop him off?

"Can we talk?" He gestures to the stairs that lead back down to the parking lot.

I turn back to Stacey, who's already wrapped up in blankets again, waiting to continue the show. I grab my jacket from the coatrack near the door, slipping my arms into the sleeves.

"Start the next episode without me," I tell her before stepping out and shutting the door behind me.

We walk down the stairs, and Dylan beats me to the bottom, offering his hand for me to take while I finish the last couple steps.

"I got the all clear from the doctor to drive again."

I want to be excited. I know the proper response is to congratulate him and be happy with him, but all I can feel is that someone just yanked a rug out from under me again. This is good. I know this is a good thing. Dylan needs to heal, and when he heals, he can return to his life, but I feel like I need to reach out and hold him in place. I need to beg him to not go out there again, because I can't face thinking that something worse could happen to him. And just thinking those thoughts makes me hate myself, because how can I be so selfish?

"That's great," I say, but the words fall flat. We're standing under a streetlight in the parking lot, and there's a tiny flurry of snow falling. It's so small that I can only see it as it passes through the light of the streetlamp before it melts when it hits the ground.

"You don't seem thrilled," Dylan says.

"I am," I lie. "I'm just tired." I try to smile and reassure him. Whether he believes me or not, I can't tell, but he lets it go.

"I wanted to come apologize," he says. "For how I acted when we ran into my dad. It's not your job to stand up for me."

"It's not, but I should have." I take a deep breath and let out a rough, heavy sigh.

Dylan smiles and stuffs his hands into his pockets. "How's Stacey?"

I shrug. "It's been rough, but brownies got her to emerge from her room."

He nods. "She'll bounce back, but this is why I wish she'd just give up on him so we can all move on."

"Yeah, but at the end of the day, he's still your dad."

"Not to me," he says roughly. My first instinct is to protest and try to defend his dad, but I realize there's nothing left to defend. I just met him, but if I were Dylan, I'd probably feel the same way. And maybe that's okay.

"No boot and you can drive," I say, trying to change the subject. "What's your plan?" I try to force enthusiasm into my voice.

He smiles and wraps his arms around me until my hands are resting against his chest. In the cold winter night, his body feels like a furnace, and I can't help but lean into him more.

"Now the real training begins." He smiles.

"Like what?"

"More hiking." He shrugs matter-of-factly.

My thoughts go back to the limp he was hiding last week. I do everything in my power to keep the smile on my face, but then it's Dylan whose smile wavers.

"What?"

He opens his mouth to speak, staring off into the darkness of the night. What's always stunned me about winter is how quiet it is. There are no bugs or animals rustling around in the night. And when there's snow on the ground, it muffles out any other noise. Tonight there are only a few inches at our feet, but it feels like we're the only two people in the world.

"Two years isn't a lot of time to finish twenty-three mountains, plus I can't just start where I left off. Not with this injury. It will be weeks before I'm back out there."

Weeks. That's all the time I have. Not months. Just weeks before the pit of worry becomes my permanent residence.

If I were a good girlfriend, this is the part where I'd tell Dylan that he can do it, but I don't. I can't get myself to say the words, because I don't want them to be true. I want Dylan to let go of this insane goal to hike all the 14ers in Colorado. And just the thought of wanting him to give up makes me hate myself more.

"I guess I'm just afraid to fail." His face drops when he says the words, and it's like I'm seeing him for the first time. He's not just afraid; he's terrified. He can't even look at me, and I can't tell if it's because he can sense I want him to fail or because he's fighting his own battle.

I don't want to see him like this. No matter how I feel, seeing him face the fear of his own failure is worse.

We're still wrapped in each other's arms, standing under the spotlight of the streetlamp. I reach out my hand, and his cheek is warm against my cool fingers. I turn his face until he's looking at me, and before he can protest, I kiss him. It's not like our other kisses, which have been casual, blissful almost. This kiss feels desperate, like my selfishness will be overpowered by what Dylan wants so badly.

He kisses me back, his lips tracing mine until it feels like my head is spinning. When I finally pull away and open my eyes, he's gazing back at me.

"You're going to do it," I say boldly, forcing myself to believe it.

He smiles back at me, his eyes full of wonder, like I've just thrown him a lifeline. But now it feels like I'm the one who needs to be rescued.

CHAPTER 19

It's the beginning of December, and despite the snow falling in steady sheets of white, we're at a pool with temperatures closer to bathwater than winter.

"Want to race?" Dylan says, gripping the edge of the pool.

The pool is now an official part of Dylan's recovery plan. It's a safe way to exercise and build strength without putting too much strain on his joints. Dylan was overjoyed that he had an excuse to get a membership to the local community center, but I would have been a little more inclined to training that didn't involve swimming.

"You know you'll win," I say, stepping into the deep end of the pool using the ladder, unlike the dive Dylan took. He already knows from our camping trip over the summer that swimming isn't my preferred method of exercise. I sink deeper with each step down the ladder.

"I've got a bad ankle and arm; you've got a chance," he says.

I step off the last rung on the ladder and fall into the water, my head dunking in. I swim back up and reach for the edge of the pool next to Dylan.

It's not that I can't swim — I can — I'm just not well practiced. Seeing me swim is closer to watching a terrified dog tread water. My head's over the water, but you'd never be able to notice with the amount of splashing.

The community center's pool is massive, with six lanes reserved for people who want to practice laps. Right now, Dylan and I share one lane, while a few other people swim up and down the other lanes.

"Okay, now what?" I ask, still clutching the side of the pool. The water on this end is six feet — too deep to touch — while the other end is only three feet. Dylan insisted on starting at the deep end so he could dive in.

"We race," he says, turning to position himself to take off. "One . . ."

"What?" I ask, not at all ready.

"Two . . ."

"Dylan —"

"Three!"

He shoots off, diving into the water and making long strokes across the pool. His focus is on his legs, and the rotation of his left arm is a little off. His dislocated shoulder hasn't been bothering him, but he also hasn't been using it. This will be the first big test for his shoulder and how it's healing.

After watching him for a few seconds, I push off the wall of the pool and begin my lap, quickly losing momentum. I attempt to copy Dylan's form as I swim, but the movement feels too unnatural to be considered correct. When I get to the shallow end, I switch to the doggy paddle momentarily until my feet are able to touch the bottom, and I walk to where Dylan is.

"Told you," I say, coming up to meet him. He's smiling, water dripping down his face as he stands in the waist-deep water.

"My mom brought me to swim lessons when I was little. It stuck." He shrugs.

"How's your arm?" I ask as he rolls his shoulder out a little.

"Tight. It feels a little weird, but nothing to be worried about."

"And your ankle?"

"Don't even notice it," he says, and then he pushes off the wall again to start another lap. I try my best to keep up, but I'm not able to keep good form and have to continually stop to catch my breath. At the end of each lap, Dylan waits for me until I catch up.

I only do a few laps with Dylan, but my body is already exhausted, so I let Dylan take the lead and have his fun. He swims for half an hour before joining me at the edge of the pool and pulling himself out of the water.

"How do you feel?" I ask, my feet still dangling in the water.

His smile answers before he's able to put it to words. "Great! This is the first time I've been able to do something physical without any sort of pain." He rolls his ankle in the water, testing it. "I have to check with my physical therapist, but he might let me start long hikes in a few weeks. Then who knows, in just a month or two I could be right where I left off."

The words throw me like they always do when he talks

174

about his recovery plan. "Yeah, but I wouldn't start hiking yet. You should probably take it easy so you don't reinjure yourself."

"I've been taking it easy," he says quickly, trying to reassure me.

"Yeah, but don't you think it might just be a better idea to make sure it's all healed and stays healed? You know, tread with caution?"

Dylan looks at me, confused. "What do you mean? That's why I've been doing all this physical therapy and training. If I just wanted it to heal, I would have sat and done nothing all these weeks. But I want to get back to my life."

"I'm just saying, more time for your ankle to heal is a good thing." I'm trying to reassure him, but I've already lost control of the conversation.

"I'm doing what my doctor says."

"But your doctor doesn't know you the way I know you." I cringe even as the words come out of my mouth.

"What's that supposed to mean?"

I bite my lip, looking off at the pool in front of us while I feel Dylan's gaze on me. "You push yourself too hard."

He shakes his head, still confused. "No, I don't."

"Sometimes you can be a little careless," I say, trying to make the words light.

Dylan doesn't say anything after that. He lets out a soft, unamused laugh and gets up.

"I'm going to go to the locker room and get changed. I'll meet you at the car."

He leaves before I have the chance to say anything else, and I silently scold myself. I should have just let it go. The conversation happened so quickly; I barely had a chance to realize what even happened. It felt like an argument, but neither of us ever raised our voices.

I make my way to the locker room, changing quickly and not bothering to deal with my hair, which is still dripping went and now covered in chlorine. Dylan's standing at the entrance to the community center, waiting for me at the double doors.

"Ready?" I say with a soft smile, hoping he's already moved on from our conversation.

"Yup." He definitely hasn't moved on.

Since Dylan's ankle is mostly healed, we've been driving his truck lately, and Dylan has gone back to being the one to pick me up. The ride home is silent, with nothing but the radio to break the tension. When he pulls up in front of my building, I turn to kiss him before opening the truck door. He kisses me back, but it's so quick, it's like he isn't even there.

"Bye." I wave softly. He gives me a quick half smile before driving away.

I let out a deep sigh before turning to walk up the stairs to my apartment. A text chimes on my phone. I toss my gym bag full of my wet towel and bathing suit into the bathroom and check the text.

It's an automated message saying my photo order is ready to be picked up. I completely forgot I ordered more prints for the café earlier in the week. I do what I do best in these situations: I stop thinking about my problems, and I start moving. Within an hour, my hair is dried and I'm at the store picking up my print, buying a frame before I bring it to Snapshot Café. I already have a few other prints up for sale, but Riley always seems thrilled when I come to drop another off. It feels like I'm here every few days now. I've only sold three prints since I moved here, but it's enough to fuel my desire to keep coming back. It's pennies in comparison to wedding photography, but I enjoy the seclusion of nature photography more than the hustle and bustle of wedding photography.

It's crowded at the café tonight, a loud murmur of voices greeting me at the door as soon as I walk in.

"Hey, I'm here to see Riley," I say when a waiter comes over to greet me.

"Sure! I'll go get her." She glances down at the frame in my hand and smiles.

A few seconds later, Riley comes walking out, all smiles as she sees me standing with photo in hand.

"You've become quite the regular," she says, putting her hand out for the frame. I give it to her, watching her expression as she looks at the photo I took on our camping trip last month. "Where was this taken?"

"Alta Lakes."

"It's beautiful," she half murmurs. "You had another sale since you were last here too. Paychecks will be ready next week." She smiles and tucks the frame into her arm.

"Oh, and I also forgot!" I pull out a box of business cards. After Riley's insistence, I got them printed off. I hand her the box.

"Perfect!" she says, looking a card over before turning back to me. "Where you going next?"

The question catches me off guard. "What do you mean?"

"Well, most of the photographers who bring their photos in are local, so we get a lot of the same things. But you've brought in ocean photos, Yellowstone, Washington. The photos sell fast because they aren't within driving distance. I assume you travel a lot."

"Just in the past couple months." I shrug.

"Well, keep it up." She smiles. "But don't forget to keep coming back so we can sell the photos. Things are about to get busy again with ski season in full swing. I'd love to have a few more prints ready in the back for when things get bought."

"How many more?" I ask.

"Ten, maybe twenty?"

My eyes go wide. "Really?"

"Yeah, you've sold enough prints to have your place here. Come back in a week with some new ones?"

"Of course," I say, still in shock. Riley walks off with a smile, my photo in hand.

The entire drive back to the apartment, my mind is working through a mental catalog of my photos, trying to count up what my best work is. There are so many photos, and there are even a few more from Alta Lakes that would be perfect, but Riley's words keep playing on repeat in my head.

Where you going next?

CHAPTER 20

"It's not that Dylan isn't talking to me. He's just not . . . talking to me," I tell Lori, feeling just as lost as I sound. It's our weekly video chat session. Lori was catching me up on the latest drama happening in college—the school is trying to shut down the soft-serve ice cream machine in the cafeteria and students are signing a petition—but now it's my turn to attempt to catch Lori up on the latest with Dylan.

"What in the world does *that* mean?"

"It means it's been two days since we went swimming at the community center, and he responds to my texts and phone calls, but he never actually says anything."

"Has he brought up what happened at the pool?"

"No. That's the issue. He hasn't brought up anything. If I don't start a conversation, then there isn't a conversation. He doesn't act like he's mad; he just acts like he doesn't care." I can feel myself starting to talk in circles, losing my breath in the process.

"Okay, first off, take a breath," Lori says, her voice level as always. "He's a guy. They don't express themselves the same way we do."

"I think he's poorly expressing that he's mad at me," I say, burying my face in my hands.

"For saying that he's not careful when he hikes?" Lori asks, confused.

"No. If I'd said that—which is what I wanted to say—things would probably be fine. Instead, I said he was careless, which is arguably the same thing, but a much harsher way of delivering the news."

"Okay then . . ." She ponders over the words. "Just go and say sorry. Explain you're worried about him, and then all will be forgiven because your overbearingness comes from a place of love."

I open my mouth to protest, then stop myself. "Right now?" I ask.

Lori cocks an eyebrow. "Either now or let yourself think and wonder about why Dylan's mad at you for the next few hours, days, or even weeks, knowing your ability to ignore a problem."

I make a face, unamused.

She shrugs. "I'm just working off your track record. Now go talk to your boyfriend. Communication is key to a healthy relationship."

I roll my eyes. "Look who's talking."

"I'm a perfect example of what not to do in romantic relationships. Now *go*." She motions with her hands for me to go out the door. We're both laughing by the time I go to end the call, but as soon as I'm alone again, I can feel my nerves start to pick up.

I grab my keys and head out the door before I can change my mind.

Truthfully, it's not that I'm afraid to say sorry to him; it's that I'm afraid I'm blowing everything out of proportion and that by saying sorry I'll only bring more attention to what happened.

When I pull up to Dylan's apartment, I don't see his truck parked anywhere, but I get out and make my way toward the entrance to the building, assuming he moved his truck somewhere else. He didn't mention going out to do anything today, but given his anger, I wouldn't put it past him to not tell me what he was up to.

I walk up the stairs and down the hall to his apartment door, knocking, but no one answers. I stand there a couple minutes, knocking and putting my ear to the door to hear if there is at least someone on the other side, but there's just silence.

I pull my phone out and call Dylan, but after a couple of rings, it goes straight to voicemail. With a sigh of frustration, I turn to leave, but when I do, Dylan and Trent are making their way up the stairs. Dylan's laughing at something Trent said when he finally looks up to see me waiting at the door.

They're both surprised to see me there, that much I'm sure of. Both boys are red in the face, but not from embarrassment — from being out in the cold. Dylan is in full hiking gear, with his winter bag, boots, and gloves, his hands gripping a pair of snowshoes. It's the entire winter hiking ensemble.

"Shit," I hear Trent say under his breath before turning to Dylan. "I'll be inside." He scoots past me and into the apartment, leaving us standing in the hall alone.

"You went hiking?" I gesture to the snowshoes.

He looks down at them and then back up at me. "I asked Trent to go with me, so I wasn't being careless." He says the words so casually that I almost don't catch the connection to our conversation from a few days ago.

"Trent hates hiking," I say.

"He knows I need someone to train with. He also knows how important it is to me."

The words sting, and they act like a slap in the face as Dylan moves past me to get to his door.

"I care," I say.

"It's hard to tell some days. You help me through physical therapy, but then you start to talk like you're trying to convince me to give up. You know how important it is for me to finish this list in two years, but you keep acting like you want me to quit before I've even started."

"I don't—"

"You do." He cuts me off. "You don't want me to do bigger, riskier hikes. Admit that for me."

I stare at him, glassy-eyed.

He shifts, whether frustrated or annoyed, I can't tell. "Tell me you want me to finish the 14er list. Tell me you're okay with me hiking these final summits."

I can't get myself to speak. Even if I wanted to, I can't say the words.

He looks up at the ceiling in frustration and drops his hand down to his side. He moves toward the front door of his apartment, ready to walk away from me at any moment.

"This is something I have to do, Marly. I thought you of all people would understand that." There isn't any anger when he speaks this time. If anything, he sounds exhausted. His voice is soft, begging me to understand.

"I don't want you to get hurt again." The words feel weak, like I'm shouting into a void.

"People get hurt, Marly. It's life. I can't stay home just so you know I'm safe."

"Of course I know that," I say, but now I'm crying. It feels like my knees are going to buckle, so it's all I can do to keep myself standing straight.

The snowshoes drop to the ground, and Dylan closes the distance between us, wrapping his arms around me. I'm not sure when or why it happened, but now I'm shaking, the sobs coming out in a hysterical rhythm.

"Breathe, Marly," he whispers. But I can't breathe. I can't stop seeing all the blood. I'm in the hospital again. Cora's crying face is in front of me. There're too many tears, and I've lost track of which tears are mine. The hospital is full of my family, all of them crying, all of them falling to pieces. And despite being surrounded by so many people, I'm alone.

"You're okay." A hand rubs up and down my back, and I hear the voice, but I'm not sure whose it is anymore. The memories attack me, an unwanted nuisance on my mind. I urge the images to go away, but they only seem to sink deeper and deeper until I fall.

"You're safe."

I'm being held together.

"Hey, look at me."

I blink, and Dylan's there, but there isn't any blood. He's watching me with a worried gaze, and when I shift, I realize he's the only thing keeping me standing.

I wipe my face, the tears coating my cheeks. When I finally come to, he sighs, looking away from me.

"I'm not mad at you," he says softly. "I'm mad at our situation."

I have Lori's words of what I'm supposed to say in the back of my mind, but the words don't feel like enough anymore.

"I know why you want me to stop," he says without looking at me. The words are chosen carefully as he speaks with slow cadence. "But I also know I need to do this for myself, and I'm going to do it with or without you."

I blink, a little stunned. "What do you mean?" I finally get myself to speak.

He looks at me, and when I see his face, I know this isn't good.

"I think we both need a break. For a little while at least."

It feels like everything freezes. How can he be holding me in his arms like this but want to go on a break? Or perhaps that's the issue. He doesn't want to hold me in his arms.

I untangle myself from his grasp and take a step back. Stepping away from him leaves my body cold and unsure.

"What?"

"I just think we would benefit from some space. You can focus on photography and take more photos for Snapshot Café, and I can focus on physical therapy and rebuilding my strength.

And then maybe . . ." He trails off, never finishing his sentence.

"And then what?"

His eyes burn into mine like he's looking at me for the last time. "And then I don't know what will happen."

CHAPTER 21

"**H**e wants to go on a break?" Lori says when I'm on the video chat with her again that night. It feels like I'm in shock more than anything else. I want to cry. It feels like my body needs me to cry, but after I left Dylan's apartment, I was numb. Nothing feels final. We aren't together, but we aren't broken up. At least it doesn't seem like we are. When I left his apartment, he walked me to the bus and gave me a hug goodbye. If things were different, it would have been a kiss goodbye, but who hugs someone goodbye after a breakup? Maybe we didn't break up?

"Yeah," I say. The emotions are there, biting at my skin, but they never come to the surface. I'm sitting in bed, my back to the headboard, while the white walls of the room surround me. The room is a blank slate. This was supposed to be my fresh start, so why does it feel so wrong?

"I guess . . ." Her words trail off. For once, Lori is speechless. "I guess wait a few days and feel it out?"

"And just sit at the apartment with his sister and pretend

like nothing's wrong?" I say, knowing Stacey already left to go to work.

"You can talk to her, Marly. You don't have to confide in just me."

"I know, but it's his sister," I say.

"But she's also your roommate. And your friend," Lori says softly.

"I know," I say. It's not that I don't feel close to Stacey. In fact, ever since the fiasco with her dad, I've never felt closer. And while I'm happy to be her shoulder to cry on, it's hard to think of it the other way around when the person I'm crying about is her brother.

There's a long beat of silence where neither of us knows what else to say.

"I was thinking of going on a small road trip this week," I say, trying to shift the subject.

"What? Really?" That picks up her attention. She sits up from wherever she's lounging about in the apartment.

"The café wants more prints, and the owner told me she likes my photos because they aren't from around here, so I figure I'm the girl for the job." And also because I now have more free time than I know what to do with.

"Where are you going?" she asks, her voice getting more and more animated.

"I don't know yet," I admit. I haven't put much thought into it. When Riley first mentioned that she wanted photos from different locations, I imagined Dylan and I would do the trip together. I haven't gotten far enough into the planning process to even make a list of places to go.

Lori is quiet, letting herself sort through the options. "Okay then," she says, and I can tell she's shifting into the side of Lori I've grown to love. She's shifting from best-friend-venting Lori to let's-plan-an-epic-trip Lori. "Where do you want to go?"

"Somewhere different. Maybe a national park? But I don't want to drive too far."

"How far is too far?"

I think about it for a minute. "No more than ten hours?"

"I'm on it!" And just like that, Lori and I spend the next couple minutes listing out all the options we have for places to visit. We narrow the list down pretty quickly, starting off with a list of all the national parks within ten hours driving distance. Then I choose my favorites based on what looks the most different from Colorado or any of the other photos I've taken so far.

"You sure you don't want to do two days of driving?" Lori says. She's pulled up photos of some of the national parks in California and is swooning over Redwood National Park. "I mean, look at some of these photos." She turns on screensharing so I can see the website browser she's pulled up. In the photos, the trees are massive, usually with a person standing next to them so you can fully appreciate how wide and tall they are. The trees are so large that it would take multiple people stretching out their arms in order for someone to wrap their arms around the trunk. She scrolls through a few photos and stops on one where the forest is misty, giving a haunted fairytale feeling as the sun peeks in from the upper corner of the photo.

"How long of a drive would that be?" I say, looking through the photos.

She opens another browser and types it into Google Maps, and I laugh when the result comes up.

"Yeah, I'm not driving twenty-three hours," I tell her.

"Just make the trip longer."

"Lori," I say in my best warning voice.

Lori lets out a sigh and closes the tab with the redwood forest information.

We shift through all our options for a few more minutes and finally land on Arches National Park in Utah. The more research we do into the parks, the more I realize how unprepared I am. Most parks require permits to stay overnight or just to do individual hikes. Those permits sell out weeks — sometimes month — ahead of time. The fact that it's December, an off-season for the park, is the only reason I'm able to sign up for permits without difficulty.

"Oh, you should do something like this!" Lori pulls up a photo of one of the large arches, and behind it is the night sky full of stars.

"I haven't tried night photography yet," I admit. I've seen countless photos of star trails, which is when you leave the exposure on your camera open long enough that you're able to capture the movement of stars in the sky. The result is usually long lines in the sky stretching over the horizon.

"Well, you should! I mean, how perfect!"

"Okay, it's decided then!" I say, already feeling a little more hopeful about the trip.

We spend the rest of the night bookmarking anything that looks like it's worth a visit. I write down the addresses of almost a dozen spots I can park the bus to camp, each of them coming with a stunning view. I save about twenty different hikes into my phone, varying in length, but most of them are around three miles. Every hike is just a short walk to get to a new rock formation, each one different from the rest. Just looking at the photos, it's hard to imagine how different the terrain will be, but an itch of excitement ignites in me.

"When are you leaving?" Lori asks after we've spent the hour planning the trip.

"Tomorrow." I shrug.

"Look at you! A couple months ago I had to beg you to go drive that bus, but now you're eager and ready!"

I smile, but there is a tiny seed of doubt in the back of my mind. Yes, it is much easier to go on road trips now, but I go because living out of the bus feels more familiar than staying home. When I'm out in the bus, I can almost ignore the fact that my parents are gone. In the bus, I can pretend the reason I'm alone is because Dylan is busy working—not because he wants space. The bus has become a tiny sanctuary.

"It's getting easier," I admit. I'm not sure why it is, but it's something I know to be true. I'm not sure when the shift happened, but now when I think about how my parents are gone, the thought no longer feels suffocating. That's not to say I don't miss them, because I do, but the pain has dulled to a point where I can breathe again. Or perhaps it's because I can pretend they're standing on the sidelines, cheering me on.

"Your dad would be so jealous of all the cool places you get to see."

I smile, thinking about how if things had gone as planned, he would have eventually convinced my mom to gift me the bus so I could travel. Knowing my dad, he probably would have used every sick day or vacation time he had to come out and visit me so he could experience all the adventures I was having.

"My mom would have loved to meet Dylan," I say. The words sting once they leave my mouth. In all the planning, I almost forgot where Dylan and I last left things, and truthfully, I wonder if this space is just temporary or if this is the end of our story.

CHAPTER 22

"You're going on another trip?" Stacey asks when I talk to her the next morning while she's making her morning coffee. She's tired, still recovering from a long shift at the hospital, but the edges of her lips are pulled down.

"Yeah, to Arches National Park to take some photos for Snapshot Café. They asked me to bring in more prints and said they like when the photos are from outside of Colorado, so I thought I'd use it as an excuse to go on a little road trip." I shrug, but Stacey just cocks her head to the side, confused.

"In December?" she asks, pouring herself a mug and topping it off with her tradition of two spoons of sugar and practically half a mug of cream. "Won't there be snow?"

Truthfully, snow isn't an element I gave much thought to. I looked into camping options, of course, but I never thought of just how cold it will be. I know the space heater in the bus does well enough to keep me warm, but waterproof against the snow? That's a different story.

"It's not ideal, but there won't be any crowds."

Stacey raises an eyebrow like I'm crazy. "Is Dylan going too?"

"No . . . Uh . . ." I remind myself what Lori said. Stacey is my roommate and friend. I'm allowed to talk to her. "We're taking a break."

She was looking away from me, her gazed fixed on her coffee mug, but her eyes dart back to me. She doesn't say anything, perhaps wondering the same thing I am. Is it weird to talk about Dylan since she's his sister?

"Are you okay?" she asks, looking over me more closely than she did before.

"Yeah. We just need some space." I surprise myself with how calm the words feel. But perhaps this is because I've gone numb. The urge to cry keeps surfacing whenever I think of Dylan, but I push it down. I've grown so used to Dylan's presence that even waking up this morning without a good morning text felt off. I didn't allow myself to think of what the absence of that text meant.

Stacey looks at me, not quite believing my words.

"When you leaving?" she asks, the creases around her forehead more pronounced as she observes me.

"In probably an hour or so. I'm just finishing up packing. I wanted to wait until you woke up to head out."

"Oh," she says, surprised. "Okay." She blinks a couple times like she needs to wake herself up. "Have fun then."

She gives me a faint smile, and then I'm off.

The drive is painfully long. Lori's in class, so I can't call her, and calling Dylan is out of the question. I listen to an audiobook, but it never catches my attention. Instead, I'm lost in my own mind, staring out at the unending road, overanalyzing every conversation I've had with Dylan since his accident.

The longer I drive, stuck in my thoughts, the more frustrated I get. My body is antsy, wanting to do anything other than sit in the bus for another second. About four hours in, I pull over to walk it off, but it only gets me more worked up. I'm pacing in front of a porta potty in the middle of a parking lot on the side of the highway when I notice another woman staring at me.

"Is there someone in there?" She points to the porta potty.

"Uh, no. Sorry," I say, moving out of her way. My face is flushed as I move. She watches and gives me a weak smile before stepping into the porta potty.

I make it a point to be on the road again before she comes back out.

Back in the bus, I feel like I'm fuming, just waiting for something to happen to put me over the edge. My brain tells me that the emotion I should be feeling right now is rejection over Dylan asking for space, but instead, all I feel is anger.

My eyes water, tears threatening to spill over, but I push them away, letting the frustration guide me forward.

It's five o'clock when I reach the entrance to the campground. Originally, I planned to try more dispersed camping, but none are as close to the park as I would have liked. Then the more research I did, I realized that because it's off-season, the sites are first come, first served, without any reservations. I'd normally be worried arriving so late in the day, but with snow coating the ground, there isn't much competition.

The landscape around is stunning. It sits in the heart of Arches National Park, a place that looks like it belongs on Mars. The rocks are endless strips of orange forming giant arches that can be seen for miles. Snow coats mostly every surface of the rugged scenery, making it softer across the landscape. Orange stone peeks out from the snow, a bright highlight against an icy pallet.

The campground has a single road that winds through the park with camping spots along the edge of the road. It's about half-full, with plenty of sites to choose from for the night. From what I read online, it's near impossible to get a camping spot last minute in the summer, but since it's the beginning of December, it's easy to find a place to camp.

I pull the bus into a spot next to a wide view of arches in the distance, feeling more out of my element than I ever have. Arches National Park is like nothing I've ever seen. While Colorado is home to the Rocky Mountains, Arches National Park doesn't seem real. Part of me feels like if I go up to the stone to touch it, the mirage will be ruined, and I'll realize it's all just a dream. But when I step out of the bus and turn around, it's more vivid than I ever could have imagined.

There aren't any bad camping spots. Instead, each spot is nestled on all sides by towering smooth orange stone. Everything is a sunset-orange color, from the gravel to the stone arches in the distance. The sky is a bright, clear blue, but in a couple hours, as the sun sets, I can only imagine how everything will continue to glow even more. It doesn't seem possible for colors like this to exist in nature.

I begin to settle into the campsite, opting not to use the pop-up since the sides are just canvas; this way when I turn the space heater on, I won't lose too much heat. There aren't any electric or water hookups, but I have the solar panels, and the bathroom is just a short walk from where I am.

The sun begins to set just as I'm settling into the campsite. I bring my camera out to take photos of the sunset as the darkness descends. The rocky landscape is all orange, so as the sun goes down, those surfaces only glow brighter. Top that with the fact that everything is coated in a fresh layer of snow, and it looks like a scene pulled out of some magical fairy tale where fire and ice can exist side by side.

There are a few others camping out around me. An RV is parked across from me, while a lonely tent is positioned in the campsite closest to the bathroom building. Voices of the other visitors echo across the landscape, but the tones are hushed against the beauty out in front of all of us. The tent has a campfire going, filling the air with a familiar, comforting scent that reminds me of the years of camping I did with my parents.

When the night sky goes dark, I retreat into the bus and start up the space heater. I close myself into the tiny space, making my bed for the night. I originally planned to make a campfire tonight, but with the snow and the night sky getting dark so early, it didn't seem worth it.

I lie in bed, closing my eyes, trying to ignore the tears that are still threatening to surface, as they have been for the past twenty-four hours. I've done so well keeping the tears at bay, but alone in the bus, they creep in, the sense of loneliness prominent.

I try to take myself back in time to when the world felt so much lighter. But when I open my eyes again, I'm here in the bus alone. And perhaps that's the most painful part of it all.

All the frustration I felt today peels off like an old layer of skin, leaving me raw and exposed. I'm alone, crying in the bus, missing my parents, wondering how it is I'm supposed to exist without them here. I wonder where Dylan is and what he might be thinking. Is it just me suffering and feeling this pain?

I fall asleep, clutching my mom's blanket to my chest like it's the only thing in this world holding me together.

CHapteR 23

I wake up freezing. Thankfully, I packed the bus with a few extra blankets since the winter weather is creeping in. I needed them all, plus my space heater, to stay warm overnight. I sit up just enough to reach across the bed and pull the curtain back. Outside, the sun is already shining over the horizon, warming up the air after a cold night. I reach out to the space heater to turn it back on after it turned off automatically overnight.

After sharing the bus with Dylan for so many nights, it almost feels weird to have the entire bed to myself, like something is missing.

I'm slow to get out of bed, my body wanting to stay within the warm sheets, but I get dressed quickly, throwing on as many layers as I can and opening all my curtains to let the light shine in. Eventually, the inside the of bus warms up again, and I'm able to take off a layer or two.

The morning is quiet, with the campers around me still huddled up in their homes for the night. I keep myself shut inside the bus as I begin to make my breakfast, which is just yogurt from my fridge, granola, and some fruit. I also dig into one of my cabinets to find a few packets of hot chocolate, which I heat up over my camping stove.

I start the morning by checking my email since I was able to figure out how to use a hot spot from my phone. At the top of my inbox is an email from Riley with the subject line, "Someone needs ski photos!"

Hi Marly,

Hope all is well! Ski season is in full swing, and I've been giving your business cards to clients who want to hire someone like you to take their photos while they're skiing. I told them about your travels and showed them some of the photos you've taken that are on display, and they seemed super interested. As long as you can ski and take photos, you're perfect for the job! Hope it's okay that I gave them your card!

Riley

I'm a mix of excited and nervous reading through Riley's email. When she told me to get business cards, I imagined getting people who just wanted regular photo sessions, not while skiing. The concept of skiing photography sounds great, but it's a whole other class of photography, not to mention something I've never practiced or had experience with before. I've gone skiing and obviously do photography, but I've never done them at the same time.

I check through my other emails to see if anyone has contacted me about taking photos, but so far there's nothing, which I count as a good thing for now. Maybe it will give me some time to do a little more research and make sure I can still ski since it's been a few years since I've tried it. While the prospect of the potential job terrifies me, I can't ignore the hint of excitement.

Once I finish checking my email, I put everything in the bus away to make sure nothing slides around while I drive. I make my way toward Devil's Garden Trail, a trail that I found multiple times when I was researching different things to see. The trail is about eight miles and will take me to seven named arches and Dark Angel, which is a 150-foot sandstone tower.

I get to the trailhead at 8:40 in the morning, and there's already a handful of cars in the parking lot, though I imagine if it were the summer, there'd be no parking at all. I park the bus before pulling out my backpack, which I've used to store plenty of food and water since the hike is on the longer side.

It's easy enough to find the trail, not because there's a crowd of people leading the way, but because it's paved, making New Hampshire look like an obstacle course. A small coating of snow leaves footprints in my wake. I'm barely a quarter mile in when I reach my first offshoot. I follow the path to the right and make my way toward the first named arches, Tunnel Arch and Pine Tree Arch. Tunnel Arch is exactly what it sounds like. I can see it long before I reach it, the massive rock jutting out of the ground. In the center of the rock is a perfectly smooth hole; the layers creating a tunnel that switches between shades of white, brown, and orange.

I take photos as I walk, never putting my camera down for more than a few minutes. There are small groups of people along the path, taking their own photos, but I'm surprised again by the lack of crowds. While it is colder, it makes me thankful for coming during the off-season. I hang back at the arch, waiting for people to leave for the perfect moment to capture my photos.

I visit all the arches on the trail: Pine Tree Arch, which is another large tunnel, though less smooth and much larger. Then there's Private Arch, which lives up to its name since I'm the only one there due to the longer walk to get to it. Dark Angel is its own spur off the main trail.

I walk half a mile down the offshoot, and soon I see the tower of stone standing tall against the horizon. It seems massive in height, with very few land formations around it, making it even more grand. Perhaps it seems all the more impressive because it's a dark contrast in the sky as the snow coats the ground.

I'm here to see the arches, of course, but when Lori and I were doing research on things to see in the area, we found out there are petroglyphs throughout some parts of the park. The petroglyphs for Dark Angel aren't officially marked. There is no map or trail to get to them, making them a true hidden gem. The only way to discover them is to venture past the sign at Dark Angel that reads "End of trail."

I tried and failed to find GPS coordinates when I was researching the hike, and the only thing I learned was that I need to go west. There're footprints scattered everywhere from people who've recently passed through looking for the petroglyphs, but I walk past the tower, making my own footprints in the snow. I wander aimlessly, my eyes trained on the rocks to spot any sort of carvings or drawings, hoping the snow doesn't hide them from my view. I keep my phone in my hand, my eyes glancing over to my GPS location to make sure I don't go too far off-trail.

I see the sign before I see the carvings.

"You've found something unique. Please preserve it."

I smile, jogging over to the sign and rounding the corner. Behind a bush, an entirely new world is uncovered. An outcrop of rock above the petroglyphs protect them from the snow, making them clear as day. Across the rocks walls are carvings of sheep, people, snakes, and other images that I can't make out. Entire scenes and stories are depicted across the walls. I step closer, the history at my fingertips seeming unreal. The carvings are thousands of years old, a moment in time preserved.

I take photos of the petroglyphs, my footing careful, like one wrong move could make it all disappear.

I'm stunned as I explore the area, seeming to uncover more petroglyphs the closer I look. I'm there for what could have been an hour, the entire landscape to myself, before I turn back.

Back on the trail, I come across Double O Arch, Navajo Arch, Partition Arch, and, finally, Landscape Arch—the longest natural arch in the world. I see it from a distance, but it only gets more and more impressive the closer I get.

The arch stretches 290 feet wide, with thin lengths of stone stretching across the sky. The longer I stare at it, the more gravity-defying it seems. When I was researching it online, a lot of questions came up as to whether the arch was still standing. When will the arch fall? Is the arch stable? I didn't fully appreciate it at the time since it said at its thinnest point it's six feet of rock. Six feet of rock felt pretty thick, but standing here and seeing the structure in person, six feet doesn't seem nearly wide enough to support the massive rocks balancing on one another. Where the structure is the thinnest, it looks like it's one small earthquake away from falling to pieces. The structure is so precarious, the hiking path that leads you underneath the structure is no longer accessible.

"Impressive, right?" a woman says to me as I take photos.

"It feels like it should be an optical illusion." I shake my head.

"It's a reminder that Mother Nature can have a steady hand when she wants to," the woman says.

"Have you hiked this trail before?" I ask, looking her over. The woman is older than me, probably closer to my mom's age than mine, and her hair is tied back in a braid, her backpack slicked over her shoulder. She exudes the sort of essence only hikers do when they're out in their element: utter bliss. Hikers have a bounce in their step when they're out enjoying a good view, and the woman radiates it.

"No." She shakes her head. "Just here to cross off a few bucket list items. I'm Dove, by the way."

"Marly," I say, smiling back.

"What about you? First time to Devil's Garden?"

"First time to Utah in general," I say.

She smiles, excited by my answer. "Oh, really? I've been in Utah for the past two weeks, soaking it all in. I was in Canyonlands National Park last week. This week is Arches. Next week I head to Colorado for Black Canyon of the Gunnison National Park."

"Oh," I say, not having realized the other two parks exist. I'm sure Lori and I saw them on the map when we were doing our research, but the names didn't click. "I just came from Colorado."

"You from there?" she asks, perking up a bit.

"No, I'm from New Hampshire, but I'm living in Colorado for a while." As I say the words, I'm only reminded of how unknown my living situation is.

"A girl with lots of miles under her belt." She smiles. "I wish I had started to travel when I was your age. I only recently started after a nasty divorce. I realized life is too short to waste your time worrying about what other people want. Now is the time to worry about what I want, which is to explore this beautiful planet."

"Do you travel full-time?" I ask.

"I guess you could call it that. I've only been traveling for two months, but I don't know when I'll stop or settle down. I work remotely, and so far, my boss hasn't asked me to come into the office." She gives me a wink, making me wonder what else there is to that story.

"I have a bus that I was living out of over the summer. I started in Washington and drove across to New Hampshire."

"And now you're back for more?" she asks.

"Sort of." I shrug. "I met a guy when I drove through Colorado, and I came back to see what would happen. Right now I'm just exploring, I guess." I laugh a little, having no idea how bad the story sounds to her. Is it weird to move across the country for someone you met while you were on a road trip? Only now do I realize just how crazy it all sounds, but in the moment, it felt like the right choice.

Dove smiles, seeming thrilled by the story. "Exploring the guy, or exploring the land?"

I smile despite myself. "Both, I guess."

"Where's the guy?" Dove asks, her voice curious.

I feel my face drop, but I try to maintain a smile. "Back in Colorado."

Dove seems to notice my change in mood and puts her hands in her pockets, training her gaze back to the arch stretching out in front of us.

"The universe has a mind of its own sometimes," Dove murmurs. "If there's one thing I've learned in the past couple years, it's that you can't control everything. Not the person you love or the clouds in the sky. But beautiful things happen when you learn to lean into the chaos." She glances over to the arch. "Like a stone archway that's on the verge of collapse."

CHAPTER 24

i explore Arches National Park with no real direction, capturing every moment with my camera. I find myself constantly moving, afraid that if I pause for too long, I'll enter a whirlwind of worrying over my relationship with Dylan. So I keep moving. The December air leaves the morning full of frost, but as the sun rises in the sky, the orange-and-copper stone underneath comes to life again for another day.

The second night in the park I practice night photography from my campsite. Off to my far right, there are no other campers, so I point my camera in that direction, setting it up on the tripod. By seven o'clock, the sky is a galaxy of stars, speckles of light against the night sky. The air is cold, and I'm bundled up in every layer I have, my breath fogging in front of me.

The trick to night photography is a slow shutter speed in order to capture as much light as possible to get crisp photos of stars. To get star trails, which show a star's path as it moves across the horizon, I need an even longer shutter, sometimes for up to an hour. The longer the shutter is open, the harder it can be to have the right conditions for the photo. With too much light polluting the sky, it will be too bright to capture the photo correctly. Campfires, cars, and cities can ruin a night photo.

I set my camera's white balance and adjust the aperture to be as wide as possible to let more light in. I start my ISO at 1600, and with a little trial and error, I hope I'll be able to lower the number more. Finally, I switch my camera's shutter speed to thirty seconds, which is how long it will have the lens exposed to take the photo.

I take the first shot, waiting the thirty seconds in anticipation. When the preview of the photo comes up, the stars are there, but the photo looks slightly grainy, and the sky is too bright. I want the sky to be dark blue, clear it's still night, so the stars pop in contrast.

I lower the ISO to 400 out of curiosity and hit the shutter button, then wait another thirty seconds. The image pops up again. This time the sky is crisp and much darker, the stars speckling across the image.

I spend the next hour adjusting my settings, playing with the different options until I get a photo that's a perfect contrast of bright stars and dark sky. The final image I come up with is so good, I capture more stars in the photo than what I can see in the sky.

Despite the cold, I stay awake longer in the darkness, drinking in the thrill of night photography. During the day, you can only capture what you can see with your naked eye. At night, there's a whole other world to explore.

I change my camera to the BULB setting, which means I'll be

able to manually start and stop my shutter. I set my ISO for 50, the lowest it will allow me to go, and make the aperture smaller. It's the opposite of what you want for night photography, but I plan on having my shutter open for an hour, so I can't let too much light in.

I connect the camera to my phone, making it possible to control the camera without needing to stand next to it. I hit the button on my phone to start the shutter. Then I wait. The time on my phone reads 8:40 p.m. I retreat into the bus and wait, pulling up a movie on my laptop. I glance over at my phone every now and then to make sure it's still connected to the camera. When I glance out the window to my tripod, a tiny green light blinks, telling me it's still capturing the image.

When an hour passes, I hit the shutter button again, nervous of what the result may be. Did I waste my time?

The screen loads from my phone, the operation slow as it brings the photo up.

The star trails are stunning, bright lines of white stretching across the frame. The photo isn't perfect — the sky is a little too bright for my taste — but it's possible that with some editing, it could be near perfect.

On the horizon, I can see a clear image of all the rock formations off in the distance, so clear that it almost looks like dusk in the photo, not late night. The sky is another show in itself. While the background is over-exposed, creating a blue-gray color, the stars leave a clear path in the sky as they make their trip across the horizon. There must be dozens of stars in the photo, some brighter than others. Together, the stars make a perfect circular path.

I go to bed eager to try again the next day.

The photography is a welcomed challenge, keeping my mind occupied enough to prevent me from calling Dylan. In the morning, I'm preoccupied with reviewing the photos on my computer, double-checking my settings, and taking mental notes on what I should change for next time. Throughout the day, I find myself picking up my phone, expecting a missed call or text message from Dylan, but the screen is always blank.

The third night in Arches National Park, I'm feeling more confident with my night photography, so I step it up a notch and change the location I'm shooting. While the view from my campsite is good, I want the photo to have something to frame it. I end up choosing Balanced Rock as my location to give the photo some visual interest.

The stars are already out by the time I park the bus in the trailhead parking lot. It's eerie getting out of the bus to walk in the dark knowing the sun won't be rising anytime soon. I'm the only one here, which was the goal, but it feels unsettling in the dark. The moon is half-full, lighting the night just enough so that I don't feel like I'm blanketed in black.

I tuck my tripod under my arm, the camera slung around my neck. I walk down the trail, hoping I'll know the best spot to take the photo when I see it. The park is dark, making it hard to make out much of anything. The entire trail is less than half a mile, so I haven't been walking long when I think I make out Balanced Rock. I can see a large mass of rock out in front of me that looks vaguely familiar to the photos I saw online.

I take a test photo on the tripod. My settings aren't correct, but it allows me to check the focus and positioning. It takes a couple tries, but eventually I'm all set. I start off with the regular night photos with a thirty-second exposure. The image comes out crisp, the stars dotting the sky. Balanced Rock is perfectly in position, a giant boulder sitting on an apex of rock. It looks like one lean to the left could cause it to tumble down.

The photos are the best night photography I've done so far. The sky is a dark blue that fades until it has a slight hint of orange at the horizon where the sun is showing through.

Finally, I adjust my settings, preparing for the longer exposure to capture star trails. It seems like a gamble to do this type of photography. I could invest an hour into a single photo, and when it's done, it could all be for nothing.

I connect my phone to the camera so I can control the shutter. With one press of the button, it begins to capture. I make my way back to the bus, feeling uneasy about leaving my camera behind. I have the entire parking lot to myself, and I'm out in the middle of nowhere, but walking away from my camera feels wrong. I considered sitting next to the tripod during the hour, but besides getting bored, I'd also be cold.

When I get back to the bus, I climb into the back seat and pull my laptop out and connect it to my phone's hot spot. I try video chatting Lori, hoping she picks up. A couple rings later, the screen loads, and Lori's face pops up on the screen, her hair in a messy bun.

"Well, hello there, night owl," she answers.

"You said I can call whenever I want," I say, laughing as she grimaces into the screen. She moves around a lot, and I catch a glimpse of her desk in the background. It's a cluttered mess of books and notes, which is very unlike Lori.

"I didn't take study breaks into account," she says, moving something around off camera.

"I can let you go," I say.

"No, no. If you called, it's for a reason." She moves to sit up straighter, pulling the laptop closer to her face.

"I'm trying out night photography."

She cocks an eyebrow. "Okay, maybe you did call me for no reason."

"Well, it was either call you or call Dylan, and this is a no-Dylan zone, so I figured you wouldn't mind."

Lori lets out a tired chuckle. "No, we can't have that happen, can we?"

"I'm starting to feel ridiculous about the whole thing," I say.

"What about it?"

I shrug. "I feel like I'm overreacting, I guess."

"About what?" she asks.

"About Dylan hiking the 14ers and getting hurt."

Lori is quiet, seeming to try to find the right words. "The best thing you can do for yourself is to learn to just let things happen. You've been trying to fix things before something even goes wrong."

"But something did happen. He had to be rescued off the mountain." I hear my words getting louder as I talk, the worry and anxiety bubbling to the surface again. I remind myself to breathe, trying to calm myself before I get more worked up.

"Right, but you keep assuming it's going to happen *again*, no matter what. So, stop assuming."

Her screen starts moving again, and her face going in and out of focus. A muffled sound comes from the other end as she moves around the room. When her screen is back in focus, she's sitting at her desk, looking down at one of her textbooks, her face scrunched up in concentration.

"I can let you go," I say, watching her.

"No, it's fine. I'm just trying to finish a project that's due tomorrow." But even as she says it, her eyes are elsewhere, her focus lost.

"I'll call you tomorrow," I say, trying to keep my voice upbeat to hide my disappointment. At the thought of being alone, I can feel my anxiety nipping at my heels again.

Lori frowns but seems thankful, her face relaxing the smallest bit. "You'll call so I can see the sunrise?"

"Of course." We talked about catching a sunrise before my trip was over, and Lori insisted that I call her on video chat so she could enjoy the sunrise too.

"See you in the morning then." Lori smiles, giving me a quick wave before the screen goes dark.

And then I'm alone again. I sit in a sea of darkness, the only visible thing the tiny green blinking light coming from my camera in the distance. I have a moment of panic, and all I want to do is run out to the camera, turn it off, and drive home—or at least to Colorado Springs, which is the closest thing I have to a home. But I let the hour pass slowly, reminding myself to breathe until the panic eases and the emotions fade. I remind myself why I'm sitting in a national park in the middle of winter: to get the epic photo. So, that's what I do, focusing on my goals rather than my worries.

Finally, right on the hour, I stop the shutter, not waiting for the image to load onto my phone before I step out into the darkness. I use my headlamp to guide the way, my pace much faster, as I'm eager to get back to my camera. I scoop the tripod up and fold it back into place before turning back to the parking lot.

Good photo or not, I'd rather be done with photography for the night.

When I get back to the bus, I get into the driver's seat, taking the tripod and camera with me. I tuck the tripod into the back and turn on the preview for the camera.

I'm stunned when I finally pull the photo up. The sky is a rich blue that lightens to a gradient the closer it gets to the horizon. Balanced Rock is in perfect focus off to the right side of the frame, and the stars have moved to create a beautiful circular pattern in the sky. I zoom in to see the details, and the trails are amazing. Some stars are bright and strong, while others are lighter and almost fade into the sky. Some even have a slight hue to them.

It's the type of photo I didn't think I'd ever be able to produce. Most people think being a photographer is just having the right equipment, but in reality, it's so much more. It's about skill, trial and error, and most of all, patience so you can wait for the perfect time to capture a memory.

I give myself a moment of utter joy, because this is what I came here for.

§

On the last morning of my trip, I wake up at six thirty, crawling out of bed long before the sun has peeked over the horizon. The sky is still dark as I put things away so I can drive. The rest of the world is still asleep as I drive the bus down the campground road.

I promised myself to make my final hours in the park worth it, and that involved saving the best for last.

It only takes me fifteen minutes to reach the parking lot for the Delicate Arch trail. I put the bus into park and grab my backpack from the passenger seat before climbing out. I'm the only vehicle in the parking lot, and I follow the trail upward to the arch. My breath is visible; this is the coldest morning on the trip so far. The cold makes the morning air feel lonelier, and I focus on my steps as they guide me to the spot where I'll watch the sunrise.

As I walk, the sky begins to grow brighter, and with no trees for miles, it's easy to navigate in the dim light. The trail is easy to follow, starting as a gradual hill that grows steeper the farther I go. The land around me is a giant smooth rock, guiding me to the arch at the top.

I'm almost a mile and a half in when I come across Twisted Doughnut Arch, a massive wall of rock at the top of the steepest part of the hike. I move upward, keeping an eye on the arch's opening until I can see Delicate Arch on the other side. Before I go any farther, I take a photo of Delicate Arch, framed on all sides by Twisted Doughnut Arch.

Once I'm at the top, the same swing of emotion that I get at the summit of every mountain flows through me. The journey was much shorter than what I'm used to, but when I look in front of me, I see Delicate Arch in the distance. Around Delicate Arch is a swirling downward slope of rock, and it sits in perfect balance at the edge of a massive hole.

The hiking trail skirts along the edge of the hole, the trail circling around until I'm brought to the base of Delicate Arch. I sit a few feet away, pulling off my backpack to bring out my tiny camping stove to heat up my breakfast.

Water begins to boil over the stove as I walk around taking photos. The air is warming when the sun starts to ascend, but my breath is still clear. I mix a pack of oatmeal into the boiling water as the sun makes its first appearance. It rises to the left of Delicate Arch, casting its light across the canyons of rock.

The world glows in shades of orange and pink, the desert landscape being brought to life. I find myself taking photos as often as I can, soaking in the few moments where the sun is touching the horizon. Then as the sun reaches higher into the sky, the oranges and pinks of the sunrise fade to blue.

I watch it all happen in front of me, taking photos until I grow too hungry to ignore the warm food. I take in the morning that way, eating oatmeal, sitting on a cold rock, watching as the sun begins its race across the sky for another day.

It's the end of my time in Arches National Park. It feels bittersweet. Traveling alone was easier than I thought it would be, but by no means was it effortless. For most people, camping means giving up the comforts of running water, a large bed, and a hot shower. For me, it means learning to be alone with my thoughts.

I pull my phone out, thankful I have a signal as I dial Lori's number on FaceTime. After a few rings, the screen changes, and her face loads. I can barely make out her features in the dark.

"Good morning," I say, my voice soft in the quiet awakening of the day.

"Already?" she says, moving around, making it impossible to see her until she flips a light on. She's squinting on the other end of the line, clearly not in the position to be awake yet.

"You're the one who said you wanted to see the view," I remind her.

"I know, I know," she mumbles, dropping her head back onto the pillow and closing her eyes.

"Isn't it nine in the morning for you?" I double-check the time zone difference in my head. "Shouldn't you be up by now?"

Lori groans and moves to open her curtain, light flooding in through the window. "My first class isn't until eleven, and I was up late studying."

I try to hold back my laugh and watch her struggle to keep her eyes open without squinting. Lori is very much the type of girl to preach self-care, but she is also the last one to wake up and get her morning routine started, no matter how hard she tries.

"Want to see the view?" I ask. I flip the camera on my phone so she can see what's in front of me, and her face lights up, her eyes growing wide.

"Oh, wow."

I turn, letting my phone scan the horizon so she can take it all in.

"Wish you were here?" I ask.

"I'm jealous, Marly," she says, her voice edging on a whine.

"You've created a monster, you know. I won't be able to settle for a normal life after this."

She smiles. "No one likes normal anyway."

"When I get back to Colorado Springs, I'm hoping I can sort through all the photos I took and pick out which ones I'll bring to Snapshot Café. I've got a few in mind, but I have to decide which ones would be best to print."

"Any word from Dylan?" Her voice is light, casual, but it leaves a pit in my stomach.

"No," I say, worried at what that means.

Lori purses her lips. "Probably a good thing. He wanted time, and you gave it to him."

I take a deep inhale, my eyes far off on the horizon.

"Are you going to go see him when you get back?"

"I don't think so," I say, even though I want to. "I don't think I should. I should wait for him to come to me, right?" The words sound more and more unsure.

Lori nods. "Yeah. Probably."

And there it is, the tiny piece of doubt that's been in mind for days. What if Dylan doesn't come to me first? What if I go back, waiting for him, but he's already moved on?

I scold myself for thinking it. Dylan wouldn't just leave me hanging like that. He'd at least come talk to me first—right? I want to reassure myself, but these days it feels like I know him less and less.

"You know what's annoying?" I say, my voice louder than I mean it to be. "The entire time I've been here, I've been trying keep myself busy so that when I finally finish running around all day, I don't realize how much I miss him." Because it's not just Dylan that I miss. I miss my parents too, and I'm keenly aware that the only time it felt easier to be on my own was when Dylan was here, and that certainly doesn't count as being alone. "And worst of all, I don't think he misses me. He's probably too worried about his leg and arm healing and when he'll be able to hike again," I admit.

"You really think that?" Lori says, her voice soft.

I open my mouth to speak, then close it again. The tears are back, blurring my vision until I push them away. "I don't know."

Lori's quiet, and we sit in silence. When I look back to my phone again, her face is frozen, her mouth open like she was in the middle of saying something. I wait for it to load, but within a few seconds, the screen goes dark and the call ends as I lose my signal.

I release a heavy sigh, shoving the phone back into my bag and packing up my stuff. For the second time now, it feels like I've had my lifeline of sanity cut off too soon. In a way, it's like the universe is telling me that I have to learn to be on my own.

CHAPTER 25

I have a cell phone signal when I get back to the bus, but Lori doesn't pick up when I call. I make my bed while I wait for Lori to call back, but even after I'm done, there's still no sign of her. I call again, but this time it goes straight to voicemail, reminding me that Lori has a habit of not plugging her phone in at night.

I resign myself to the fact that her phone is dead as I start the GPS and begin the drive back to Colorado Springs. Eventually, I hear a text come in as I'm driving, and when I get to my first pit stop of the day, I see the message from Lori.

Forgot to charge again, sorry! In class now. Call later?

I frown, realizing it will just be me and my thoughts for the rest of the day. The drive continues, just as uneventful as the drive there, though this time my frustration has turned into a feeling of dread and defeat.

I'm about two hours in when my phone goes off, but it's an unknown number.

"Hello?" I say.

"Hi, this is Marcus Watson. I'm looking to speak to Marly Price."

I try to place who Marcus is in my mind, but nothing comes up.

"Yes, speaking," I say, still trying to remember who he is.

"I'm from Beaver Creek Resort. I was given your card from a colleague of mine. We're looking for a photographer who can work with us throughout the rest of the ski season. We have private sessions that get scheduled on a weekly basis where a photographer works one-on-one with skiers to take photos of them when they're in their element. We're looking for someone who'd be able to come in to work on the weekends. The job includes a season pass to the lifts, and you're welcome to stay at one of the rooms here at the resort when you're working. Would you be able to come in for a trial run tomorrow?"

Marcus speaks clearly on the other end of the line, but it takes me a moment to compose myself enough to give a response. When Riley said she gave my card to a few people, I imagined I'd be working one-on-one with people here and there, not a seasonal job.

"I would love to. What time?" I eye my GPS as I drive. I'm about four hours away from Colorado Springs, but now I'm wondering if I should just drive straight to the resort. It will be a longer trip, but then I'd have the chance to at least practice skiing again before the job interview.

"Could you make one o'clock work?"

"Yeah, that sounds perfect," I say, pulling off the highway at the next exit I see. I need to change the GPS and figure out if there's a place near the resort I can park overnight.

"Perfect. Is the email on your business card a good place to send the rest of the information for the resort?"

"Yes, that's fine."

"Great, then I'll see you tomorrow."

Once the call is ended, I give myself a moment to maintain my composure. My first instinct is to call Lori and Dylan, but Lori's still in class, and Dylan is off-limits. After a few minutes of deep breathing, I change the destination on my GPS to Beaver Creek Resort. The call happened so quickly that it doesn't seem real, but after a few more minutes of driving, an email comes in on my phone from Beaver Creek Resort.

I'm practically beaming as I drive, trying to stop myself from opening the email. When I get to the next rest stop, I put the bus in park and start scrolling through what Marcus sent me.

I didn't think of asking questions when I was on the phone, but Marcus sent over the entire job description, what my pay would be, and some of the perks of the job: a season ski pass, a place to stay while I'm working, and free rentals if I need them. The hours are just two days a week with six hours of skiing each day. Then I'm expected to edit and submit the photos to clients within a week.

The skiing alone sounds exhausting, but I can't contain my excitement. When I arrive in Beaver Creek, Colorado, I stop by one of the outlet stores to buy new ski clothes and other winter gear, like gloves and goggles.

With a brand-new jacket, pants, gloves, and hat, I head out to the resort to get in a practice run before my job interview tomorrow. The slopes are moderately crowded by the time I emerge with my rented gear. I expected the skis to feel foreign when I put them on since it's been so long, but as I push myself off through the snow, old muscle memory comes back, and I glide across without too much trouble. It's a euphoric feeling to be on skis again. It's been at least three years, maybe more.

My parents took me skiing as soon as I was able to walk. It was a hobby my mom loved, and she was more than eager to pass it down to me. We skied as a family almost every winter, though we went less and less as I got older.

As good as it feels to be in the skis again, I move toward the bunny slope for a few practice runs before I get ahead of myself.

The bunny slope is riddled with beginners who struggle to walk across flat ground in their skis, never mind going down a slope. I go down the slight hill without struggle, coming to a perfect stop at the bottom.

I move on to the main ski lift, getting in line for the one that will take me to the easiest trail besides the bunny slope. The sky is clear blue when I get to the top, making the views of the mountain stunning as the landscape rolls out in front of me. Snowcapped summits reach out into the distance, and with one small push from my right leg, I begin to make my way down the slope.

A rush of wind goes across my face as I ski, but I don't feel cold. I wind side to side as I descend, practicing my turns as I go. I almost want to laugh when I make it to the bottom with perfect ease.

I ski for the next two hours, working my way up to harder

and harder slopes, shocked by how easily everything is coming back to me.

The next morning, I wake up sore from the waist down, but I hop out of bed and begin reviewing the email Marcus sent me the day before. I ended up parking the bus at a truck stop lot near the resort, so I'm eager to head back.

It isn't a job interview in the traditional sense, because I'm not even meeting with Marcus. I'm meeting with Tristen, one of the ski instructors who had the idea of hiring a photographer in the first place.

I supposed to meet Tristen at the lifts at one o'clock, and I stand there waiting in full ski gear, having no idea what I'm doing.

"Are you Marly?" someone says, coming up from behind me.

I turn in my skis and see a guy who looks to be only a couple years older than me in a neon green jacket. He smiles at me when I turn, his eyes on the camera around my neck.

"Yes! You must be Tristen."

"The one and only. I assume you know how to ski?" he asks, eyeing the rental skis at my feet.

"Yes. Nothing too fancy, but I've been skiing since I was little."

He seems satisfied with my answer and turns toward the ski lifts. "Well, let's get started then."

I move to catch up with him. He gestures for me to follow as we make our way toward the lift. We sit together as it scoops us up off the ground and toward the summit of the mountain.

"Today is going to be a bit of a trial run," Tristen says,

adjusting one of his gloves while we sit. "I've been trying to convince Marcus to hire a photographer for years. We get all sorts of skiers here, and some of them have been coming to me and asking if we have a photographer. That's where you come in. Marcus isn't sold on it yet, but he will be if we find the right person for the job. All you need to do today is show me what you've got. Pretend I'm someone who hired you to take my photos. We've got one hour. Work your magic."

"Oh," I say, a little taken aback by Tristen's approach. "Did you want me to take photos of anything in particular?"

"Anything that looks good," he says, and that's all the encouragement I need.

We spend the next hour together, and I direct him where to ski, moving ahead of him to make sure I get to my photo spot before he does. It makes me thankful I arrived a day early to check out the slopes myself. It makes my test run go flawlessly, because I already know which slots on the slope are most photo friendly and where I can sneak off to the side to take a photo without getting in the way of other skiers.

Tristen is easy to direct, eager to get his photo taken. His skiing skills are far better than mine, and toward the end of our session together, I tell him to use some of the jumps on the mountain to capture photos of him midair.

Our hour is almost up when I capture my last photo and meet him at the base of the mountain. I pull my camera out and let him preview some of the photos.

"These look great," he says, eyes wide as he flips through the images. "Can you send these to Marcus tonight?"

"Sure, they won't take too long to sort through and edit."

"Perfect! You do that, and I'll get you a job by tomorrow." He hands me my camera back, and I can't help but smile with him. He can't be serious, can he?

By the end of the job interview, Tristen seems more excited than I am. I'm not sure how I expected the interview to go, but definitely not like that, and definitely not that well. Most of all, it feels like this is the type of photography I'm meant to do. While wedding photography makes money, it brings me more stress than joy. Photographing while skiing feels fun more than anything else.

Everything feels too good to be true, so I've been bracing myself all day waiting for reality to come crashing down. When I sort through the photos that night, it feels like a dream. I do minor edits, removing other random skiers from the background and fixing the white balance and coloring on the photos.

I email Marcus just like Tristen told me, attaching only the best photos. When I hit send on the email, it doesn't feel like fate that I found this job; it feels like something I've been working toward the entire time without realizing it.

CHAPTER 26

I spend another night in my bus, parked beside a huge truck stop. When I wake up the next morning, I have a renewed sense of excitement and am already eager to get a phone call from Marcus. Tristen promised my photos were good enough that Marcus would have to offer me the job, but I remind myself it could be a long shot.

I'm on the road again in no time, trying to stop myself from getting my hopes up too much for a opportunity that seems too good to be true.

Until recently, I didn't even know jobs like this existed, but now that I do, I can't imagine myself doing anything else. I've been taking photos for years, but never have the results been as exciting as what I did yesterday. The thought of going back to photographing weddings seems like a migraine waiting to happen.

Stacey's home when I walk through the front door, curled up in a blanket with a glass of wine in one hand. Her hair is tied up in a messy bun, her eyes transfixed on the TV.

"Hey!" I say, stepping through the door with my bag. Stacey perks up as soon as she sees me, honing in on the excitement.

"Good weekend?" she asks, putting her glass of wine down on the coffee table.

I can't stop myself from grinning. "I just got back from a job interview where I'd be a photographer for a ski resort in Beaver Creek."

Her eyes go wide. "I thought you were going to Arches National Park?"

"I did. I was driving back when I got a call from one of the managers saying someone had recommended me to them for their photography job. He asked me to come in for an interview and trial run."

Stacey is just as stunned as I was when I first got the call. "When is it?"

"Yesterday. I drove straight to Beaver Creek and did the interview. He's supposed to be calling me soon."

"What exactly will you be doing?"

I launch into detail of what the job will be like: lots of skiing, taking photos, and nights at a resort where I have a room all to myself. I pull my camera out of my bag to show her the photos I took for the interview, and we go through them all one by one. Eventually, we reach the photos from Arches, and we start to sort through those while I tell Stacey all about the trip.

Before I know it, a couple hours have passed, and we've both shifted to sitting on the couch talking while the TV drones on in the background. For a moment, it feels like I'm back home with Lori having one of our girls' nights in.

I pull myself away from the TV to get snacks, and I notice my phone is blinking with a new notification. I see Marcus's email, and I can't open it fast enough. I can barely contain my excitement as I glance over the words, skimming far too fast to make sense of the sentences. Until I see it: *I'd like to offer you the seasonal position of ski photographer starting December 29th.*

"I got the job," I say quickly, turning to Stacey. Her eyes are still glued to the TV, but she blinks, coming back into focus.

"What?"

"I got the job!" And this time I shout as I say the words.

Stacey gets off the couch and closes the distance between us to give me a hug. "I'm so happy for you!" she says, a huge grin on her face that probably mirrors my own. "How do you want to celebrate?" She glances around, looking for something, but her attention is withdrawn when there's a knock at the door.

We both pause, and I pull away from our little celebration to answer the door. I open it just a crack before I recognize who it is, and once I do, I feel myself straighten before I open the door all the way.

"Hey, are you looking for Stacey?"

Dylan smiles slightly when he sees me, which makes my stomach twist into a knot. I'm nervous — more nervous than I've ever been to see Dylan — because I don't know where we stand anymore.

"I was actually hoping to talk to you," he says, his voice quiet.

I blink, unsure of what's happening.

"Can we talk?" He motions behind him, taking a half step back.

I glance over at Stacey, who's taken a few steps closer to the door. She keeps her distance, but it's clear she's listening.

"Sure," I say, reaching for my jacket, which is hanging on the coatrack. I slip it on and give Stacey a quick smile before I join her brother outside and down the stairs.

It's cold tonight and only getting colder as time goes on. I let Dylan lead as we make footsteps in the slush that's been left behind on the shoveled sidewalks around the apartment complex.

"Is that a new jacket?" he says, eyeing the coat I bought for skiing.

I can't help but smile as I hold one of my arms out to glance at the fabric. "It is. I, uh . . ." I wonder how to bring this up. "I got a job offer to work at a ski resort, so it felt appropriate to get the proper gear."

"What? That's amazing!"

Even in the dim light, I can't help but notice how happy he is for me. If it were another time, I'd reach out and kiss him, right here, right now. But instead, I'm left to admire from afar.

"What will you be doing?"

"I'll be a photographer for the skiers. I ski down ahead of them and wait to take the perfect action shot." I brush my hands out in front of me, pretending I'm holding my camera.

Dylan's face erupts into a wide grin, and he stops walking. I don't notice right away, so I stop a few steps ahead and turn to look at him. He's still grinning when he shakes his head, looking at me like I'm his favorite person in the world. It takes everything in me not to close the gap between us and wrap my arms around him.

"I never had a doubt you'd find your place here," he says.

The words feel so intimate and personal that I look away, suddenly self-conscious of all the attention.

I have to hold back a smile as I look down at my shoes. "Thank you," I say so softly it's nearly a whisper.

When I glance up again, Dylan is watching me, his eyes full of thoughts he hasn't spoken yet. Finally, after a moment of stillness, I break the silence.

"Why did you want to see me?" I ask. It feels like I need to brace myself for his words. I know what I want him to say, but the doubtful part of me concedes that there isn't a way he'll ever say the things I want him to.

"I missed you," he says softly. I feel like his words can't be true. How is it he could be feeling the same things I have been the past couple days? "I wasn't sure if you'd be home or not, but I wanted to see you."

The words come out shy, like he's afraid of how I may respond.

"But what about what you said?" I fight the urge to run into his arms, forcing myself to come face-to-face with the thing that tore us apart in the first place.

Dylan lets out a sigh that's so quiet I think I imagined it. "I still want to finish the 14er list," he says, and I feel my heartbeat thud faster. "But I'd prefer to do it with you rather than without you."

The words echo between us, and I feel myself reaching, wanting so badly to say yes, to fall into his arms again, but I find myself only asking questions.

Just how far is he still willing to push himself?

Dylan takes a few steps forward and reaches down for my hands. I didn't realize how cold they had gotten until his warm fingers wrap around mine.

"Please tell me you've missed me as much as I've missed you."

His face is so close to mine that his warm breath fogs in the space between us. My eyes are trapped in his gaze, and I find myself leaning forward without meaning to, our bodies acting as magnets.

I never make the decision to kiss him. I just know one moment we're standing with our lips only inches apart, and the next moment there's nothing between us anymore.

As soon as our lips meet, he releases my fingers, curling his hand behind my head to bring me closer. My mind is reeling as we kiss, wondering if this is okay. Should we be kissing when it's so clear we don't agree?

But I want to. I want to kiss Dylan and be with him as he hikes. I want to be the person who meets him at the final fourteen-thousand-foot summit, kissing him to celebrate an achievement so few people in this world can accomplish.

I let myself believe we'll be okay. I let myself believe that I can do this. I can learn to let go. To stop worrying.

I kiss Dylan, convincing myself that it will all be okay.

CHAPTER 27

"**C**ome on, you two. Dinner is ready!" Stacey shouts from the kitchen almost as soon as we enter the apartment. We just got back from another day at the community center for Dylan's physical therapy in the pool. The scent of chlorine wafts off us, the tips of Dylan's hair still damp from the pool. He puts my bag down before helping me out of my winter jacket as it leaves a trail of quickly melting snow in its wake.

Dylan takes my hand and pulls me over to the table. It's been a week since we got back together, and it feels like things are back to normal. My new job starts at the end of the month, and I help him work through his physical therapy exercises almost every day.

Stacey is running circles around our little apartment kitchen. Despite all the night shifts she works, she's started to lean more into cooking as a hobby. She claims it's a stress relief, which I'll never understand, but if it means home-cooked meals for me, I'm all for it. Today she insisted on making sure dinner was ready when we got back from the community center, so the casserole is fresh out of the oven by the time we step through the door.

"Sit, sit." She motions us toward the table and hands Dylan a spoon to scoop himself a serving.

"This looks great, Stace," Dylan says.

"Introducing my cheesy tortellini bake!" She makes a grand gesture with her hands before sitting across from us.

Dylan hands me the serving spoon, and I get my own scoop. The casserole looks delicious, with tortellini, cheese, and ground beef all in a creamy red sauce. When I take a bite, it's even better than it looks.

"Marly, are you going to go home for Christmas?" Stacey asks, scooping herself a serving. It feels like all color drains from my face, my eyes catching on the calendar Stacey has hanging in the corner of the room. It's December 21st.

Aunt Cora called me more than a month ago, asking what my plans were for Christmas and if I'd be coming home or staying in Colorado for the holiday. I brushed it off, eager to throw that holiday away and be done with it before it even began.

Of course, I've seen the Christmas decorations and heard the music, and the snow is a constant reminder of the looming date. But I ignored it all, distancing myself from the holiday, which is riddled with family and tradition.

It will be the second Christmas without my parents, but that doesn't make it easier.

"Are you going home?" Dylan says softly. He reaches for my hand under the table, his thumb rubbing over the top of my hand.

"Um, I haven't really thought about it," I say. Lori asked

if I was flying home the last time we video chatted, but she didn't mention Christmas, so I never made the connection. I just assumed she wanted to make time to hang out in person again sometime soon.

"If you're in town, you can spend it with us." Stacey's chipper as she talks, but Dylan eyes me warily.

"We just do a gift exchange and a big dinner with too much food. It's usually just the three of us, but we can make room at the table for a fourth," Dylan adds.

For a moment, I start to feel dizzy. Memories of Christmas come running through my brain. All the memories are similar, my parents and I aging little by little every year. The traditions were always the same: breakfast in the morning, gift opening throughout the afternoon, and ending the day baking countless types of Christmas cookies. For years and years, it was always the same. Until last year. But the memory of last year is vague. Christmas the way I know it has been on pause, like my brain is waiting for my parents to come back to continue where we left off.

"You can fly home if you want to," Dylan says when I take too long to reply.

My face feels hot, and when I look over at him, he stares back at me, eyes pleading for me to say something.

"I don't think I want to fly home," I whisper.

"Well, Christmas with the Ellises has never failed to disappoint," Dylan says, his voice light.

"We mostly spend all day watching bad movies. Not even Christmas movies," Stacey says.

I remind myself to smile, and Dylan gives my hand a gentle squeeze.

"What's in this casserole anyway?" Dylan says, shifting the conversation back towards our meal.

Christmas never comes up again. The rest of dinner, Stacey catches me up on the latest show she's been binge-watching. I relax into my seat again, letting my mind wander away from the holiday. It's when Stacey gets up to put the dishes away that my mind returns to the conversation.

"I saw my physical therapist yesterday, and he wants me to start doing my regular exercise routine." Dylan says the words excitedly, perhaps thinking the news will cheer me up.

I glance up, trying to hide the shock and fear that come with that news. When I don't respond right away, Dylan continues.

"He said I can start doing longer hikes again, and if I don't experience any pain, I can start adding on more and more distance and elevation. My shoulder is going to be the only issue, I think. It's taking way longer to heal than the ankle. But as long as I avoid heavy packs, I should be fine."

"Hard to imagine your shoulder can heal when it has to support such a large head," Stacey says, joking with him as she sits back at the table, our plates now cleared.

Dylan attempts to kick her from under the table but only ends up hitting the leg of the table, jostling everything.

"Don't hurt your good leg too." Stacey laughs.

Dylan rolls his eyes before turning to me. "What do you say? Want to join me for a hike?"

My brain immediately goes to the last time we hiked together, when it was supposed to be just a short walk. Dylan struggled even on flat ground. How will he do on harder terrain? I know I should be supportive and feel excited to be able to do the things we used to do together again, but all I feel is sheer and utter terror at the thought of Dylan getting hurt.

"I can't. My job starts next week," I say, thankful for the excuse.

"Maybe I can do some hiking on my own while you're busy during ski season. Then when you have weekends free again, we can get back out there."

My stomach drops, and I try to ease the anxiety away.

"I don't know, Dylan," I say, the apprehension clear.

"Don't you miss it?" he asks, knowing I haven't gone on any big hikes since I got to Colorado. I've done plenty of short, small hiking trips, but nothing like I'm used to doing.

Stacey gets up from the table, eager to take a step away, making herself busy cleaning dishes in the sink.

"Not all of us live and sleep the mountains, Dylan," she says, trying to ease the tension.

"I miss it," I admit.

"Come on, help me pick out my first hike back." He stands up and motions for me to follow him, but I stay seated.

"Dylan, I don't think it's a good idea for you to go hiking yet." I try to keep my voice even, but I can't look at him as I talk, afraid I'll lose my nerve.

"What do you mean?" he asks with a light laugh.

"I just think you need more time to heal."

"I'm healed. I've talked to my doctor and my physical

therapist. They said I'm fine to start hiking again." He's raising his voice; perhaps he doesn't notice it, but I do. And so does Stacey.

"I'll be in my room if you guys need me," she says, abandoning the dirty dishes in the sink. She has to walk past Dylan to get to her room, and his eyes linger on her a moment before they snap back to me.

"What am I missing, Marly?" he asks me.

I stare at the table, feeling his gaze on me. "You've gotten hurt twice while hiking," I say.

"We've already gone over this," he says, frustrated.

"I think you're just pushing your luck trying to hike these massive mountains."

"I'm not hiking them yet. I'm training for them. That's the whole point."

"But that's the goal, isn't it? To finish the 14ers in Colorado in two years."

"Of course, and you know that. That's why we went on a break. I thought us getting back together was you understanding that this is something I need to do."

"With or without me," I whisper.

"You know I want to do it *with* you," he pleads.

"But you're so goal oriented that you'd rather push your luck than err on the side of caution." I hate myself as I say the words, but I can't stop the downward spiral.

"Marly," he says.

I look up, and his head is tilted to the side, annoyed, like I'm missing something obvious.

"You went hiking when you knew it would rain," I remind him.

"Then I'll never go hiking if the forecast says rain!" He throws his hands up in the air. "And then what about when I broke my leg? I slipped on ice. Are cold temperatures unsafe too?" he says, raising his voice again.

A voice in my head wants to tell him, yes, cold temperatures are unsafe too. That's one of the many things that kills hikers every year, but I don't say that.

"I just want you to be safe," I say, my voice soft, hoping Dylan will lower his in response.

"I'll be safe. I don't know what to do to make you believe me."

"Then don't go. Wait until spring maybe."

Dylan turns his back on me, annoyed as he lets out a deep sigh. "Why are you acting like this?" He throws his hand in the air. "You can't control me and what I do just because you're afraid I'll get hurt."

I sit at the table, practically sinking into the chair. I bite my lip, fighting to keep myself together. I don't want to have this conversation. Not now.

"I thought we were over this, Marly."

I shake my head. "No, we just stopped talking about it." I think back to how he came to the apartment to talk to me about it. He made it very clear that nothing had changed for him, that hiking these mountains is just something he has to do. And I let him assume I was okay with it. I wanted to be okay with it.

"Then let's talk," he says, his tone struggling to stay even.

"Hiking makes me happy, and next week I'm going to go on a hike with or without you. And then maybe a couple weeks from now I'll do a bigger hike. And they'll get more challenging until I can go right back to where I left off."

"Why is that list so important to you?" I say. The words feel like a plea as they come out of my mouth. I realize I'm crying. But I know why it's so important. I know this isn't about the physical challenge or just checking mountains off a list. It's about finishing what his grandfather started. Even as I say the words, it feels unfair to be challenging him in his goal.

"Why is it so important that I *don't* finish that list?" Dylan counters.

"Because I love you!" I shout, the words rough and dry against the edge of my throat. They come out like an angry bark rather than a soft declaration. "Because I'm terrified that you'll get hurt and I'll lose you. The only way I can feel *sane* is if I know you're safe. Because the thought of losing anyone else I love *hurts*."

I'm standing now. My hands are shaking, and Dylan is staring at me, wide-eyed.

"I don't want to be hurt anymore." I try to shout the words, but I'm too tired, and they come out soft. It wasn't supposed to be this way. This isn't how you tell someone you love them for the first time. I know the words to be true — I've known it for a long time — but I never intended for the words to come from my mouth. It came out as a reflex, or perhaps a cry for help. In a way, I've always known, the feeling growing until it was impossible to ignore. But I never allowed myself to admit it, because to love someone is to allow yourself to get hurt by someone.

"Marly, I—"

"Get out," I say before he can complete his sentence, too afraid to hear what his response is. Anger, embarrassment, and fear collide until I'm a fury of emotion.

"What?" he says.

"Please *leave*," I beg, pointing to the door. I look past him at the small Christmas tree Stacey set up in the corner of the room. It's barely two feet tall, and I didn't even notice it until now. It has tiny decorative ornaments with white lights strung throughout. I focus on one of the small purple ornaments while I listen to Dylan make his way across the room and out the door.

There's a soft click, and I release a sob the instant he's gone. I want to allow myself to collapse; to lie on the floor, and sleep there but I don't.

"You okay?" Stacey says, poking her head out of her room. Her eyes rake over me, and I feel like if I don't respond, she'll come out and hug me.

I take a moment to breathe, wiping the tears away. "I'm fine."

Her eyes stay on me, but I turn away. A few seconds later, her arms wrap around me. The touch makes me fall to pieces, and another flood of emotion envelops me.

"Why won't he listen to me?" I ask when I'm able to calm down.

"He's listening, Marly, but you can't change who he is," she says gently.

240

I glance up at her, my eyes feeling puffy and tired. She frowns, watching over me, unable to help. Because I know she's right. I know he hears me, but he can't give up the part of himself I'm asking him to, the same part of him that I fell in love with in the first place. So, why am I unable to let it go?

CHAPTER 28

i end up buying a plane ticket to fly home on a red-eye flight December 23rd. It departs at 9:48 p.m. and lands around 4:36 a.m., but I'm thankful to have found a plane ticket on such short notice. In my rush to leave, I text Dylan to let him know that my aunt wants me home for Christmas. It isn't a complete lie. When I called Cora to let her know I'd be home, she was ecstatic, promising me the guest bedroom at her house would be ready when I got there, but remind her that I have a bed at Lori's apartment waiting for me.

I want to call Dylan to let him know I'll be gone, but I can't deny the fact that every time I think about it, I lose my nerve and a rush of emotions bar me from speaking. I'm not mad at Dylan; I'm mad at myself for not being able to let things go. I can spend all day telling myself that I'm okay with Dylan hiking again, but the moment it becomes reality, every nerve in my body stands on end like it's fight or flight.

You okay? Dylan texts me after I tell him I'm flying home for Christmas.

Yes.

Do you need a ride to the airport?

No.

I keep my answers short, hoping it will be enough to stop him, and it does.

I also text Lori that I'll be home, and it's barely ten minutes later that I get a call from her.

"You're coming home?" she says into the phone, her voice an octave higher than usual.

"I'm actually about to leave for the airport now. It was kind of last-minute." My voice falls flat, missing all the excitement Lori has. She picks up on it immediately.

"Is everything okay?"

"Yeah, just . . . Christmas." I shrug.

"Okay," she says, still trying to read into what else I'm not telling her. "Text me your flight number and what time you land. I'll pick you up."

And just like that, Lori goes into rescue mode. It feels like I've shot myself in the foot, flying home. No matter what, I won't have my parents this Christmas, but now I also won't have Dylan. I wanted to call him after our fight, but I couldn't get myself to. I'm mostly embarrassed by what I said and how I said it. It's not at all how I envisioned telling Dylan that I love him, and instead of it being a sweet declaration, it came out as a shouting explosion.

I manage to sleep on the plane, time passing in a blur until I'm standing inside the airport at the pickup location while I wait for Lori's car to pull up. Outside, snow has just begun to fall. The sky is still dark, the airport crowded with people traveling for Christmas. It was a miracle I was able to find a flight in the first place.

Outside, there's a line of cars waiting to pick people up, and when I see Lori's sedan in the distance, I run outside, bracing myself for the cold. I weave through the crowd of people to her car before opening the passenger door and throwing my duffel into the back seat.

"Welcome home!" Lori says with a smile. The car is dimly lit under the airport lights, and I smile weakly. It's almost 5:00 a.m. by the time I crawl into her car, and Lori somehow looks like she's wide awake and ready for the day.

It's Christmas Eve. I'm back home, but nothing feels right.

Lori notices. She pulls the car forward and away from the airport, but she glances over to me occasionally as she merges back onto the highway. It's not until we're on the highway in the flow of traffic that she directs her full attention to me.

"Okay, spill," she says. "What's going on?"

"It's 5:00 a.m., and I'm running on four hours of sleep that may or may not have happened while I was on an airplane." I yawn, already wondering if there'll be enough time in the day to take a nap.

Lori sighs and pushes further. "I get that, but I was more asking why you suddenly decided to buy a plane ticket and fly home."

I smile in a nervous way. "I wanted to come home for Christmas?"

"Marly," Lori says in her don't-give-me-that-bullshit voice.

I shift in my seat and take a deep breath, realizing the sooner I tell her, the better.

"I told Dylan I love him," I say.

"What?" Her voice is high with excitement, but I can feel her energy drop almost instantly when she notices my mood. "He didn't say it back?"

I lean against the window, my chin resting against the palm of my hand.

"I didn't give him a chance to react. When I said it, I more or less screamed it at him in the middle of a fight. I didn't even mean to say it. It just came out."

"Wait, so what happened? What exactly did you say?"

I sigh, shaking my head. "I don't even know. I don't remember how the conversation began. I just started freaking out. He started talking about pushing his training more, and I just lost it. At some point I just shouted that I loved him, as if that were a good explanation for why I was acting so erratically."

Lori lets the words settle before responding. "And then what happened?"

"I asked him to leave."

"What? Why?"

"I don't know," I say, letting my face fall into my hand. "Because I was embarrassed. I didn't mean for it to happen that way."

"How did you mean for it to happen then?"

I shrug. "I would have preferred that the conversation never came up again, I guess."

"But if that's how you feel, wouldn't you want him to know?"

"That I love him, or that I don't want him to go hiking?"

"Both," Lori says.

I sigh, leaning my forehead against the cool glass.

"I'm not ready for that conversation yet," I admit.

§

The plan is to spend Christmas Eve with Aunt Cora, who insists that Lori comes along as well. We've become a matching set over the years, a bond that only grew closer after my parents died. Lori normally spends Christmas Eve with her father's side of the family, but her parents wanted she come with me to Cora's house.

After picking me up from the airport, Lori drives me back to her apartment where I crash on the bed in the spare bedroom — or, I guess the bedroom that used to be my room but is now just full of my furniture. I told Lori I could move my stuff out if she needed to find a new roommate, but she claims she prefers the single apartment life.

After I sleep for four more hours — this time in a bed — Lori and I make our way over to Aunt Cora's house.

I set the table for Cora, eyeing the two chairs Lori and I will be in, mindful of the fact that it's usually my parents who sit there.

Their absence is a giant black hole in the day, sucking everything around into it. Each time I try to throw myself into the present, helping Cora chop vegetables or playing with my little cousins, I keep expecting to see my mom out of the corner of my eye or hear my dad's laugh from the other side of the room.

Christmas Eve at Cora's house was always a tradition, but now I can't help but wonder what the point is. Why bother if we aren't all here?

"Need help?" Lori asks. She's placing a basket of bread in the middle of the table.

"No, I'm almost done," I say, putting the last set of utensils out.

A Christmas song plays loudly behind me, and I turn to it. My little cousin Lex is seated in the middle of the couch in the living room, blanket in one hand, cookie in another. Her eyes are glued to the TV that's playing *Elf* for the third time since I've flown home.

Lori looks around the room, her eyes falling to the Christmas decorations. Cora always goes big with Christmas. She finds the biggest tree that will fit in her house and makes it the focal point of the living room. The fireplace is a masterpiece, with a tiny Christmas village on the mantel and all the windows are lined with garland. It's the same set of decorations that's out every year, but it feels like it's been too long since I've seen them.

"Did I come here last year?" I ask.

Lori looks at me, confused. "No, I don't think so. I think you stayed with my family the entire week. Some of your family came to our house actually."

I nod my head, but nothing clicks in my memory.

"I don't remember Christmas last year," I say.

Lori frowns. "It wasn't a good year."

"What do you mean?"

"You just seemed numb. Everyone came to visit to try and cheer you up, but it's like you shut yourself out from the world for a couple days. My parents had you sleeping at our house for a couple weeks so they knew you were okay."

"Really?" I knew I had slept at their house, but I had no idea how long, only that the days had seemed to morph together.

"You don't remember?" Lori asks.

I shake my head. "I barely remember anything from last year." There are flashes and images of moments from that first year without my parents, but I remember the feelings more than the moments.

The ache of my parents' absence was constant, like a fresh bruise I was hyperaware of, wanting to ignore but constantly touching. Life was happening around me, but I was surrounded by a sea of static, unable to hear or see anything that wasn't my own grief.

"Marly, can you come here a minute?" Cora yells from the kitchen. Lori turns to sit with Lex on the couch, and I make my way over to Cora. Her smile is bright when I step into the room, and she motions for me to come closer as she talks in almost a whisper. "Upstairs are a few boxes with the kids' Christmas pajamas. I forgot to wrap them. Do you think you can handle that for me?"

She gives a quick smile, and I nod back.

"Where is everything?" I ask.

"In the closet. Thank you so much; you're a lifesaver!" she says quickly before returning to setting everything up for dinner.

I make my way up the stairs quietly to avoid being detected by my cousins. Everyone's matching pajamas are stashed away in a bag in the upstairs closet. I drag the wrapping paper out and get to work, hiding away in Cora's room. I'm wrapping the last set of pajamas when Cora steps in, looking relieved when she sees everything wrapped.

"Thank you so much!" she says in a hushed tone. "I'm terrible at making sure everything is wrapped. Your mom and I used to set an entire day aside every December to wrap presents. I can't seem to get myself to sit down and do it alone, so now I end up panicked on Christmas Eve."

"If I'm around before Christmas next year, I can help you wrap things," I say. My mom loved wrapping presents every Christmas. She handled most of the wrapping in our house, but I didn't know she did it with Cora.

Cora smiles gently. "I'd like that."

We each grab a handful of presents, and I start to walk to the door, but Cora lingers.

"You know how you were asking a couple months ago about selling your parents' house?" Cora says, her words hesitant.

I turn, the presents still gripped in my arms, but I don't say anything.

"I know I keep telling you not to sell it because you might want it someday, but I don't think it's my job to be deciding things for you. Do whatever you want with the house. It's not fair of me to make you hold on to the house when you don't want it."

I'm stunned to hear the words. I only ever brought up selling the house when Cora was insisting I move back into it. But living in it again seems like a nostalgic nightmare. How could I live in a place where I'd be constantly reminded of who was missing?

"I love the house," I say, having trouble trying to tell Cora what I mean. "But it's hard to be there without them."

Cora gives me a small knowing smile.

"I didn't want you to sell the house because I didn't want to see someone else living there," she admits. "But after you moved, I realized that maybe selling the house is exactly what you need. Maybe what we both need." She smiles, her eyes downcast. She's never talked about what it was like to lose her brother—my dad. She was always too focused on making sure I was okay. But now it's clear she's been hurting just as much as I have.

"Thank you," I say. The thought of selling the house gives me a mix of relief and panic, and I'm not sure which of the two emotions is stronger.

Cora grips the presents in her arms and makes her way across the hall and back downstairs.

"Your parents would be proud of you. You know that, right?" she asks as we walk back into the living room.

I glance over, surprised. "For what?"

"For following your dream. Traveling." She pauses and seems to think about her next words. "Moving on, even when it's hard."

The words take me by surprise. Cora talks about my parents a lot, but always about memories, like they could still be alive. She's always been careful to avoid the topic of their deaths.

I give a tight smile, unable to say anything.

"The holidays are harder without them, but I know they'd be so incredibly proud of you." She bends down to put the presents under the tree, and I do the same. My little cousins notice and begin to flock around the tree.

"Present time?" Tiffany says, reaching for the one I just placed at the edge of the tree.

"Not until after dinner," Cora says, ushering the kids back and leading them to the dining room. She glances over her shoulder as she walks away, giving me a soft smile.

The evening goes on in a blur, with plenty of food and presents throughout the night. The entire night feels off, like there's a gaping hole everyone's choosing to ignore. Sometimes I'm able to get caught up in the moment, smiling as one of my cousins shows off a new pajama set, but then I remember who isn't here, and a pit forms in my stomach. My eyes wander to a family photo in the corner of the living room. It's a group photo from a birthday party where everyone in our extended family was in attendance, my parents included. They're standing in the far back corner of the photo, and I'm just barely able to make them out.

We eventually leave Cora's house and go back to Lori's apartment, which is decorated from head to toe with cheap dollar store decorations. It's Lori's first Christmas in her own apartment, and she wanted to go big. Since she didn't have the budget for going big, she took a trip to the dollar store, buying them out of every Christmas decoration. The result is an apartment that looks like Christmas threw up on it. The garland is too short, the ornaments look better from afar than up close, and she used wrapping paper to wrap anything she could get her hands on — including her coffee table.

"I told my parents we'd be at their house at 8:00 a.m. Is that okay?" Lori shoves her coat into the closet.

"Yeah, that's fine." I close my eyes, rubbing my temples.

"You okay?" Lori's voice comes closer, and I feel the couch shift next to me.

I shake my head, leaning into the couch. I can feel myself breaking, being ripped from the inside out. It feels like a fresh wound again, impossible to heal.

"Hey," Lori whispers as her arms wrap around me. I curl in on myself, and it feels like someone is pulling me apart piece by piece until there's nothing left. I can see my dad in a Santa hat, passing me a present while I stay wrapped up in my blanket. And my mom is in the kitchen, elbow-deep in a bowl of mashed potatoes, asking me to help. Each memory is like a whip against my skin.

I thought it would be easier this year, but the grief feels like it only gets heavier. It's like a part of me is waiting, hoping that with enough time, my parents will come back. Then, when reality sets in, I lose them all over again.

"Do you really not remember last year?" Lori asks.

I shake myself back to the present, pushing the tears away and sitting up.

"I think I just kinda checked out." I try to laugh it off, but the sound comes out choked. "If I could do that again, that'd be great."

Lori shakes her head. "The only way it will get easier is if you deal with it."

I nod in a sad, ironic way. "Don't worry, I'm dealing with it whether I want to or not."

My phone rings, and Lori and I both jump, surprised by the sound. I pull it out of my pocket, shocked when I see Dylan's name on the screen.

"Have you talked to him since you left?" she says, her eyes huge and watching.

"No," I say, my hand frozen, unsure of what to do. "I've been avoiding him."

"Answer," Lori says, her eyes on Dylan's name on the screen.

I fumble with the phone, rushing to answer before it goes to voicemail.

"Hello?" I say, but my voice is hoarse.

"Hey."

My stomach drops when I hear his voice on the other end. I feel shattered, but his voice is like a warm touch of familiarity.

I eye Lori, and she gives me an encouraging nod.

"Hi."

Dylan pauses, nervous in a way that's foreign to the Dylan I know. "I just wanted to call and say Merry Christmas . . ." The last words linger like he was going to say more but then changed his mind.

"You're a day early," I joke, but I sound just as nervous as Dylan does.

"I know. I didn't want to disturb you tomorrow in case you were with family and—" He stops there, catching his words and regretting them.

"I was with Cora today. Tomorrow Lori and I are going to be with her family," I say. Lori watches, her eyes trained on me.

"Oh, good." He pauses, and I expect him to say more. "Um, Merry Christmas."

"Merry Christmas," I say, and then the line goes dead. I put the phone down, and Lori raises an eyebrow.

"He called just to say Merry Christmas?"

"I guess so." I throw the phone onto the coffee table.

Lori glances from me to the phone.

"What?" I ask.

She shakes her head. "Nothing, I guess."

CHAPTER 29

I fly home on the twenty-eighth, eager to shed the Christmas memories and get ready to start my new job. For a long time, I thought I'd gone to Colorado to chase a boy, but going home for Christmas made me realize I went to Colorado to start fresh, even if it was only temporary. I didn't want the memories hidden behind every corner. I needed a place where I could exist without the weight of grief sitting on my shoulders.

I spend the almost seven-hour plane ride thinking about home, trying to define what the word means. For over a year, I've felt displaced. I went from a dorm room to an apartment to Lori's family. Even Cora's and my grandparents' houses, bouncing around until I ended up in the bus, moving from state to state every couple days.

I had no anchor, and it didn't occur to me that I had found one when I met Dylan. In the short amount of time I've known him, he's been the one to ground me and pull me back down to earth.

Regardless of how Dylan feels, I know I love him, but what

terrifies me is why. I'm scared that my reason for loving him is out of grief, that maybe I got too caught up in the moment to really understand *who* Dylan is. Maybe I only understand what I need from him.

When the plane lands, my eyes are puffy and red. I feel like I'm on the verge of crying, but I hold myself together, navigating back to the bus where I left it in one of the airport's many parking lots.

When I walk through the apartment door later that day, Stacey greets me.

"Hey! Merry belated Christmas," Stacey says, poking her head out of her bedroom when I walk through the door.

"Merry Christmas," I say back quickly, beelining it for my bedroom. I can hear Stacey behind me, watching as I make my way over to the closet and grab my ski clothes and stuff them into my bag.

"How was your trip?" she asks, leaning on my doorway.

"Good," I say, the word coming out automatically.

"We missed you for Christmas."

I try not to let the words have any weight. Instead, I focus on packing everything I'll need for my first week of work.

"I'm heading to the ski resort for the weekend. I'll be back Sunday night like usual."

"Oh," Stacey says.

I pause when I turn and see the frown on her face.

"My first day is tomorrow," I tell her.

"I know. The twenty-ninth. I just forgot, I guess."

We sit in silence as I finish gathering my things.

"Are you and Dylan okay?" she asks, her voice curious but not prying.

I put my stuff down and look at her. In truth, I don't know what to say.

"I don't know," I admit.

Stacey nods absentmindedly.

"I'll be back Sunday," I say, pulling my bag over my shoulder and walking toward the exit.

"Dylan wanted to talk to you," she says quickly. "He was going to stop by later tonight."

"I'll talk to him when I get back," I say. I grasp the door to open it, but Stacey reaches out to stop me.

"Marly." She looks over at me with the same face Lori gives me when she tells me to stop bullshitting her.

I drop my hand by my side and glance down. She lets out a frustrated sigh.

"I heard the whole conversation, you know." She crosses her arms across her chest. "I didn't want to, which is why I left the room, but when you're both shouting at each other, it's impossible not to hear."

I keep my gaze down, embarrassed. "I'm sorry," I say, because I'm not sure what else I should be saying.

"I don't want an apology; I want you to talk to my brother. He's barely said a word since you left, and I'm sick of seeing him sulking. He wants to talk to you, but he can't even get ahold of you because you left without warning."

"I was going home for Christmas," I say quietly.

"You planned to spend Christmas with us," she says just as

softly. "Or at least it seemed like you were considering it. I know things have been rocky for you two since Dylan's accident, but just talk to him."

"I have to go to work." I glance at the door. "But I will talk to him. When I get back though."

Stacey drops her arms and steps out of the way, having said her piece.

"See you Sunday," she says, her words sounding deflated.

Dylan calls me when I'm driving—probably because Stacey told him where I was going—but I ignore the call. I promise myself that come Monday, I'll go talk to him in person. My feelings are too all over the place to talk to him now.

I get to the resort late that night, and I check in at the front desk to get the key card to access my room. As soon as I step through the door, I collapse onto the hotel bed with all my things still stashed away in my duffel bag.

When I pull my phone out, a voicemail notification is waiting for me.

"Hey, Marly. Stacey said you had to leave to go to work." He pauses, and the line goes quiet. "We missed you at Christmas. Talk soon."

The message ends, leaving a whirlwind of emotions in its wake. In the quiet of the hotel room, I start crying, all the built-up emotions from Christmas and the chaos and confusion I feel over Dylan spilling over. The sobs erupt, and my head spins as I bury my face in the white hotel sheets. It's the first time I've been alone in almost a week, so I give myself permission to feel each and every emotion.

§

I'm skiing ahead of my third client of the day. It's also my last client of the day. He's a snowboarder who wants photos of himself midair when he goes over some of the jumps scattered throughout the slope. As I ski down, I make it a point to avoid the ramps, but I pull off to the side and nestle myself into a corner, waiting to take the perfect photo.

The mountains are a stunning white, and the skies are crystal blue, not a cloud in sight. If I took my goggles off, everything would be too bright, the sun reflecting off the white surface. The mountains in Colorado are massive, making the ski slopes back home look tiny. The stark white poses the biggest challenge to me today, making it imperative I get the white balance right so the photos don't end up overexposed and washed-out.

I take my camera out and focus on the ramp. A minute goes by, and I see my client coming down the mountain, his bright red jacket a clear indication I have the right guy. I pull my face toward the viewfinder and put my finger over the shutter. When he takes air on the ramp, I put my finger down, my camera capturing multiple frames.

I select the preview display and smile, looking at my work.

We do a few more runs down the mountain, and I make it a point to direct my client so he knows which angles will look best. Before I know it, my work for the day is done, and I head to the employee lounge.

I'm sitting on a bench pulling my ski gear off when Marcus comes up from behind me.

"How'd it go?" he asks, wearing a suit that makes me look comical as I pull off layer after layer of snow-covered winter clothes.

I reach down to where I placed my camera on the bench next to me and pull up one of the photos before handing it to him.

"Nice work! How's it feel out there?" He smiles as he hands the camera back to me.

"Great. Barely feels like work." I can't help but smile as I pull off my thermal layer sweatshirt.

"That's what I like to hear." And with that, Marcus walks off with a smile of approval.

My second day of work goes by just as quickly as my first, though the weather is cloudier, making the photos slightly less impressive for the angles where I'd normally have the rocky Colorado horizon in the background. After I finish my second day, I pack up my things and make my drive back to the apartment.

I'm dreading my arrival the entire time, still not ready to face Dylan and whatever else may be waiting for me. But when I pull into the parking lot, I'm relieved to not see his truck waiting for me.

"Hey!" Stacey perks up when she sees me walk through the door. She turns off whatever show she was watching and moves her full attention toward me. "How was it?"

I smile, dumping my bag at the entrance of the apartment. I had to check out of my room at the resort before my shift started, so I haven't been able to shower, but even so, it feels good to have been out in the cold and moving my body again. Everything from my hips down is sore, but it's a good sore.

"Great. I have three clients a day, and then I just have to make sure they get their photos edited and sent to them in a week."

"Can I see some of them?" she asks.

"Sure." I cross the room as quickly as I can with how sore my legs are and dig through my duffel bag for my camera. I pull up the photos before passing it to Stacey.

"These are great," she murmurs, sorting through each photo. I watch over her shoulder as she looks them all over, but a call comes in on my phone. Dylan's name pops up on my screen.

I hit the end button.

"Was that Dylan?" Stacey says, glancing over.

"Yeah, but I'm not ready to talk to him just yet."

"You know you can talk to me, right? Just because he's my brother doesn't mean I'll rat you out if you trash-talk him. In fact, I'll probably be the first to trash-talk him." She gives a stiff laugh.

Stacey hands me the camera, and I take it, placing it on the couch next to me. I consider Stacey a friend—maybe not as close of a friend as Lori, but she's no stranger.

"You said you heard the whole conversation, right?" I ask.

Stacey gives me a quick nod, and I groan, still embarrassed.

"Then you know I told him I love him?"

"Yeah," she says quietly.

I let my head drop back against the couch. "It's not that I don't mean what I said. I just . . ." I pause, struggling to admit it. "I wonder sometimes if the feelings are circumstantial."

Stacey stares at me, confused. "What do you mean?"

"What if I only love him because he's the only thing that's made me happy since my parents died?" I force myself to say it, but it feels like a weight off my chest to finally admit it.

"He's not the only thing that's made you happy. In fact, it seems lately he's had the opposite effect seeing as you've been avoiding him."

I raise an eyebrow, and she shrugs.

"He says you won't answer his calls."

"If I do love him," I say slowly, testing the words out, "then why can't I let him do the things that make *him* happy?"

"Because you're scared," Stacey says simply.

The tears come without warning, and I have to fight to keep them at bay. "I keep wondering what the point of loving someone is if you're going to lose them."

Stacey shifts beside me. "What drew you to Dylan in the first place?"

I blink, feeling a tear fall, and I think back to the first time we met, when we hiked Ouzel Lake Trail in the summer.

"He was a hiker," I admit, feeling a little silly about it. He was also cute, but I don't tell Stacey that.

"Then you went on a hike just the two of you. What made sparks fly?"

We were hiking Mount Elbert, and I had a panic attack, but instead of getting frustrated with me or brushing the situation off, he talked to me about it.

"He pushed me to do better." Physically, mentally, emotionally. Dylan was always there on the sidelines, pushing me when I thought I couldn't do it anymore. He helped me hike Mount Washington without my dad. He's forced me out of my comfort zone so many times that I've lost count, and I'm a better person for it.

"You push him too," Stacey says. "I know you don't see it, but I do. The old Dylan didn't have girlfriends. He had a line of girls he flirted with until he got bored. He doesn't open up to other people, but he opens up to you. You probably know more about him than I do."

I let out a small smile. "Then how do I stop worrying?" Logically, I know the odds of Dylan getting hurt while hiking aren't high, but it feels like every time he steps outside, I risk losing him forever.

"Marly, you lost your parents. That doesn't leave you without scars," Stacey says gently, shaking her head. "I don't know what will help, but you have to decide if falling in love is worth the risk of losing love. And you have to ask yourself if you're willing to live a life without risk."

CHAPTER 30

I manage to avoid Dylan for the rest of the week. He gave up on calling and went back to texting, and then he eventually gave up on texting too. I was worried he'd corner me in my apartment, but Stacey reassured me that Dylan wouldn't come to the apartment uninvited. I make it through the week and am eager to drive to Beaver Creek to ski and put my focus on anything but Dylan.

When I come back from working all weekend, I find Stacey and Janet sitting at the table, their focus on something in front of them. Stacey's head pops up when I walk in.

"You're back!" she says, voice chipper. "My mom and I are testing out the paint-by-number kits we got for Christmas."

"They're looking good." I walk over to get a closer look. Stacey's looks like it's supposed to be a sunflower. She already has the yellow bits painted in. It looks like she's working on the green of the grass next. Janet's looks a little more complicated, her colors are all over the place, but it looks like the painting is supposed to be a lighthouse when it's finished.

"Lots of skiing this weekend?" Janet asks.

"Stormy Saturday, but today was perfect," I say, trying my best to put on a smile, but it feels odd to see Janet again when I have no idea where Dylan and I stand, though I have no one but myself to blame for that.

I pull a chair out at the table to join them until Stacey goes to the front door, grabbing her jacket from the coat hanger.

"Where are you going?" I ask, feeling a bit of panic to have her leave the table.

"Picking up Chinese food. I ordered you your usual. Figured you'd be hungry when you got back."

"I'll go with you," I say, moving to get up.

"No, I'm fine. I'll be back in ten minutes. It's just down the road."

She ushers herself out the door, and before I know it, I'm left alone with Dylan's mom.

"We missed you at Christmas," Janet says.

"Oh, uh . . ." I struggle.

"Dylan said you guys haven't really been talking?" Her words are light, not pushy at all, but I feel like I've been cornered into a conversation I don't want to have.

"Yeah," I say, leaving it at that.

"He seemed upset about the whole thing," Janet says, soft, understanding.

"Really?" I relax in my seat again, curious now.

"He said you don't want him hiking anymore?"

"Oh." I feel a part of me deflate. "Yeah, I guess that's been the running issue."

"The boy is as stubborn as they get. It never goes well when you tell him what to do." She laughs.

I sit in my chair, hoping the conversation will end soon.

"I feel the same way, you know," she continues.

"You do?" I ask, perking up, but then I push the excitement away as soon as it formed. This doesn't change anything for me and Dylan.

"Are you kidding me? Every time he goes on a hike or any sort of adventure, I'm worried sick, and that's before his first accident. But I wrote it off as just that. An accident. I've tried talking to him, but I'm afraid the more you tell him not to do something, the more he digs in."

I nod, understanding all too well.

"Here's what I've learned." She reaches across the table and gives my hand a gentle squeeze. "When you love someone, you have to trust that they have the instincts to take care of themselves. The more you try to hold tight, the more they feel they need to prove you wrong."

I nod, knowing she's right, but I have no idea how to put the words into practice.

Janet leans back, folding her arms on the edge of the table. "It's harder when you've lost someone from not holding tight enough."

I almost want to correct her and tell her that she's wrong. I lost my parents because I held them *too* tight. They died in a car accident coming to visit me. If I hadn't insisted, they'd still be alive.

I push the thought away, waiting for the familiar guilt to

subside. I glance up at Janet, and she's frowning, lost in her own thoughts as well.

"The phone call I got the day my dad died was my worst nightmare. I'd been talking to him for months, trying to sway him from hiking, to convince him to take things back a notch or two. His health wasn't what it used to be, and I was worried something was going to happen one day, but my dad insisted he was fine. Said I was a worrywart. So, I let it go."

She pauses, caught up in some memory.

"He died doing what he loved. I use that thought to comfort myself. I don't think he would have wanted it any other way." She pauses, a slight smile coming through at the corner of her lips. "And Dylan? Dylan is my father through and through. He's got the type of focus that can't be broken. It's something I've always admired about him, but when it comes to how that mindset might affect his safety . . . that's where I worry."

"You want Dylan to stop hiking too?" I ask.

"Yes, but no." She looks over at me and sees my confusion. "I would love for him to have safer, less risky hobbies, yes. But this is who he is. Hiking grounds him. Gives him purpose and something to prove. And ever since my father passed away, he's only become more determined to finish what my father started."

"The Colorado 14ers," I say.

"That's the one," she says, laughing to herself. "My ex-husband, Dylan's father, thought my dad was ridiculous for trying to reach for that goal. Said it was a waste of time and that it didn't prove anything. I'm afraid Dylan took that as a challenge."

"Is that why he's so determined?"

She shrugs. "Maybe. I'm sure it's part of it. But I think Dylan is still upset about losing his grandfather. Those two were inseparable. He's kept it together in the past couple years, but I know it was hard on him to lose his grandfather right in front of him like that. I can't imagine what it would have been like to be there alone, having no way to help him."

She looks up at me, sympathetic.

"I know it doesn't make much sense, why he cares so much, but I think it's his way of grieving. Some people go to graveyards, other people hike mountaintops."

I let out a short laugh. Janet looks up at me, curious.

"Dylan insisted I hike the same hike my dad and I did every year before he died. He packed photos of my parents into my backpack." I pause, having no clear way to describe it. "It was the only type of memorial I've experienced where I felt like they were truly there watching over me."

She smiles and looks down at her half-finished painting.

"He never looks at photos or brings up memories of my father. At first, I thought it was because it was too hard for him, but then I realized it's because the mountaintops are where he feels closest to him. That's where his memories lie. So, I let him be. It's his way of grieving, as odd as it may sound."

"Can I ask you one thing?" I ask.

She sits up, her attention on me. "Of course."

"How do you stop worrying about him?"

She nods, unsurprised by my question. "You can never truly stop worrying when you love someone. That's the price of love.

What you can do is remember that it's not your responsibility to make sure someone else is safe. Maybe when Dylan still lived under my roof, but not anymore. Just like it wasn't my responsibility to keep my dad safe. He was an adult. He made his choices. It took me a long time to come to terms with that."

CHAPTER 31

dylan stopped calling me. It's my fault. I've avoided every call and ignored every text message, yet I still find myself pacing, wondering why he hasn't tried to get in contact with me. I've picked up my phone multiple times to call him to apologize, but I never tap on his name to start the call.

I start to wonder if we're broken up. Neither of us have talked about an official breakup, but we'd need to talk to each other in order for that to happen, and right now conversations aren't exactly our strong suit.

It's Friday morning, and I arrive at the ski resort early to take advantage of my season ski pass and spend time skiing for fun rather than work. I'm only a couple runs in when I make my way toward one of the chairlifts and see a familiar face.

"Stacey!" I shout. She turns, her bright pink jacket making her pop against the snow. When she sees me, she smiles, starting to move toward me.

"I was hoping I'd find you!" She's a little ungraceful on her skis, leaning too much into them as she walks rather than letting them do the work.

"You didn't tell me you were skiing today." As I'm talking, I look past her, my eyes catching on a blue jacket — Dylan's jacket. I can feel my face freeze when I spot him. He doesn't notice me until he's already walking toward Stacey. I can tell the moment he recognizes who I am, because he stops in his tracks for a fraction of a second before continuing.

"Hey," he says, smiling to try to rein in his confusion. "You guys going up this lift?"

Awkward silence hangs between us. Seeing Dylan shocks me, not just because I've been avoiding him, but because I didn't think skiing would be an option for a long time because of his injuries.

"Yeah," I say. It's undeniable at this point since we're only a couple feet away.

Dylan turns to get in line, and Stacey follows, motioning for me to come too.

"What are you guys doing here on a Friday?" I ask.

Dylan's the one who turns to speak to me. "Stacey's off from work. I'm playing hooky. Would rather be hiking, but Stacey said the only way I'd get her up a mountain is if it involved skiing down."

Our turn in line comes, and I hang back, letting Stacey go. She gives me a what-are-you-doing face and pushes me forward. I don't have much time to react before the lift comes, and I rush to get into position. The chair slides under both me and Dylan until we're sitting and lifted into the air.

"Sorry," I say softly once we're in the air. I look back quickly, and Stacey is smiling in the chair behind us by herself, giving me a mischievous wave.

"You're fine," Dylan says with a hearty laugh. "I saw your bus in the parking lot, so I figured I'd find you eventually."

We sit in silence for a few seconds, watching the skiers go down the mountain as we make our way upward. I'm not sure if that means he's glad we've run into each other or if he had just resigned himself to the fact that it was inevitable.

"I was hoping to run into you actually," he admits. "I wanted to talk to you about the last conversation we had."

I can feel my face go bright red, so I'm thankful for my helmet and ski goggles.

"Dylan, I really—"

He cuts me off. "Do you regret what you said?"

I glance over, and though it's hard to tell while he's wearing goggles, I can see how much he hangs on my words.

"I regret the way I said it." I pause, taking a deep breath. "And maybe the timing of *when* I said it. But I don't regret the words. I meant that." It comes out shaky. I'm not saying anything directly, but he knows exactly what I'm referring to.

He glances away from me, avoiding my gaze when he says his next words. "You didn't give me a chance to respond. You haven't even answered my calls or texts since then. And then Stacey banned me from coming to the apartment until further notice. I've been waiting for you to come find me, but you never did."

"I know. I'm sorry. I just . . ."

I wanted to push him away because I couldn't stand the

thought of losing someone else I love. But I can't say the words. I try to think back to all the worry and what little things have pushed me over the edge, and I'm filled with anger.

"You were keeping things from me." The words start off soft, but they build, and any last bit of emotion I was holding back comes out at once. "I've been trying to help you train and get back to normal life, but you went hiking with Trent without telling me."

His face shifts, like I've slapped him across the cheek. "Because that's what I've had to do my entire life. I've always had to hide things around my dad. I didn't mean to do it to you too, but when you were so worried, I just thought it would be easier if you didn't know."

"It wasn't," I say, feeling myself getting emotional, my face and body hot under all the layers of clothes. "All it did was make me wonder what else you were hiding from me. And how am I supposed to trust that you're not going to push yourself too hard when you can't be truthful about simple things like what you're doing to train?"

The ski lift reaches the top of the mountain, and Dylan braces himself. I straighten in my seat, ignoring the tears that threaten to spill over.

"I never meant to lose your trust," he says, standing as his skis touch down. He slides across the snow and to the edge of the trail, waiting for me.

"I'm not your dad," I say when I slide up beside him.

He opens his mouth like he's about to say something, but then he stops himself. "I know," he says softly, nodding his head.

Stacey slides in beside me, her legs a little unsteady.

"I'm going to take it slow on the way down. Don't feel like you need to wait for me." She takes a deep breath, her eyes on the packed-down trail in front of her, and with one push, she starts down the mountain, her progress slow and careful.

Dylan is the next to leave, and he gives me a tentative smile before pushing off. I follow shortly after, trailing close behind him. He's good at skiing. He glides left and right down the slope, steering around other people on the mountain effortlessly. My eyes follow him, worry coursing through me as he makes sharp turns, but he never falters. If he's still injured, it's impossible to tell. I lose track of him at one point, but when I reach the base, I'm happy to see him waiting for me, his gaze trained on me as I come to a stop.

I'm smiling when I pull up, but I don't slow down fast enough, bumping into Dylan softly. I laugh at the small collision, and as his arms come out to steady me, our ski poles tangle.

"I'm sorry for not telling you about going on the hike with Trent," he says quietly, and I right myself.

I forgot where we had left off in our conversation, and it felt like we were just hanging out again. It takes me a few moments to reorient myself. "It's fine," I say.

We make our way toward the chairlift together. I wonder if we should wait for Stacey, but Dylan leads us forward.

"Are we okay?" he asks.

I glance over at him, curious about what he may mean exactly.

"Next!" the man staffing the chairlift shouts at us.

We move forward, taking position before the chair scoops us up and we're pulled forward.

I think of Dylan's question as the chair lifts us into the air, and I have to fight to keep myself seated where I am and not scoot closer to Dylan. I thought I missed him before, but seeing him now only makes it more obvious how much I crave to be near him.

I filter through the words in my mind, trying to figure out what I should say, but Dylan beats me to it.

"I don't want to go back to the way we were. I don't want to go back to not talking to you or seeing you. I miss you, Marly. I've been missing you this entire time. It's why I tried calling you so many times, but when you didn't answer, I didn't know if that meant you wanted me to stop. So . . . if you're done, I need to know."

I suck in a breath, and when I look at him, I know what I've been wanting to say. "I don't want to give up on us. And I don't want to be the thing that stops you from pursuing your goals. I want to be the person beside you, cheering you on."

"Then let's do that." He smiles, but when I don't smile with him, it fades.

"I've been trying to," I admit. "All I've ever wanted is to cheer you on, but every time you talk about getting back to crossing off these massive goals, I start to panic, and I can't—" It feels like my chest is getting tighter. I remind myself to breathe. "I can't stand the thought of you getting hurt again."

He reaches an arm around me, his hand rubbing up and down my back. In our full ski gear, there's a cloud of space between us and all our layers, but the gesture is there.

"Then we'll take it slow," he says softly. "For my sake and yours."

I smile, but it still feels like there's a tiny wedge between us. "I've sorry for how . . ." I try to find the right word. "Controlling I've been."

Dylan leans back, leaving an arm draped around my shoulders. "Sometimes you gotta let the rubble fall, Marly. Some things are out of our hands, and we just have to have a little faith that it's going to be okay."

"But what about your goal of finishing the list in two years?"

The question makes him pause. "I still want to. I'm going to try, but it's not the be-all and end-all anymore. Obviously, it would mean a lot to me to be able to finish the list before my grandpa's eightieth birthday, but I don't want to be so consumed by the goal that I ignore the person who loves me."

I feel myself stiffen, and Dylan lets out a soft laugh.

"What? I thought that'd be a good segue into something you said a couple weeks ago."

I cringe more. There's no avoiding it now.

I lean my head against his shoulder, the movement natural and automatic. He shifts beside me, leaning away, and I panic.

"Marly," he says.

When I turn to face him, he lifts my ski goggles until they're resting on the edge of my helmet. He kisses me before I have the chance to respond, his lips warm and nose cold. The tips of his fingers skirt across my cheek, tracing my smile as I lean into his touch.

"In case you were wondering," he says, pulling away until we're just inches apart, "I love you too."

I'm unable to control my smile. "I was hoping you'd say that."

The ski lift jostles as we get to the top, and we pull apart with wide grins. We stand right as the snow meets the bottom of our skis and slide down to a level portion out of the way of the ski lift. I pull up beside Dylan where he's waiting for me.

"You never mentioned you could ski," I say.

"You never asked." He shrugs and smiles, and I wonder what else there is to discover about him. It feels like I have a lot left to uncover.

Dylan pushes himself forward, glancing back at me as he makes his way down the mountain. He smiles in a way that feels like a challenge, and before I know it, I'm zooming down the mountain as well, racing to keep up with him. I want to reach out and grab him, tell him to go slower and not take the turns too sharp, but there's no need. He beats me to the bottom, grinning from ear to ear when I catch up with him.

"You working this weekend?" Dylan asks as we move back toward the ski lift.

"Yeah," I say, and his face drops a little. "But I was hoping to venture out into the mountains soon, just not on skis."

His smile is back, and I know I've hooked him.

"I was hoping to find someone to go hiking with." I glance over with a sly grin, feeling a bit like we're back to our old selves.

"What did you have in mind?"

CHAPTER 32

We ski together for the next couple hours. When we run into Stacey again, she's wearing a smug grin, like she accomplished something. Dylan and I talk each ride up the lift, picking up whatever conversation we left off on.

The idea to go on a hike together came out on impulse, but it felt like a peace offering. Even with Dylan's injuries, I feel like the hike will be more of a challenge for me than for him. I watched him ski all day, and there were no signs of him being hurt. He moved without fear, and if he had any pain, he never said anything. Every now and then I'd feel a bit of panic, watching as he made sharp turns, but with each run down the mountain, the anxiety eased until there wasn't any. It was like there was a tight knot in my stomach, and each time I saw him ski a flawless run, it untangled itself until it disappeared completely.

My shifts Saturday and Sunday feel slower than usual. I have my normal number of clients, but I'm antsy, ready to be off the slopes and get on my computer to research hikes for Dylan. My mind still wanders to a place of worry, but each time it does, I push the thoughts away, reminding myself how my eyes followed Dylan down the slopes all day without injury.

When I wrap up with my last client of the weekend, I pack my things from the resort as quickly as possible before driving the bus back to Stacey's apartment. She's gone when I get back, working her shift at the hospital.

I sit curled up on the couch, barely able to keep my eyes open as I start brainstorming hikes. I start off writing short, easy hikes but then quickly cross them off knowing that's not the point anymore. I have to trust Dylan.

So, I aim for bigger and write down a list of mountains Dylan has mentioned he still has left on his list to complete. I look them up online, but each one only seems more challenging than the last. Perhaps this will be pushing him too hard.

I give up my search, promising myself I'll figure something out in the morning.

When I'm eating breakfast the next day, I scroll through the names of summits, and my eyes keep falling to one: Sunshine Peak. The name stands out to me, but I'm not sure why.

I search the summit to pull up the trail information and then immediately realize why it's so familiar. This is the mountain Dylan's grandfather died on. They both hiked almost to the top but never reached the actual summit.

I research the trail more, collecting as much data as I can. It's 11.9 miles with 4,553 feet in elevation gain. And not only that, but the last road we'd need to drive to get to the trailhead is closed in the winter.

I dismiss the idea of doing the trail. It's too long and steep and will only be harder to access in the winter. But as I'm looking at more trails, I keep finding myself going back to Sunshine Peak.

I'm still scrolling when Stacey wanders from her room to get breakfast. She brings a bowl of cereal out, coming to sit down.

"You're going hiking?" Stacey says, looking over my shoulder.

I have the map for Sunshine Peak pulled up. I've been trying to see if there's a way to hike just Sunshine Peak. The most popular route takes you to Redcloud Peak first, then Sunshine Peak. Maybe we could cut out miles and elevation by avoiding Redcloud and just hiking Sunshine. There's a second trail that takes you straight to Sunshine, but the trail is steeper, with more challenging terrain.

I push my laptop back, feeling a little hopeless. "I wanted to, but the odds aren't looking good."

Stacey looks from my laptop back to me. "Does this mean you've finally stopped avoiding Dylan?" She says, one eyebrow cocked upward.

I give her a look, warning her I know what she's up to.

She smiles a wide grin, taking a bite of her cereal. "You're welcome."

"You know, you're not supposed to meddle in other people's relationships."

"Oh, please. You're both too stubborn to go talk to the other person. I knew you could work it out if I got you in the same room together." She pauses to take another bite. "Or on the same chairlift."

I roll my eyes, pulling my laptop back to me. "Well, thanks.

Now I'm trying to figure out how to hike this mountain in the middle of winter."

"Sunshine Peak?" Stacey says, looking closer at my screen. "Is that the one my grandfather hiked?" She doesn't mention the full history of the hike; we leave it unspoken.

"I want Dylan to be able to complete it. Maybe it will help him feel some sort of closure."

Stacey pauses, her gaze unblinking. "Yeah, maybe," she says, voice hushed.

"Only issue is that no one hikes it in the winter. There are a few trail reports here and there, but that's it." I pull up a tab on my laptop, showing her the websites where people can submit information about a trail after they hike. Hikers can say how much snow there was, if the trail was broken in, or if there were any icy spots. Most of the reports say the trail was unbroken and snowshoes are recommended. While I don't mind breaking trail when I need to, snowshoeing 11.9 miles might be more than Dylan and I can handle right now.

"Well, not everyone posts trail reports." Stacey shrugs.

I pull up another tab, frowning. "The access road to reach the trailhead parking lot is closed in the winter. You need to park at Mill Creek Campground, which is five miles one-way; so that's ten extra miles onto an already 11.9-mile hike."

"Oh," she says, looking down at her food.

I sigh, restarting my search, sifting through the list of mountains. Maybe Dylan and I can start smaller, something he's already hiked for the sake of getting back out there. We'll hike Sunshine Peak, just in the spring.

"Trent has a snowmobile," Stacey says suddenly. I look up at her, confused. "He and Dylan use it all the time. I'm pretty sure Dylan's used it in the past to hike in the winter when roads were closed."

"Really?"

She nods, taking a mouthful of cereal.

It would make the trip manageable. If the trail is broken in, then the most challenging part would be the amount of elevation. I know Dylan has covered more in a day, but I have no idea how much he can handle right now.

"How much hiking has Dylan done since his accident?"

"His doctor gave him the all clear after Christmas, and he's been out every weekend since then. He does all his strength training during the week and then long endurance hikes on the weekend. It's obnoxious. It's all he does, which is why I made him go skiing. Plus, you know." She shrugs. "You."

"How many miles can he do?"

She tilts her head, staring at the ceiling. "Nine miles? That was his most recent hike. He went on Saturday and dragged me along with him."

"How much elevation gain?"

She makes a face. "I don't know."

I frown, and Stacey gives an exasperated sigh, taking her phone out to look up the trail.

"It has 2,651 feet of elevation gain," she says, putting her phone back into her pocket after having checked the trail info.

"Do you think he could cover 4,553 feet in elevation gain?"

She cocks an eyebrow. "A normal person probably couldn't,

but I'm sure Dylan can. He doesn't even act like he had an injury."

I save the trail info on my laptop. Now I have a plan, or at least the start of one.

CHAPTER 33

Later that week, I show up at Janet's house, feeling a bit in over my head. I put her number into my phone after Dylan had his accident, but I haven't used it much besides coordinating when we were taking shifts to help Dylan after he got hurt.

I texted her asking if there was a day I could come over and talk to her, hoping it didn't seem strange or out of the blue. She responded to my text, telling me to come over Wednesday night. At the time, I responded back eagerly, but now that I'm sitting in her driveway, I'm panicking.

Her house is small, just a little cottage-looking thing in the suburbs outside of Colorado Springs. It looks like in the summer it would be the type of house you'd expect to have a perfect floral garden leading you to the front door, but right now there's at least a foot of snow coating the grass.

When I ring the doorbell, she's there almost instantly, greeting me with a smile.

"Marly, come on in." She ushers me inside, taking my coat and hanging it in the closet. Janet's decor reminds me of a summer beach house. It's decorated to feel like a cozy summer cottage despite the roaring weather conditions outside the front door. There are seashells decorating the shelves, and the walls are a pastel blue. "I assume your visit is for a particular reason?" She sits on the couch, and I follow close behind.

"Yeah, Dylan and I have been talking." I rehearsed exactly what to say in my head, but hearing it out loud, it sounds less graceful than I hoped it would. "I wanted to take him on a hike, something special." I pause. This is the harder part. "I was hoping we could finish hiking Sunshine Peak since he didn't get to finish it last time."

She gives me a slow nod. "He's been avoiding that one," she says.

"He has?"

"He had a hard time with my father's death. In a lot of ways, he struggled more than I did, though he would never say it. Stacey's offered to do that hike with him many times, but he always refuses."

That catches me off guard. Stacey loves to hike, but she isn't one to volunteer to do challenging peaks. She prefers to keep her miles and elevation gain low. I'm surprised Stacey didn't mention anything when I was researching the trail info.

"Do you know why?" I ask.

"I don't think he wants to go back there. I have a feeling he's leaving it for last. A grand finale. Final goodbye. Whatever you want to call it."

I frown, realizing my plan isn't such a good idea after all.

"I didn't know that," I mumble. I feel foolish now, sitting in his mom's house trying to put together the one hike he's been actively avoiding.

"I think it's a good idea," Janet says, her voice sure. "It will challenge him in a way he's never been challenged before."

"Yeah, but I don't want to force him to do it, especially if it's because he wants to save it for last."

"I think you'd be surprised how easily *you* may be able to change his mind."

I look down, a little embarrassed.

"And besides, I think this mountain is exactly what he needs. Perhaps he's been frantically trying to cross all these mountains off because there's only one in particular he's trying to get to." She gives a small knowing smile.

She gets up from the couch and walks into her kitchen. I hear her rifle around before she comes back, a small burlap bag in her hand. She holds it out, the bag jingling like it's full of glass.

"My father left pretty clear instructions after his death. No memorials or graves. He just wanted his ashes scattered across the places he loved. Only issue is, he didn't specify *where*. Dylan wants to scatter them across the seven peaks he never got to finish. Some of his ashes have already been scattered on some of his favorite hikes, or in places where we have special memories, but we saved enough for the seven peaks. Dylan's goal is to complete the same peaks my dad already completed, then finish the list, spreading his ashes on each summit." She reaches into the bag, taking out one glass bottle. "If Dylan is one thing, he's symbolic."

She stretches her hand out, extending the tiny bottle to me.

I take it in my hands, the glass cold against my fingertips. It's small, maybe three inches tall and about an inch wide. The glass is clear, letting me see the gray ashes within. It feels oddly intimate to see and hold it, like it's something for private eyes only. The one thing holding the ashes in is a small cork at the top of the bottle.

"You should keep it for now. I need to talk to Dylan first, make sure he wants to do the hike." I try to give the bottle back to her, but she shakes her head.

"I think this is what he needs to stop feeling the pressure of finishing the list."

My hand drops, fingers wrapping around the glass. I have no idea why Janet is trusting me with such an important piece of her family, but I hold it close. I have no idea if Dylan will budge and agree to the hike—or if the hike will even be manageable—but when I leave Janet's house that night, my plan is surer than ever.

CHAPTER 34

i don't have time to see Dylan again until Monday. We've been keeping in contact since we went skiing, but nothing more than a few texts here or there. After he finishes work, he picks me up from Stacey's apartment for dinner. I greet him at the door before he's able to knock.

"I've been promised a hike?" He smiles as soon as he sees me. I told him I finally had a plan and that I'd tell him tonight at dinner.

"Let's eat first." I walk through the door, slipping my coat on as I go.

The entire drive to the restaurant, I can tell he's itching to ask questions, fighting to hold back. He glances over at me every now and then, perhaps wondering if I'll change the subject to the hike I've promised. He's like a little kid on Christmas morning, waiting for permission to start opening presents. If he had any concern I'd go back on my word, it's gone now.

I wait until we're seated and have had our orders taken before I bring it up.

"Here's the hike I have planned." I pull out the map I printed and unfold it across the table. Dylan leans forward eagerly. His eyes trail over the map, the excitement leaving his eyes when he makes out the details.

"Sunshine," he says, his voice level.

My first thought is regret. He was so eager for the hike until he saw exactly what my plans were. I wonder if I should have had a backup plan, but now it's too late.

"I wanted to do something meaningful," I say. "The same way you made my hike without my dad meaningful."

Dylan stares at the map a little longer, his eyes trained on the labeled points.

"I was going to leave that one for last," he says. He leans back in his chair, his face pulled down. I want to fix it right away, to do whatever I need to in order to make his smile come back, but that's not what he needs. What he needs is the same push I did when we hiked Mount Washington.

"I know," I say, and he looks up at me, his eyes full. "I talked to your mom. She told me about how you want to complete all his unfinished peaks and save Sunshine for the final peak. But maybe we should do that one now."

I let the words hang in the air, but Dylan doesn't say anything.

"I think it would help you feel closure after everything." I keep my words light and gentle, but he shakes his head.

"I don't need any closure," he says, his voice rough.

"Then why do you look so upset right now?" I ask. Once I say the words, Dylan blinks, looking away. I reach into my pocket and pull out the tiny jar of ashes, holding it in my hand for him to see. "Your mom wants us to scatter his ashes."

He looks up, and it's like he's been hit by a train. His face reveals a sort of agony I've never seen, but I imagine it's similar to what I looked like after my parents died.

"You should do it." I put my hand out, offering the ashes, but he doesn't take them. Instead, he shakes his head, looking down.

I pull my hand back, slipping the jar into my pocket and zipping it up. Dylan lifts his head with a sniffle, a red glint in his eyes.

"I want to save it for last," he says, but the words come out uneven.

"Okay," I say. "But I need to know why."

He looks back at me, perplexed. I've never been one to push. It has always been him pushing me, making me face my issues. Now it's my turn.

"Because it will be more special that way."

"Maybe," I say, offering agreement. "But maybe you'll feel better now if you do it first. If you redo Sunshine, you'll have your grandfather with you on all the remaining hikes."

Dylan isn't looking at me, his eyes focused on the condensation forming on his glass of water.

"Can I be honest with you?" I say the words matter-of-factly, like we're having an entirely different conversation.

He looks up.

"I didn't want to hike Mount Washington. In fact, I didn't even want to go on that road trip, never mind be dragged to

North Carolina against my will."

He cringes a little, both of us remembering how upset I was.

"But at the end of the day, I was thankful that you, Lori, and the rest of my family pushed me to do things I *never* would have done on my own. I became stronger that way, and I want the same for you."

He opens his mouth to speak, then shakes his head. "It's not the same."

"Yes, it is," I say slowly. "Let me do for you what you've done for me."

"I haven't trained enough for this hike," he says, grasping at an excuse.

"You know that's not true," I challenge, catching him off guard with my response.

"What happened to being overly cautious?"

"I still am, but I know you're strong enough."

He looks at me, his eyes doubtful.

"I'm sorry for how I've acted. I saw how determined you were, and it terrified me. Not just because I've lost people I've loved already, but because that determination is what kills hikers. It's when you're so summit focused that you don't notice the dangers around you. When you got caught in the storm, that was all I could focus on."

He nods. "I know," he says, a layer of confidence slipping away from his exterior. "But I know how dangerous it can be. I only need to get caught in a storm once to realize how quickly things can go wrong."

I smile, knowing he means it. "So, do the hike," I challenge.

He takes a deep breath, his eyes refocusing on the map.

"It's not an easy hike," he says, his eyes following the lines of the trail.

"Good thing we're not beginners."

He looks at me and smiles in a tired sort of way, but he's shifted. He doesn't pull away from the challenge; he's ready to walk directly toward it.

"What's the plan?" he asks, and I know I've won.

"The access road is closed in the winter, so Trent is going to let us borrow his snowmobile so we can drive the access road to the trailhead."

He raises an eyebrow. Technically, it was Stacey who talked to Trent about borrowing his snowmobile, but the result is the same.

"You want to hike this in the winter?" he asks.

"Only if the conditions are good. I'll watch the weather to make sure there's no recent heavy snowfall, no high winds, and no low temps, and maybe we'll even get a blue-sky day if we're lucky. And I'll check trail reports to make sure we're not the ones breaking trail."

Dylan lets out a strained laugh. "I think it's possible you're even crazier than I am."

I panic, thinking maybe this isn't a good idea. Maybe now it's me who's letting my vision sway us away from the very real risks. Or perhaps Dylan is right, and you only need to get caught in a storm once to have a little caution instilled into you.

"It's not a race to the top. It's a game of patience waiting for the perfect opportunity. We need the snow, temperature, and trail conditions to be on our side."

He glances down at the map, pulling it closer. "Okay, I'm in."

CHAPTER 35

t he weather is never perfect. Weeks pass, and it's never the
conditions we're waiting for. If the weather is good, there's
two feet of fresh snow on the mountains, making it so we'd have
to break the trail. If there are recent trail reports, the temperature
is below zero with high winds. If there are no winds, there's
snowfall. It's a constant rotation of conditions, none of them
falling into place nicely.

We check the weather and trail conditions every day, waiting
for something to line up. It's March now, and it feels like waiting
is pointless. We've been hiking together, but only smaller hikes
to prepare our bodies for what's to come. While Dylan trains
physically, for me the training is all mental. Each small hike
we go on, my eyes are trained on him, the knot of anxiety ever
present, but with each hike we do, it grows smaller and smaller.

I keep waiting for him to ask to hike a different 14er, one
that's easier to conquer in the winter. But he never brings it up
despite the fact he's losing time to finish the list in two years.
He's settled into the idea of Sunshine being his next peak.

We meet every weekday to strength train together and then choose a longer hike once a week. We start to fall into a rhythm that feels like we're back to our old selves. With each day we spend together and each challenge Dylan endures, I can feel myself breathing easier, any doubt of his safely slowly melting away. It's clear preparing for the hike makes Dylan happier, the way he seems lighter on his feet the farther we go. At first, I thought it was because he was feeling more like himself, but then I realized he wanted to see me training beside him. We're a team again, constantly pushing and pulling each other forward.

"What about Friday?" Dylan asks, pointing to the weather report for that day. The summit forecast is sunny blue skies with a high of twenty-five and a low of ten. Temperature-wise, it's probably as warm as we'd want it to be. If it gets too warm, the top layer of snow on the trail will melt enough that our feet will sink in with every step. We'll need it cold enough to keep the snow frozen, but not too cold that it's dangerous.

"Friday might be okay. It hasn't snowed in a week, so there's nothing fresh on the trails, but even then, I don't know if someone has hiked the trail since the last snowstorm."

Dylan looks over my shoulder as I sift through a few different trail-reporting websites. The most recent report we can find is from two weeks ago, before another foot of snow was deposited.

"Maybe we can try," Dylan says, looking back at the weather again. Winds are a high of five miles per hour—a rarity, especially in the winter.

I stare at the screen longer. "What if we get ready and assume we're hiking it? We'll head out with the snowmobile. If we get there and the trail is broken in, we'll hike. If it's not, we'll turn back and at least say we enjoyed the day driving around on the snowmobile." I feel a little knot of worry in my stomach at the thought of it, but it's easier to push the doubt away now.

"Sounds like a plan." He smiles.

§

It's dark as we unload the snowmobile from the trailer on the back of Dylan's truck. We work in headlamps, illuminating our way through the darkness. It's 4:30 a.m., and the plan is to start hiking in the dark to be at the summit before ten. The sooner we're off the mountain, the safer.

"All good," Dylan says, tossing the straps he used to secure the snowmobile into his truck. He hops onto the snowmobile and turns it on, rumbling the entire forest. It comes to life, the lights illuminating the trees around us. The machine seems loud enough to wake up anyone nearby, but we're alone out here.

I pull our hiking bags from the truck and strap them together. I secure my bag around Dylan's and put both bags on my back. We brought only one snowmobile since there's enough room for two people, but the only way to take our bags is to put them both on my back.

Our bags are heavier than they would be on a summer day. We're both equipped with extra clothing, emergency blankets, sleeping bags, gloves, hats, water, and food. For climbing gear, we each have snowshoes secured to our bags. Though we hope to not need them, they will prevent us from falling into the snow if the trail isn't broken in. If the trail is packed down enough to walk on, we each have a set of microspikes, which are metal spikes we can secure to our boots. The spikes will make crossing ice easy without either of us having to worry about slipping.

"Ready when you are," Dylan says, seated on the snowmobile. I finish securing his backpack to me, twisting side to side to make sure his bag and my bag are secure. In total, I have probably thirty pounds on my back right now.

With the heavy gear strapped on, I'm thankful to be able to sit on the snowmobile and take the weight off my back. Though the bags are heavy, the backpacks center the weight perfectly on my hips rather than my back.

I wrap my arms around Dylan and scoot up farther. "Ready."

He revs the engine, and we're off. We follow a trail made by cross-country skis to the access road. Dylan pauses at the entrance. The gate stops cars from driving, but there's just enough space to the right of the gate for the snowmobile to enter.

We aren't the first ones down the road, which is encouraging. There are other tracks from snowshoeing, skiing, and possibly another snowmobile. The tracks muddle together, and it's impossible to tell how old they are. I'm hopeful as we drive that maybe this means the trail will be broken in.

The map said it was five miles from the campground to the trailhead, and we drive down the road in the dark for what feels like forever. Eventually, Dylan comes to a stop in front of a sign, and I get off the snowmobile, peeling the backpacks off and letting them tumble to the ground. Dylan gets up, pulling the keys out of the ignition. He takes a few steps toward the start of the trail, pausing at the entrance into the trees. I follow, pointing my headlamp into the darkness.

The trail is patted down. There is a clear narrow trail made, a line down the middle leading into the trees. It's just wide enough for one person to walk, and the edges of the trail are much higher where the snow is still fresh and untouched.

"Wow," I say. I was mentally preparing for needing to turn around. After watching the trail reports for so long, I started to settle with the fact that people don't hike Redcloud or Sunshine Peak in the winter. It just isn't practical with the road being closed. But there it is: a broken-in trail.

Dylan is quiet next to me, his headlamp pointing down the path. I can see his breath fog out in front of him.

"If the trail isn't broken in all the way, we might have to turn back, but it's looking good," I say, turning to get our bags. They're both on the ground still, mine attached to his, and I undo the buckle. When I look up, Dylan is still standing at the edge of the trees.

"You okay?" I leave our bags on the ground, walking up to meet him.

I try to keep my head pointed away from him so my headlamp doesn't shine into his eyes, but I can see the emotion brimming under the surface. His face is in a scowl, trying to maintain composure, but I can see it slipping.

When he still doesn't respond, I reach out with my gloved hand, wrapping my fingers around his upper arm and giving it a small squeeze. He turns abruptly, his headlamp moving fast. He keeps his face level but looks down at me.

I see countless emotions floating over his face: happier memories of the last time he got to hike with his grandfather, and, of course, the tragic moments of that same day. This is the thing he's been fighting so hard to avoid, right here in front of him.

I take a step forward, closing the distance between us, wrapping my arms around his torso. We're both wearing so many layers it feels more like hugging a cloud than a person, but I feel his arms come up around me, his warm breath at my temple.

Doubt creeps in, heavy and strong. I wonder if coming out here was a smart idea, if maybe I should have listened to that voice in the back of my mind that urged me to sway Dylan away from hiking. Worst-case scenarios run through my mind, giving me glimpses of everything that could go wrong. The panic eases its way back into my mind, threatening to undo all the hard work Dylan and I have been putting in the past couple weeks.

I fight the urge to speak my worries, knowing that if I said we should turn around, we would. Dylan is fighting his own battle, his confidence wavering—not because it isn't safe, but because the memories around the hike are too hard.

When I close my eyes, I promise myself to take a very realistic view of the hike. When I open them again, I realize the weather and trail are on our side; it's just the mental battles we need to fight.

I push the worries I have away, taking a deep breath. Today I need to be the one to push Dylan.

Moving our bags, I sling mine over my shoulder before

handing Dylan his.

"This is going to be a lot harder than I thought," Dylan says, and I know he isn't talking about the physical challenge of the hike.

CHaPteR 36

despite the path to the trail being broken in, we both wear our snowshoes to stamp the trail down more. The path starts in a valley between the mountains, making the incline slow and steady. It isn't until we're three miles in that the real climb starts and the flat walk is exchanged with a steep hike. As soon as we start ascending the trail, we make regular stops to strip off layers of clothing to avoid sweating.

That's the real challenge hiking in the winter. It isn't about the climb; it's always about the cold. Maintaining core body temperature is everything. Beginner hikers don't know when to add or remove layers. Wait too long to add a layer, and you've lost body heat. Wait too long to remove a layer, and you're sweating. The last thing you want is to be damp in below-freezing temperatures.

In many ways, the snow makes the terrain easier. With the right gear, climbing across an icy surface is easy. Spikes on the bottom of our boots make it so we can walk without fear of slipping. Even my snowshoes, which are designed for hiking, have bars that lift up to elevate my heels to make my footing even when I walk uphill.

Dylan leads the way. He's wary at the start, but the longer we hike, the faster he powers forward, propelled by his goal. The only way I know something is off is that he doesn't talk. Normally when we hike together, it's a constant conversation, talking about anything and everything to make the time go by. Now he steams forward in silence, his focus on something he doesn't share.

As we walk, the sun creeps up. It takes an hour and a half to cover the first three miles, but we're slowing when the incline starts. While Dylan leads, I glance at my watch, keeping an eye on our pace and progress. In order to do this hike today, we need many conditions to line up to keep the hike low-risk. By some miracle, each factor turns in our favor.

Three and a half miles in, the incline doubles again. We're above tree line, the snowy mountains stretching out far ahead of us. It feels like another planet. Everything is shades of white, blue, and purple. There's not a cloud in the sky, making the mountain range wrap around us in every direction for as far as our eyes can see. All the mountains are snowcapped, but the rocky surface is still visible. Big boulders peek out from the snow, too massive to be covered.

I'm down to only two layers. Despite the cold, I can feel myself sweating just the tiniest bit. I unzip the outer shell of my puffy jacket, letting the cold air flow in enough to keep me from sweating.

"You okay?" Dylan stops, waiting for me.

I adjust my backpack, trying to open my jacket a little more. "All good." I give him a thumbs-up.

The sun is beating down on us, but it provides little warmth. Instead, it brightens the snow. The surface around us would be blinding if not for the ski goggles we're both wearing.

We move upward in our snowshoes, trekking poles in hand. The incline becomes so steep that we begin to use the poles to reach forward, dragging ourselves upward.

When it seems like we can't move upward any longer, the path finally levels. We're at Redcloud Peak, the last summit Dylan's grandfather hiked.

Dylan stops first, his deep breaths visible as the air steams in front of him. I take a few more steps until I'm right next to him. He turns and smiles when he sees me, his grin wide, mouth hanging open. He pulls his goggles off, eyes squinting against the brightness of the day. The air is still, with only the occasional gust coming through.

This is what he lives for; that much is obvious. Whatever struggle he had at the beginning of the hike is gone, replaced only with a euphoric sense of exhilaration.

I stand next to him, my breathing heavy from the climb, and he kisses me. I'm taken by surprise, but Dylan has one hand under my chin, guiding me to him.

"What was that for?" I ask, a little dazed.

"A thank-you for making me come back." He grins as he looks down at me, the mountains opened wide around us.

He pulls his backpack off, reaching in to find another layer of his jacket. It doesn't take long for us to get cold again since we've stopped moving. We both add another layer, and I pull my camera out of my bag to take photos. I make it a point to work quickly. I wear a thin pair of gloves as I take photos, but I know we can't be at the summit for too long. I take as many photos as I can, knowing that when we get to Sunshine Peak, my focus will be on Dylan.

Dylan watches me, and each time I glance over, his smile lightens more and more. While we may have covered the majority of the elevation for the day, the hardest part of the hike still lies ahead.

I stuff my camera back into my bag and grab my last layer to wear. The trail goes downhill again before it will send us back upward, so I dress accordingly, needing to keep myself warm.

We put our backpacks on and adjust our snowshoes, putting the small metal bars down so our heels are level with the ground again.

Dylan's gaze is trained on Sunshine Peak. From Redcloud Peak, it seems too close. It's impossible to think that we still have about a mile and a half to go when it looks like the summit is right in front of us.

"Ready?" I ask, standing straight after making a few more adjustments to my gear.

When he looks over at me, his face is stone. He gives me a quick nod, slinging his bag over his shoulder.

We continue forward, but the farther we go, the more we realize how fresh the trail is. It's still beaten down by previous hikers, but not by much. Each step Dylan takes, his feet sink in, even with the snowshoes. The slope takes us downward, making it easier, but I begin to wonder if it's time to turn back.

Dylan keeps going, his feet sinking a couple inches with each step. We've only been walking a handful of minutes when he stops.

"Maybe we should turn around," he says. It's perhaps the first time I hear worry in his voice, but this time I'm not sure if it's because we're getting closer to where his grandfather passed or because he's genuinely worried about the snow.

A part of me wants to concede, take the warning and go. This is what I wanted after all. I needed to know that Dylan would be able to turn around to keep himself safe when he's hiking, but how much risk is still in front of us?

My dad and I broke trail winter hiking many times. It's grueling work and why most people wait a day or two after a big storm to hike in hopes someone else will do the hard work of putting down a trail.

I glance across the horizon around us. The weather is still ideal, with minimal wind and bearable chill. When I look at my watch, we're ahead of schedule, so I do what Dylan would have done for me.

"Are you cold?" I ask, beginning the risk assessment every hiker takes when they contemplate turning back.

"No," he responds quickly.

"Are you tired?"

Confused, he looks at me and shakes his head.

"How's your ankle?"

"Fine," he says quickly.

"Then let's go," I say, stepping around him, my feet sinking in. I make my way forward, remembering how hard it is to be the person in the lead. I turn around and see Dylan still standing in the same spot, his eyes wary. "You coming?" I say, my voice light, trying to keep our spirits up.

"Marly, come on," he says, his voice low. His body turns away from me slightly, back in the direction we came from.

"Why?" I ask.

He doesn't say anything, the corners of his mouth tugged down. I turn around, a hard task in snowshoes, and go back to where he stands. I watch him, but he won't meet my eyes. Anxiety radiates off him in a way I've never seen before.

"Dylan," I whisper. He looks up. It's almost impossible to read his face with the sun glare coming off his goggles, but he steps back, wanting to turn around. "Give me one good reason to turn around. I know you, Dylan, and if this were any other mountain, you'd be leading the way." I try to put as much confidence into my voice as I can, but seeing him physically begin to retreat makes me second-guess myself.

"We can come back another day in the summer," he says softly.

I reach out and touch his cheek, the only exposed skin on his body. I can't see his eyes through his goggles, which makes saying my next words easier.

"We can come back in the summer if you want," I say. "But we're also going to finish this today."

"Marly—" he starts, but I cut him off.

"If the roles were reversed, you'd be dragging my ass up this mountain. I'll break trail, and you can follow. But I need you to do this."

He looks past me, at the snowy trail that'll lead us up Sunshine Peak. It's in our sight, just over a mile away. We're too close now to turn back.

"What happened to not wanting me to hike?" he asks, his voice a little lighter, even if I can still hear the anxiety.

"I remembered that I love you because you're just as crazy as me, so it's time to embrace it." I pause, realizing that the sense of anxiety, the fear of us getting hurt or something crazy going wrong, is still there. It's the type of fear that reminds me that I'm not unbreakable. But danger in life doesn't mean I'm supposed to stop living.

He smiles. The worry is still there in his eyes, but he's tucked it away in exchange for bravery.

"Okay," he says.

I lead the way, always checking back to make sure Dylan isn't far behind. It doesn't take us long to go down to the valley between the two summits, and then we're going uphill again. We pause to take off layers to avoid sweating and adjust our snowshoes for the uphill climb.

The closer we get to the summit, the harder it is to lead. There are snowdrifts obscuring the trail, mounds of snow formed from the wind making us disoriented. I catch myself wandering off-trail, going around the drifts rather than straight through them.

I pause when I realize I've gone too far, the snowdrifts making it hard to spot the correct direction. Above tree line, the trail is marked with cairns, large piles of rock every couple feet. But wind carries the snow so high that the cairns become buried, making it impossible to orient myself.

"Over here!" Dylan shouts a few feet away. He points in a direction to my far right, and I see a pile of rocks.

I make my way back to the trail, eyeballing the summit. It won't be long now.

"Let me lead," Dylan says, stepping in front of me.

I'm about to object with some excuse that maybe with his ankle I should keep breaking trail, but his stride is faster and more confident. He knows this trail.

I follow Dylan for ten more minutes before he pauses.

"I think this is where we were when the helicopter landed," he says softly when I come to stand next to him.

I'm not sure how to react after Dylan speaks, but he doesn't give me the chance. Instead, he turns away from me, making his way up the summit, closing in on the final bit of elevation. He puts his head down, never looking up as he ascends, like some force is pulling him forward.

I try to pick up my pace to follow him, but I'm slower. I can see him the entire time, the only thing giving me comfort as he moves farther and farther away. Even with him in my sight and knowing he's safe, a tiny twinge of anxiety settles in my stomach, but I push it away. I force myself not to panic, keeping my eyes on him as he moves faster until he finally reaches the summit.

He throws his head back when he gets to the top, turning to view the expanse in front of him. Though he's still a distance away, it looks like he may be gasping for breath.

I widen my strides, urging myself to close the gap between us. The closer I get, the more I hear them: his sobs.

When I'm only a few feet away, I throw my backpack onto

the ground before yanking my jacket out and putting it over my other layers. Then I go to Dylan, his cries feeling like my own.

"Take your backpack off," I whisper. He lets me unclip the waist and chest straps, and I guide it off his back. Once his bag is on the ground, I pull his final layer of jacket out and encourage him to put it on, slipping his arms into the sleeves like he's a little kid.

I don't look at his face as I work, afraid it will be the thing that tears me apart.

"You're okay," I say, wrapping my arms around his waist. His arms lock around me, and all I can feel is him. His heartbeat is loud, his breathing ragged as he cries a sort of pain he's had locked away for years.

His arms are tight around me, like he's afraid I'm going to float away if he loosens his grip.

Around us, the world is still. There's nothing quieter than the world after fresh snowfall. For this moment, it feels like we're trapped in our own space.

I'm not sure how long we stand there. There's a tiny gust of wind, but neither of us is cold, trapped in our own private cocoon of warmth. After a few more minutes, his breathing slows, and he loosens his grip. He takes his goggles off, rubbing his face.

I lean away, looking up at his face. His eyes are bright red, tears smeared across his cheeks. His gaze is far away, his face stone. I pull my goggles off and toss them to the ground before wrapping my arms around his neck. The bright snow is blinding around us, the sun reflecting off every surface of the mountaintop. He tightens his grip around my waist, burying his face into my neck. His breath is at my ear, and I can feel him shaking, trying to hold back tears.

I wait for him to still before I move back toward my backpack. I reach into one of the small, zippered pockets and reveal the tiny jar. When I turn to Dylan, his eyes are focused on it.

I hold it out, waiting for him to take it. He reaches out with his gloved hand, staring at the contents inside.

"Marly," he says softly, an objection in his voice.

I move forward, taking one glove off my hand. I take the cork out of the jar.

He takes a deep, heavy breath, watching the uncorked jar. Then he takes the jar from my hand and tips it on its side, the movement slow and careful.

The ashes come out slowly at first, almost impossible to see. A few fall to the ground before the wind picks up and carries the ashes across the mountain range. When the jar is empty, Dylan tightens his grip before dropping his hand. He reaches out with his other arm, drawing me to his side.

We stand there for a long time, watching the horizon open up in front of us, and I can only imagine Dylan's grandfather summiting every mountain along the horizon.

There's a sense of peace as we stand at the top of Sunshine Peak, and as Dylan pulls me closer, I know everything's going to be okay.

epilogue

After many long phone calls with Aunt Cora, we came to the decision to sell my parents' house. It was a mix of things that made me want to finally sell the house, but most of all, it didn't feel like home anymore. After four months of putting the house on the market and signing piles of paperwork, the house is sold — or about to be once I sign the final piece of paperwork.

"Is there anything left to pack up?" Dylan asks on the drive to visit the house one last time. We flew back to New Hampshire together, and Lori is letting us borrow her car while we're visiting. We're here for a week to visit friends and family and do the last bits of paperwork, and then we return to Colorado.

"I don't think so. The moving company should have gotten it all. I'm just going to do one final sweep through the house."

We pull into the driveway, the real estate sign is still propped up in the lawn. Otherwise, the house looks exactly the same from the outside. The snow from the winter is long melted, and the flowers that line the walkway are back in bloom. When I step out of the car, Dylan meets me at my door, offering his hand, and I take it.

I unlock the front door, a sad sense of nostalgia hitting me. This will be the last time I step through the door.

The house is empty when I walk in. Our couches, tables, and chairs have been loaded up and packed away in a storage unit. The house is hollow, and it feels stranger and more unfamiliar the farther I go.

It feels like an ending, but not in the sad way I expected. It's a relief, seeing it all packed away. It's like I've been trying to close the door for months, but something was always blocking my way. Now it feels complete, like a piece of my life has been wrapped up and stored away for safekeeping.

I grip Dylan's hand as I walk from room to room. We make silent progress through the house. I check every cabinet and corner, making sure nothing was left behind or forgotten. It isn't until we've completed our lap around the house that I pause.

I'm waiting for a sense of doubt or regret, but it never comes.

I can feel tears burning in my eyes, and Dylan wraps his arms around me. I feel sad, of course, over all the reasons someone should be sad selling a childhood home. But walking through the house only made me realize the house never held the memories in the first place. I did.

Seeing it empty made it clear.

I lean my head against Dylan's chest, my gaze falling on the empty living room. With a shaky breath, I pull away from Dylan, and we make our way back outside. The door clicks softly behind me as I say goodbye to the house for the last time.

When we get to the car, I reach into the back seat and grab my camera.

"I'll be right back," I say as Dylan buckles his seat belt.

I take a few steps away from the car, making sure I can get a full view of the house. In all the years my parents lived here, they never once took a photo of the house. Maybe it's because when you live in something every day, you don't appreciate it as much as you should.

I look into the viewfinder of the camera and put the house into focus before I press the shutter button, a final moment of thanks.

"Ready?" Dylan says when I get back into the car.

"Let's go home," I say, and for once, it feels like I know where home may be.

Support the author!
REVIEW THE BOOK ON AMAZON!

Book 3 Coming Soon!
Stay tuned for Lori's story.

Subscribe to Mandi Lynn's Newsletter:
https://bit.ly/MandisNewsletter

Subscribe to Mandi Lynn's YouTube channel
to watch as the book is created:
https://www.youtube.com/user/mandilynnwrites

Feeling inspired to go on a hike?

I hope this book helps inspire you to start exploring the outdoors, however I'd like to remind everyone how important it is to practice responsible hiking. This means keeping your safety in mind and practicing leave no trace principles.

Before you go hiking, do proper research to know the terrain you will be covering and what the weather will be. Always bring your hiking essentials and know how to use them:

- Warm clothing
- Map
- Compass
- Fire starter
- Headlamp
- Water and food
- Knife
- First aid kit
- Rain jack

Learn more about hiking safety at HikeSafe.com

See some of the author's hiking adventures by subscribing to her second YouTube channel, DustySnowBoots.

https://youtube.com/@dustysnowboots

Want to Go on Some of the Hikes Mentioned in this Book? You can find all the Trails Listed Below!

- Chapter 7, The Keyhole and Longs Peak via Longs Peak Trail
- Chapter 16, Seven Bridges Trail
- Chapter 23, Devil's Garden Trail
- Chapter 24, Balanced Rock:
- Chapter 24, Delicate Arch Trail
- Chapter 35, Redcloud and Sunshine Peak:

acknowledgements

This story took lots long hour to craft together. Never have I re-arranged and deleted entire chapters as much as I have for this book. With that said, I owe a lot of thank you's to everyone who's helped me along the way to bring this book to life.

To my alpha and beta readers, Allyssa, Nicole, Lacy, Jessame, Teresa, Heather, and Allison. You all got to read the manuscript in its earliest, and perhaps ugliest version. Thank you for the immense amount of feedback that allowed me to craft the story into what it is today.

To my copy editor, Natalia Leigh. Your attention to detail is amazing. I cannot thank you enough for whipping my book into shape.

To my proofreaders, Mimi Strzelewicz, Carolyn Trottier, and Bethany Atazadeh. Thank you for being the final set of eyes to catch all the little details!

To Brittany Wang and Bethany Atazadeh (again) who helped me mastermind every little detail leading up to release.

To my husband, who gladly plays video games so I can work late into the night undistracted — though I think he's happy for the excuse.

And lastly for my readers, who time and time again pick up my books and fall in love with these characters as much as I do. It's because of you I have the privilege to call this my job.

aBOut tHe autHOR

Mandi Lynn published her first novel when she was seventeen. The author of multiple books, Mandi spends her days continuing to write and create YouTube videos to help other writers achieve their dreams of seeing their books published. Mandi is the owner of Stone Ridge Books, a company that works to help authors bring their books to life through cover design and digital book marketing. She is also the creator of The Book Launch Planner Series, a collection of planners designed to help authors write, publish and market their books. When she's not creating, you can find Mandi exploring her backyard or getting lost in the woods.

WWW.MANDILYNN.COM

@MANDILYNNWRITES

Made in the USA
Middletown, DE
04 January 2023

20548748R00196